PARADISE

LOST

Praise for *This Side of Paradise*

"What will hold teen readers is the horror of a parent prepared to do anything, even kill, in order to clone the perfect family."

—Booklist

"An entertaining, suspenseful thriller with a genuinely chilling villain. Good fun."

—Kirkus Reviews

"Layne's tale is a heady mix of conspiracies, alternate identities, and sinister underground laboratories with a creepy schizophrenic villain that readers will love to hate. Recommend this title to thriller fans who will enjoy the ride."

—VOYA

"Every page is an adventure in this fantastic story. The writer takes us from strange and compelling to eerie and off-the-wall scenarios that literally keep you hooked until the very last page."

—Feathered Quill Book Reviews

"Layne exposes the deficits of a Utopian society with a unique and alarming twist that adolescent readers will particularly enjoy."

—ALAN Review

PARADISE LOST

BY STEVEN L. LAYNE

PELICAN PUBLISHING COMPANY
Gretna 2013

First printing, January 2011
First paperback edition, January 2013

The word "Pelican" and the depiction of a pelican are trademarks
of Pelican Publishing Company, Inc., and are registered in the
U.S. Patent and Trademark Office.

Library of Congress Cataloging-in-Publication Data

Layne, Steven L.
  Paradise lost / by Steven L. Layne.
    p. cm.
  Sequel to: This side of Paradise.
    ISBN 978-1-58980-590-3 (hardcover : alk. paper)—ISBN 978-1-45561-
775-3 (pbk. : alk. paper) [1. Robots—Fiction. 2. Utopias—Fiction. 3.
Science fiction.] I. Title.
  PZ7.L44675Par 2011
  [Fic]—dc22
                                2010038316

Cover and interior art designed by Nathan R. Baron

Printed in the United States of America
Published by Pelican Publishing Company, Inc.
1000 Burmaster Street, Gretna, Louisiana 70053

I am often asked by students around the world to identify *my* favorite authors for young adults and to explain *why* they are my favorites. I have given the same answer for the past fifteen years: Neal Shusterman, Margaret Peterson Haddix, and Joan Bauer. I have given the same reason for fifteen years: The hearts that guide their hands are worthy of medals.

So . . . to Neal, to Margaret, and to Joan, with deep gratitude for those you have inspired and for those you will inspire. You have surely worked your magic on me.

Acknowledgments

Talk about fun! This book has been a tremendous joy for me to write, and I have grown to care about these characters more than I had imagined possible. What began years ago as a book written on a dare from a reluctant reader has certainly gained incredible momentum. I would be remiss not to say that my treasured friend and colleague Val Cawley, who was teaching right across the hallway from me when I wrote the original *Paradise,* has remained just as involved in this book—and it is all the better because of her dedication to the characters and to me.

Thanks to my homegrown editorial crew: Val Cawley, Lori Sabo, Sue Roberts, and Joy Towner, who are ever so helpful as I try to turn in a manuscript that is as publication-ready as possible. I would also like to give a nod to the tremendously talented Nathan Baron—the graphic designer who works so closely with me on the jacket art of my young adult titles. I make him crazy, but he secretly loves working with me; at least that's what I tell him. I must send a huge shout-out to the wonderful folks at Pelican Publishing who truly define teamwork each time we bring a new title forward. And to Jamie Fredericks, Beverly Johnson, and their team at the Courtyard by Marriott in West Dundee, Illinois— thanks for taking such good care of me on my writing retreats!

Several 2009-2010 student groups helped pilot this novel and provided feedback along the way. My gratitude to . . .

Dr. Karen Biggs-Tucker and her fifth-grade class from Wild
Rose School in St. Charles, Illinois; Mrs. Valerie Cawley and
her seventh-grade class from Butler Jr. High School in Oak
Brook, Illinois; Mrs. Jodi Keithley and her fifth-grade class at
Des Moines Christian School in Des Moines, Iowa. Mrs. Peggy
Short, Mrs. Desiree Streib, and Mr. Miguel Gonzalez and their
seventh-grade classes from Sky View Middle School in Colorado
Springs, Colorado.

Everyone who knows my dynamite wife, Debbie, and our great
kids, Grayson, Victoria, Jackson, and Candace, realizes that I
couldn't do what I do without their tremendous support and love.
I also deeply appreciate our extended family members who are
always pushing me forward. I will also say, mostly for my wife's
benefit, that I work better when I have a collie in my study with
me—thanks to faithful Shelby who could give Lassie a run for
her money. A special shout-out to my niece Alexa, who read the
book right off of my computer every chance she was given, and
to Sage Hoyt, a true fan (with a very famous dad) and the book's
first "true" reader.

Finally, my gratitude is to the Maker of all things for allowing
me the life, the time, and the talent to craft stories that I hope
will entertain the young—and the young at heart.

Chapter 1

Chase Maxfield has been in school with me since kindergarten. He wasn't the kind of kid who got noticed back then, and I can't say things improved over the years. One look at him would lead you to suspect his favorite color was gray—better yet, white. When Chase Maxfield was your lab partner in chemistry, he was likely to have trouble getting you to do something as simple as hand him a beaker. Why? Because you didn't hear him the first time, and you didn't see him the second time—even though he was standing right next to you. If there was a "most likely to go unnoticed" award at Davenport High, Chase would have been the sure vote-getter, and everyone knew it. Until the first day of my senior year, that is, when I saw a transformation that rivaled any "extreme makeover," televised or not, that the world is likely ever to see.

Jori and I were headed down the main hallway at a slow and easy pace. When the economy tanked and her dad lost his job last spring, the appeal of housing prices in Davenport sent the McAllister family scurrying in our direction with no complaints from my brother Troy or me. This year I was showing up for the first day of school sporting something a whole lot more interesting on my arm than a new watch; I wanted everybody to get a good look at Jori walking the halls with me. Unfortunately, the crowd's attention was already riveted on my younger sibling, a guy who's never known a stranger and who loves the spotlight.

"Ohhhh, Troy!" I heard the cackle of Bunny Fewtajenga's

unmistakable voice. "That was incredible! I mean a complete back flip right here in the hallway—and without a mat—you could have been killed!"

"Or given three weeks detention." The crowd parted just enough to allow Jori's sister Julie to make her way over to Troy.

Bunny regarded Julie coolly, then inched closer to Troy and grabbed his left arm with both hands. "Guys like Troy Barrett don't worry about the rules. At least that's what I've heard. Is it true, Troy?" She leaned into my brother in a vain attempt to become his co-conspirator and loudly whispered into his ear for all to hear, "'Cause that's the rumor, Troy. That you don't care about rules."

The crowd had grown larger. Troy, normally so relaxed in a big group, was clearly one nervous boy right now. He had little to fear though because Julie wasn't the shy type. The kids at Davenport High didn't know her yet, so they certainly didn't know that she and Troy had been an item all summer long, but I had a feeling by the way her eyes were targeting Bunny's that everybody was about to find out. "There is *one* rule that Troy cares a whole lot about. And it's one of mine," Julie cautioned.

"Oh, and what's that?" Bunny countered.

"Don't touch the merchandise unless you're sure it's available." Julie grabbed Troy's other arm firmly, and in one fast and unexpected burst of power, Jori's little sis left Bunny empty-handed. "And in the case of Mr. Barrett here, there's zero availability."

A rising "Ooohhhh!" erupted from the crowd. "Catfight!" someone else called, and the girls might have gone at it, too, had Chase Maxfield not arrived on the scene at precisely that moment.

His hand was on my shoulder, moving me to the side so he could step through, before I did a triple-take. "Excuse me, Jack," was all he said, and the comment wouldn't have been such a big deal from anyone else. But Chase Maxfield didn't move anybody out of the way for anything. He didn't talk to most people period.

Jori looked at him admiringly, and I felt a twinge of jealousy. "Who's *that?*" she questioned. It was clear he'd commandeered her attention at least for a minute. More amazing than that, though, was the fact that as soon as he stepped into the center of the group, he effortlessly drew all of the attention away from my brother. And that is something I had never seen happen. Not anytime. Not anywhere. Nobody had ever reigned over Troy . . . until now.

"What's up guys?" Chase tried to hoist himself onto the window ledge but didn't make it. On his second attempt he met with some success although it was still a bit awkward; he looked great, but he was clearly struggling to act cool. "The . . . uhhh . . . the bell's gonna ring soon, right? So are we gonna be good little boys and girls on the first day of school, or are we gonna have some . . . some fun?" The entire speech came out as if a studious egghead was desperately trying to impersonate a rebellious jock.

"Chase?" Bunny was the first to find her voice. I suspected most of the crowd was trying to remember his name, but Bunny made it her business to know everybody. Those who did recognize Chase, like me, were trying to reconcile an irreconcilable transformation. "Chase Maxfield?" Bunny was going to do the work for us—clarify if what we were seeing could possibly be real.

A dazzling smile made from perfectly white teeth marched out of his mouth, took a bite out of the crowd, and hung on tight. He looked like he had left Mt. Olympus a few minutes before arriving at school. "Hey, Bunny! Yeah, it's me, Chase."

She began stammering. "But you . . . you . . . you're just so . . ."

"Ripped!" somebody yelled. And it was true. Somehow, beanpole Chase suddenly had muscle. A lot of muscle. And that wasn't the only difference. His hair was dyed or streaked—something that looked movie-star cool. A survey of his clothes broadcast the message that he now spoke fluent Abercrombie whereas before it had been more of a cross-dialect: Target and Wal-Mart.

Seconds after Chase confirmed his identity, the crowd became toddlers, each waiting for a turn on Santa's lap, and Troy was suddenly scoring a "0" on the High School Hottie register for the first time in his life. He couldn't take it. "Hey! Anybody want to hear about the time I . . ."

"They have other things to occupy their thoughts right now," Julie said with a concerned glance toward both Chase and the crowd. "Besides, Mr. Barrett, you and I need to have a little chat about *Bunny.*"

"Bunny? Bunny who?" he questioned innocently.

Julie's eyes flashed.

"Ohhhhh, *that* Bunny! Oh, well, you see Jules, she was . . . uhhh . . . she . . . she was president of the student body when she was in middle school, and uhhh, and then she was freshman class president last year. How about that?" He clapped his hands as though he'd just thought of some terrific news that Julie was sure to love. "I bet she's going to run for president of the sophomore class this year at Davenport High! I think she's into politics, Jules. Don't you think?"

Julie's face was Mt. Rushmore. She didn't even blink.

Troy danced nervously from one foot to the other and continued babbling. "She's just . . . well, I'll tell you about Bunny, she's sort of . . . You know what's really funny, and I'm sure you're gonna find this quite humorous, Jules . . ."

Julie had her hand on her hip, one eyebrow arched, waiting for him to create a coherent sentence. "Troy! She's clearly after you."

He interrupted her. "Jules, she's just trying to get to know the student body!"

"Well, *yours* is one student body with which she's going to be a little less familiar than she might like," was Julie's clipped response. She marched him off in the opposite direction, but I saw her glance back one more time. Her eyes met Chase's, and suddenly it seemed that time stopped. They studied each other, and in that moment, I became certain they knew each other very well, which seemed incredibly unlikely. The McAllisters hadn't been in town that long. Neither of the sisters would have had any reason to know anyone at Davenport High well at all, so Chase's metamorphosis from toad to prince shouldn't have even registered with Julie. So why did I see a look in her eyes that reflected disappointment? She shook her head almost imperceptibly from side to side and turned quickly away from him.

I was so attuned to the two of them that I didn't see or hear anything else. I could feel Jori's faint tugging on my arm, but I tuned her out.

There was something unnatural going on here. Chase's new Hercules-come-to-life exterior was completely incompatible with his socially awkward interior. It was as if he'd become a different person on the outside but the inner-geek remained untouched. More than anything, it was the look I saw in his eyes when they met Julie's that troubled me. It wasn't jealousy or even anger. No, it was fear. And it struck me, though I couldn't be absolutely sure, that he wasn't so much afraid *for* Julie, as he was afraid *of* her.

My grandmother rounded the access road to Sunny Days Retirement Home on two wheels and at what I was sure had to be twenty miles an hour over the speed limit. I kept quiet, though. I had learned a long time ago to stop lecturing her about safety or speeding.

"Jack, sports cars are made for adventure," she had told me one afternoon when I tried to point out the perils of drag racing. She had been trying to goad some college boys, who had handily beaten her in a race already, into giving her a chance to redeem herself. Her little red sports car and the two competing cars were resting comfortably at the park while the racing teams lounged on some picnic tables. "Come on fellas! Best two out of three—whadayasay?"

"Gram!" I had pleaded with her. "They won fair and square. Let it go. How about we ratchet the excitement level down a few notches and grab some ice cream?"

"Look, Jack," she had fussed with my windblown hair, "at my age, you never know how many adventures you have left—so

I'm determined to create my own. As long as you don't get in the way—you're welcome to come along. Start dragging me down, though, and I'll have to dump you."

I decided it might not be the best image for an up-and-coming high school senior to be dumped by his own grandmother, so from that day forward I began tightening my seat belt and biting my tongue. I assume our tongues are intended to last a lifetime, but driving with Gram is convincing me that I'll be looking at a tongue transplant by the time I'm twenty-five. She peeled into the parking lot of Sunny Days and skidded diagonally to a stop near the front doors. I winced. The tongue would be bleeding from this one. "You head on in, Jackie-boy, and see if the troops are getting organized for the Road Rally! I'm going to check in with some of the drivers who are here early, and then I'll join you," she said casually.

"Got it, Speed Racer!" I exited the car just before she put the wheels in motion again to find a legitimate parking spot. Anyone who'd ever met my grandmother would have to agree that she was one of the unrecognized wonders of the modern world. At seventy-three, she acted more like seventeen; her hearing aid was the only telltale sign of her age. She had loads of cash from a business empire she and my grandpa Amos built together, so she certainly didn't need to work. Yet here I was, entering a retirement home that she and her best friend, Florence Petrillo, had purchased so they could appoint themselves co-social activities directors. Gram and Florence treated it like a real job, and three days a week come rain or shine, one of them showed up for what could be nothing less than a two-hour extravaganza for the residents.

The decision to purchase Sunny Days had come about earlier in the year when two of Gram and Florence's longtime friends, the Emmerstine brothers, moved into the retirement home. Within a week Gram had heard nothing but complaints from "the boys," as she called them. When you're Gram's friend and you're unhappy, she takes action. She had decided to investigate and presented the results of her research to Troy and me over dinner.

"Boys, Sunny Days Retirement Home is a dud when it comes to action. Dear God in heaven, they had Waldo and Wendell making 'apple people' in a craft class today. Why these are vivacious young men with a lot of living left in them—and they're being treated like kindergarteners!"

Troy poured honey onto two hot dogs he'd just nuked in the microwave, took a bite from each dog, and started to talk while chewing, but Gram shot him a warning look. He swallowed in the nick of time and then quickly attempted to make his point. "Gram, Waldo Emmerstine's in a wheelchair, and he's gotta be close to eighty or something. I'm not sure 'vivacious' is really the best descriptor."

"Troy Barrett! Have you ever seen that man get around? Why he can do things with a wheelchair most people couldn't dream of accomplishing with two legs. Now he and his brother Wendell are absolutely right about that place. It's dullsville. Florence and I went over their yesterday to check things out for ourselves."

"Oh?" I grinned. "So you two are speaking again?" Florence Petrillo may be my grandmother's best friend, but Troy and I think of her as Gram's friendly enemy. Truth be told they couldn't live without one another, but their insatiable competitive streak leads to some pretty serious fireworks now and then. The week prior, neither would speak to the other because they'd both shown up to local tryouts for a national reality show without telling the other. Neither of them made it past the first round of auditions, but each was incensed that her "best friend" had kept it all a secret. Gram had stomped into the living room that afternoon in an absolute rage. "That Florence Petrillo is a no-good, two-faced, back-stabbing old crow! I don't know why I was ever friends with that woman!"

Troy and I remained calm. We were accustomed to these bimonthly rants about Florence, but we were careful not to let Gram know how humorous we found them. We also knew that Florence's granddaughters, Mia and Tia, were likely listening to a similar eruption from their own grandmother.

"You are friends with her because you have *been* friends with her ever since she beat up the third-grade boy who pushed you off the swing when you were a little first grader," I pointed out. We'd heard the story a hundred times. Over the years, Gram's version of this great tale of heroism had placed Florence firmly in the same category as various highly regarded U.S. generals and presidents as well as several movie stars and Olympic athletes.

Troy chimed in. "You are friends with her because she was the matron of honor at your wedding, because she was in the waiting room while your son was born, and because she never left your side for the sixteen days Grandpa was dying in the hospital."

My turn. "You are friends with her because you have vacationed all over the world together, because you share each other's clothes, and because your cell numbers are only a digit apart."

Gram had plopped into her favorite chair. "Well, she *did* leave the hospital once when Amos was dying. You probably didn't know that, but she did. And don't you ever let her tell you any different. She left me there. Alone. My supposed best friend."

Troy and I looked at each other and repeated the words in unison to a story we had heard often but which Gram continued to insist she had likely never told us. It was always the same story but depending on the status of the friendship, the blueberry scones that made an appearance at the story's end were either incredibly delicious or absolutely tasteless. Troy nodded at me, and we began. "Florence left the hospital for two hours and eleven minutes. You remember because you were watching the clock. She drove to three different grocery stores to find the rarest of ingredients so she could follow a recipe that your sister, Favorite Aunt Millie, got from a Sherpa with whom she and her faithful dog, Mr. Whizzer, were exploring in the eastern Himalayas. Florence then carefully followed the recipe to the letter to make your favorite blueberry scones and serve them to you in the hospital while they were still warm." I don't know about Troy, but I always felt the need to say "Amen" whenever we completed this particular recitation.

"Those scones were dry as dirt," Gram proclaimed, "I hardly touched them!" Troy and I had debated for years whether we should ask about the likelihood of a Sherpa making blueberry scones but decided to leave well enough alone. Favorite Aunt Millie's tendency to stretch the truth gave her stories zest, and we'd been told countless times by Gram that her sister abhorred stories lacking such an essential component. Besides, Gram assured us, "I'd never get Millie to admit it happened any other way, and you both know it."

The falling out with Florence had been seven days ago, so

apparently they had patched things up and not told us, which was the way these things usually happened. "Well, of course, we're speaking again. Florence apologized." Troy and I both cocked our heads toward her and waited. ". . . and I might have mentioned that I was sorry, too. Anyway, that's all in the past. Florence had the ingenious idea that we pretend one of us was a potential client for Sunny Days and the other was just her friend coming along to listen and take notes."

"And *who* played the part of the 'potential client' for a retirement home?" Troy looked at me with a mischievous smile.

"Well, Florence, naturally."

"Reeeeaaaally?" I didn't buy it. "Florence just agreed right off the bat that she would pretend to be the one who was interested in moving into the retirement home?"

Gram fluffed her hair, which is always an indication that she's not telling the entire truth. Her sister isn't the only one with a habit of adjusting the facts. "Well, Jack, Florence can't help the fact that she looks so much older than me. It only made sense that it would be her."

I stared her down without saying a word.

"We flipped for it, and she lost, okay? But the point is that we spent three and a half hours there, and while most of what we were told was the absolute truth—jived with everything Waldo and Wendell said about the place—the spiel about activities wasn't grounded in an ounce of reality. Engaging outings—that's what they call trips to the pharmacy and the mall. And 'Music Night'! Do you know what they call 'Music Night'? It's people picking a title from a hymnal, and everyone singing off key with no accompaniment."

Troy hopped up from the table and cartwheeled into a handspring. "Hey, speaking of hymnals, do you guys know what's really funny? You put the words 'under the bed' after the title of a hymn during church and try not to laugh during the sermon. It's a stitch! Seriously. Like *Whispering Hope* . . . under the bed, or *Nearer My God to Thee* . . . under the bed! He doubled over in laughter. I love that one!"

"Troy," Gram sounded exasperated, "I taught you that three years ago when we had that new minister—the one who always ran the church service over by thirty minutes." She looked away dreamily for just a moment. "He sure was *cute*. Too bad he married that boring organ player, Franny HoHum."

"*Hodrum* not HoHum. I've corrected you on that before, Gram." When Gram gets something in her head one way—good luck changing it. "And she was not boring. She was very nice. She just wasn't all that fast at the keyboard."

"Seeing as how people were falling asleep at weddings during the bridal march, Jack, I'd say 'slow at the keys' is an understatement. The focus of our conversation, though, is on the fact that Sunny Days is not a hotbed of senior activity, and Florence and I are seeing to it that things get changed."

"And just how, o' great and wise grandmother, do the two of you intend to do that?" I queried in a mystical voice.

"Oh, we're buying the place: fifty-fifty. She owns one half, and I own the other. By the end of the week, the deal will be all sewn up, and then we're appointing ourselves co-social activities directors. We'll plan events for the residents together, and then one of us will actually do the implementation work every other month. It'll be wild!"

"Cool!" Troy was unruffled as usual.

"GRAM! You're just going to BUY a retirement home because you don't like the hymn-sing on 'Music Night'?" I probably shouldn't have been as surprised as I was.

"Now, Jack Edward Barrett, don't you take that tone with me. I will not have my friends condescended to like they're a couple of drooling toddlers. Waldo and Wendell and all of the other people at Sunny Days are full to the brim with life. When Florence and I take over, these people aren't going to know what hit them."

And she had been right. In a matter of months, Gram and Florence Petrillo had turned Sunny Days into the place to be among retirees from cities as far as ninety miles outside of town. There was a waiting list of people who wanted to get in, and the local television stations and newspapers regaled in weekly tellings of the unique "goings-on" at Davenport's most exciting retirement facility.

I walked up the paver brick path of Sunny Days and glanced at the large number of flowers someone had probably planted back in early May. I wondered how many other high school seniors would be spending the late afternoon of their first day of school at a retirement home. This, though, was my legacy. Gram insisted on community service well beyond the high school's requirements, which should have ended halfway through the sophomore year for me. I began my stint at Sunny Days in June, so the staff and residents pretty much knew me by now. How was it, I thought as I mindlessly signed in at the reception desk, that I was here with the AARP crowd, and Troy was browning in a lifeguard chair at the city pool? I took some comfort in the fact that he'd be serving up some hash early on

Saturday morning at the downtown shelter while I'd be sleeping in until ten.

My wage-earning endeavors were confined to Saturday afternoons shelving books at the library and to my meager lawn-care/snow-removal business with Mrs. Petrillo as my only customer—that is when she and Gram weren't fighting. It had become an understanding between Florence and me that I was fired whenever Gram made her mad, but that I would be immediately rehired when they made up. I lost track of the number of times the two of them were fighting just before payday. Collecting a paycheck from a seventy-five-year-old who refuses to come to the door because she's mad at a woman you're related to is a unique skill—one I clearly do not possess.

As I made my way into the community room, which opened into a large dining area, I heard the familiar voices of Gram's biggest fans, the Emmerstine brothers.

"She's a comin'! She's a comin' I tell ya! I see Jack!" Waldo Emmerstine's wheelchair nearly popped a wheelie as he prepared to leave the dining hall.

"She won't be here for another twenty minutes, you old fool!" Waldo's brother, Wendell, picked up the false teeth lying on the tray beside his half-finished apple tart and popped them into his mouth. "And when she does get here, it'll be *my* good company she'll be seeking." Wendell smoothed back his nearly full head of snow-white hair and carefully rose from the table.

Waldo wheeled over to his brother. "Well, if she ain't a-goin' to be here for another twenty minutes, then what are you in such a confounded rush about? Worried, maybe, that she's gonna accept my marriage proposal, ain't ya?"

Wendell looked slyly at his brother and grinned. Before any of the other residents knew what to say or do, the two elderly men began moving with surprising speed toward the community room, and I stepped back to keep from becoming road kill. They had no more than settled in and begun to quarrel again when Gram's voice stopped them.

"Now, if you handsome young men are going to be arguing all afternoon, I'll have to ask you to leave!" Her eyes sparkled as she greeted the brothers each with a warm embrace and a kiss on the cheek. Then, she knelt beside the wheelchair, settled the oversized tote she called her makeup bag on the floor, and removed a wrapped package from it. "When I saw these on the Home Shopping Network, I just knew you had to have a set, Waldo. Happy Birthday!"

Waldo looked up at his brother with a cocky smirk. "Why, Katy-gal, the only present I want from you is an 'I do' in a church, lickety-split!" He spoke with lighthearted affection as he unwrapped the gift.

"Old fool," muttered Wendell under his breath. "Kathryn wouldn't marry you if you was the last . . ." Gram shot him a warning look that effectively silenced his grumbling just as his brother lifted the lid of the box. Waldo looked suspiciously at the slender handles and what looked like cut stone pieces attached to them with leather straps.

"They're tomahawks!" Gram said with delight. "Three different sizes, too! The target is on back order for another few weeks, but I thought we could start practicing on one of those beat-up old closet doors in the activity room after the Road Rally today! You have to keep those arm muscles strong, Waldo. You know what the doctor said."

Howard Breen, assistant director of Sunny Days, rushed over just as Gram was discussing her gift. He took one look at the weapons in Waldo Emmerstine's lap, and the color began to drain from his face as it did almost every time Gram arrived at the home. Howard was generally at odds with Gram and Florence over safety issues. I pitied the man. He had been assistant director for fifteen years, and the fallout of any disaster would be his. He'd had a perfect record until the Dynamic Duo bought the place and turned his world and his safety record upside down.

No one had been irreparably injured, and Gram was always quick to point that out. However, that was of little comfort to a man in Howard's position. I sometimes wondered why they didn't fire him, but I think both Gram and Florence knew that he was really good at his job. He just wasn't adjusting to them as quickly as they'd hoped. Seeing as how I had known them all of my life and I was still adjusting to them, I felt a strange kinship with Howard.

"Mrs. Barrett! This is highly irregular. I know that you mean well, but tomahawks are most definitely not included on our residents' list of approved assets." He reached for the package in Waldo's lap, "Mr. Emmerstine, I'll just take these out of your way and—ohhh—I just remembered! Sara," he called to one of his staff . "Sara, do you have Mr. Emmerstine's gift from us?" Sara quickly arrived as if she'd been cued in advance and presented a small wrapped package, which Waldo greedily tore into.

"Yeeeehaaawww! This is one exciting birthday," he hollered removing an egg-shaped piece of plastic from the box. "What in tarnation . . . ?" Waldo fussed for a moment until Wendell reached over his shoulder and pulled the two pieces of plastic apart to reveal a light brown egg-shaped piece of Silly Putty. I shuddered to think what Gram was going to say when she realized that the staff's birthday gift for Waldo amounted to a predecessor of Play-Doh. Wendell handed the gift back to Waldo who looked quizzically at it for a moment and then said, "Well, candy's always good, Howard, candy's always good!" And before anyone could stop him, Waldo scooped up the putty and popped it into his mouth.

"WALDO!" Gram screamed.

"MR. EMMERSTINE!" Sara and Howard stammered along with me.

But Waldo's mouthful had gone in too quickly and immediately began to cause trouble. He had somehow managed to get at least a portion of it lodged in his throat within seconds, and he began wheezing and gasping in no time.

"CALL 911!" Howard's voice rang out dramatically toward the main office, and, still holding Gram's gift box, he knelt down in front of Waldo. "Mr. Emmerstine, hang on! Hang on, now. Help is on the way."

Wendell did not appear to be the least bit flustered by his brother's dilemma. He took two steps toward a sofa table and picked up one of the infamous Sunny Days hymnals, then stepped back into his previous position behind his brother. "Old fool!" was all he said as he raised the hymnal with both hands and used it to unceremoniously slap his brother on the back with considerable force.

"Ffffffffththhhhtttttt!"

A large chunk of saliva-covered putty rocketed out of Waldo's mouth and landed in Howard Breen's hair! Nobody moved.

Then, Gram knelt down for just a moment, took the box with the tomahawks from Howard's hands, stood again, and placed it back into Waldo's lap.

She tugged at her tight-fitting sweater anxiously and appeared to be searching for words. Finally, she said, "You are quite right, Howard. They were not on the residents' list of approved assets . . . until about ten minutes ago." She held out her Blackberry. "I sent Florence a text on my way in, and . . . oh, lookee here, Howard!" She knelt on the floor beside him again and showed him her Blackberry. See right there under T? Tomahawks as clear as day. Mind you, it's not correctly alphabetized, but I'll handle that later. Florence is getting older, you know, and spelling's always the first thing to go."

"Whooo, boy! I'm gonna have me some fun with these!" cried Waldo, and he looked right at Howard Breen as he said, "Don't mess with me, Howie, or I'll scalp ya! Heh! Heh! Heh!"

The rest of the afternoon was smooth sailing as we assisted the Sunny Days residents in a highly spirited road rally and returned on time with no casualties—much to Howard's amazement. As the residents were seated for dinner, Gram began mapping out plans on an easel for a massive Twister marathon, and the audience cheered. My cell vibrated, and I saw that it was Troy.

"So, what's up, Sun God? You calling to rub it in?" I teased.

"Jack, how fast can you get to the pool?" His voice was intense.

"I'm with Gram, Troy. That ought to answer the fast question, except she's laying out some of her future plans with the crowd here. I'm not sure how soon she'll be done. What's got you all hot and bothered anyway, Mr. Lifeguard? They run out of suntan oil?" I wanted to hear the edge come out of his voice. No luck.

"Jack, get in the car. Now. Tell Gram you need to run an errand or tell her the truth for all I care, but I need you to get over here."

I could feel my frustration growing exponentially. "Troy, it'd be kind of hard to tell her the truth since you haven't shared with me just exactly what that might be! What's going on? You haven't sounded like this since . . ." I didn't want to go there. I didn't want to think about how our lives had been turned upside down a year ago. How we had lost our mother—and our father, too, depending on how you looked at it.

"Jack, Chase Maxfield is here . . . at the pool. He's been doing incredible stuff all afternoon off the boards and . . ."

I relaxed. "Let me give you some advice, Little Bro. You are not always gonna be the number one ticket in town. It's a good thing for you to take a back seat for once and . . ."

"Jack, would you *listen?* That's not it, okay. That's not the issue. The stuff he's doin' is flippin' unbelievable!"

"So, maybe his folks paid for a coach or maybe . . ."

"There was no coach, Jack. C'mon, Man! We're talking about Chase. When we left school for summer break, he could have blown away in a strong breeze, and now he's ready for the Olympic diving team? What coach does that in twelve weeks? He's drawn a huge crowd of interested bystanders, Jack, and one of them looks *scary* familiar. You get my meaning?"

The hair on the back of my neck stood on end, and my gut tightened. I didn't want to have this conversation. I had my nice normal life back, and I wanted to keep it that way. "I don't know, Troy. Okay, I'll admit it's a little freaky, but Chase Maxfield is not the first person to ever . . ."

"I saw him, Jack."

I nearly dropped the phone. The room was spinning. Why? Because my brother's voice was deadly scary, and because without him saying another word, I knew exactly who he meant.

"Jack, are you there? Did you hear me? I said I *saw* him. He was watching Chase. I know it's not possible, but I know who I saw, and I'm right, Jack. I know I'm right."

My mouth was so dry I didn't think I could speak, but my hoarse voice finally muttered a few words of explanation that I knew he wouldn't buy. "Troy . . . you've been in the sun all afternoon. The mind. You know, your mind can play . . ."

"Jack, would you get over here?" I'd only heard his voice sound this desperate once before. A year ago. I closed my eyes and leaned against a pillar for support. "I saw him, Jack. He was here. Today. For just a minute . . . and then he was gone. Jack, Mr. Eden's alive."

Chapter 2

What to do, what to do? He glanced impatiently at his watch. The call would come soon; he just had to be patient a little longer. He reached out and fingered the picture frame on his desk, angling it backward so the sun lit up the amazing woman in the photo. Looking into her eyes always calmed him—but not as much as seeing her in person. It was Tuesday. He would see her later today, for dinner. But what should she wear? He hit the intercom feature on his phone. "Constance?"

"Yes, Sir," came the prompt reply.

He sighed with satisfaction. It was a comfort knowing that she would always answer. Immediately. Constance was an amazing administrative assistant because she never left her desk without permission. And since she was rarely given permission, she was generally at her desk. Her boss might have exacting standards, but Constance Oswald was conditioned to keep him happy. "I'd like to see her this evening, Constance. It's Tuesday." He sounded a bit nervous—just as he did each time he brought the subject up. She noted the tremor in his voice but said nothing. He wouldn't like it if she noticed, so she pretended she did not.

"I can arrange for that, Sir. Do you have a preference on dress?"

He paused to consider. "Formal. And I think green would be nice."

"I'll be sure that it's green, Sir. Do you have a shading request? Perhaps mint?"

"No. No, mint is too pale. I'd like something more vibrant,

Constance. Perhaps, emerald? Yes, I believe emerald would be *perfect*."

"Of course, Sir. She'll be in emerald green. I'll note that for the future."

He looked at the picture again with soft eyes. "It should always be emerald green, Constance, because it goes so well with her auburn hair."

Their phones simultaneously lit up with an incoming call. He was anticipating this call, but of course, he could not answer his own phone. His finger reflexively stabbed the button to disconnect the intercom—a clear signal that Constance should now turn her attention to the caller. A moment later, she buzzed him.

"Call for you, Sir."

He reached greedily for the receiver. Speakerphone was more his style, but in this case, he wanted to tangibly feel his involvement with the call. "See that I'm not interrupted."

"Yes, Sir."

He didn't bother with a greeting. "Is it done? Is the Emissary in place? Good. Is the Barrett boy aware?" A devilish grin crossed his lips. "Excellent. How about the younger one? What did you find out? Lifeguarding, ehhhh? You know, my friend, a lot of tragic accidents happen each year near the water, don't they? I certainly hope he takes his job seriously. And what about the girl? A hospital gift shop. You don't say?" He ran his finger across the top edge of his desk searching for dust that wouldn't dare to show itself. "That's ridiculous! I'm not worried about an old woman meddling in my plans. She can be easily taken care of if it becomes necessary. Stop worrying. You give her too much credit. What? No." He shook his head at the insanity being suggested. "NO! I can't bother with those things personally at this point. It's too soon for me, much too soon. For now, a few sightings will have been enough to engage them. We need to have patience. Let the Emissary complete the first phase. There's too much going on right now for me to be away . . . but I agree. I do agree that a personal visit is in order. Ahhhh, yes, there's nothing quite like a visit—*from family*." He reached for the photograph again. "It just can't be me. Not me . . . not yet."

Chapter 3

Gram seemed to believe the story I made up about Troy losing his ride home. She tossed me the car keys and continued with her explanation of exactly how "partner elimination" was going to work for Twister. She held the rapt attention of her audience, and for a brief moment, the good humor and joyful spirit of Sunny Days Retirement Home enveloped me. And then I walked out to the car and thought about where I was going. My phone signaled that Jori was calling, and the bottom dropped out of everything. Gram had programmed a classic love song called "I've Got You Under My Skin" as Jori's ring tone on my phone. I could easily remember the day Jori first played the whole song and told me it said everything she'd ever wanted to say to me. I was on cloud nine.

"Hey! Have I told you lately how much I love hearing that song when you call?"

"Jack, someone's following me!" Her voice was bordering on hysteria, which was not at all like Jori. "I've been trying to tell myself it's not happening, but I'm sure I'm not imagining it."

"Jori, where are you? I'll call the police, and then I'll be right there."

"I'm in the parking garage at the hospital. Jack, please don't hang up. Stay with me. I'm going to try to get back inside the building, but . . ." She gasped suddenly. A quick intake of air like she'd either seen something terrible or been discovered by someone.

I couldn't hang up now; it would be like abandoning her. I

left the parking lot of Sunny Days the same way Gram entered it and pretended the speedometer was invisible. St. Anthony's Hospital, where Jori worked in the gift shop, was ten minutes away. I was going to make it in five. "Jori! Jori, what's happening? I'm coming!"

"Jack!" She croaked into the phone. I pictured her crouched low behind a rear automobile tire or perhaps even lying under a car. "Jack, hurry! I . . . umm . . . I think I saw . . ." She started to cry softly.

"Jori! I'm flying. Stay hidden. Are you hidden? I'll be there. Who is it? It's a guy, right?" It was always a guy in the movies. "Has he seen you?" No response. Now that I thought about it, what a dumb question. How could he be following her if he hadn't seen her? "Jori! Jori, please say something!"

"Jack!" she was whispering. "Just hurry. Hurry, please! Jack, *I saw him!*"

A flash fire erupted throughout my nervous system. Those were exactly the words Troy had used! But they didn't have to mean the same thing, I reminded myself. So why were my hands suddenly shaking at the steering wheel? I sailed through two stoplights just as they were turning from yellow to red—what Gram calls "taking a light on pink" and which she insists is "perfectly legal in the eyes of the law"—a view she has managed to persuade at least half of the traffic cops in Davenport to share. "Okay. Okay, so we know it's a guy." I saw no advantage whatsoever in following up on the implication that we did, in fact, quite likely know exactly who the guy was. "That helps because we're going to nail him. I'll get you out of there, and we're going to go to the police, and they will nail this creep." I had to keep her talking, keep her from allowing fear to completely paralyze her. Still, this was so unlike her. Jori was a black belt in karate; Julie had told me stories of her sister taking down guys twice her size for just making the wrong comment. Why had this particular guy spooked her so badly? Maybe it was because the parking garage was darker than outside. Still, it was only dusk. It couldn't be too dark in there. Maybe he had come at her when she wasn't anticipating it and she'd been thrown off guard. That could be it. And now she was just angry at herself for not being more aware and frustrated at her own lack of a G.I. Jane-type response. My car hit the garage ramp as I called into the phone again. "I'm here, Jori, I'm here. Where are you?" I hit my brights. I wanted to send all the light I could into the dim garage.

"Level 2, K. I'm lying in the bed of a white pickup. Jack, hurry!"

The minute I exited the ramp at level 2, I saw the truck. No hunting, no searching the aisles, there it was. I had her in my arms in no time, and as I held her, my eyes darted continuously all around, but I didn't see anyone. "It's okay, Jori. It's okay." She clung to me, which was 100 percent all right, but I felt a little guilty for enjoying it under the circumstances. A group of people exited the elevator and headed down the aisle toward us. They were singing and laughing, and their good cheer seemed to beat back the gloom. She released her grip slightly and stood facing me.

"Jori, did you recognize him? Did you see what he was wearing? When we get to the police station, you're going to need to tell them as much as you can remember." I was speaking calmly because I knew it would be important for her to review the details while they were still fresh in her mind.

She grabbed the edges of my coat, leaned into me, and began

to tremble. "You want to know what he was wearing?" Her words were escaping between halting sobs. "I can tell you exactly what he was wearing, Jack. He was wearing a black trench coat and a hat—just like the last time we saw him. He looked just like he did on the night he died."

Troy was miffed. I was majorly late getting to the pool, and by the time I did arrive, there was no sign of anyone, let alone Mr. Eden. The entrance gate, which closed electronically at day's end, was still open, and I shot through quickly—thinking it might be coming to life any second. Troy was netting some gunk out of the pool with a skimmer, which I'm sure was one of the less attractive features of his job. He looked at me and put his eyes right back on the task at hand. "Remind me, Jack, to call someone else if I ever need any real timely help? What happened? You stop to buy Girl Scout cookies from every fourth grader in Davenport?"

"Ha! Ha! Very funny, Troy. Why don't you get some new material? How long are you gonna throw the Girl Scout thing in my face? It's okay to be nice once in awhile—especially to Girl Scouts. After all, I was . . ."

"An Eagle Scout, I know, I know. We all know. Trust me. But c'mon, Jack. Eighteen boxes of Thin Mints?"

"Troy, that was like eight months ago. Can you give it a rest?"

"I'm just sayin' it was a little excessive."

"What was excessive, Little Bro, was you chowing down the contents of seventeen out of the eighteen boxes I bought.

Besides, I had to help her. She hadn't sold a box all day, and she looked like she was about to cry."

"Jack, you are such a sucker! That's a gimmick, you dope. How do you think I was the top magazine subscription seller in elementary school from first grade through fifth? We sales folk salivate when a bleeding heart like you answers the door. Ha! She and her fourth-grade cronies probably laughed themselves silly the minute you closed the door."

"Not true! You didn't see her. She was a very sweet little girl. She had pigtails! I couldn't very well say no to her."

"Well, those were some very sweet Thin Mints, too," he countered, "and I couldn't very well say no to them either."

I cracked up then and so did he. Our fights never last longer than ten minutes.

He walked to the other side of the pool and went to work helping a combination of bugs and leaves make their exit from the water.

"So, where's the crowd?" I asked. The place was dead. "The gate's still open, so where are the people?"

"Aaah, something's up with the gate timer. I think it'll close at eight—don't ask me why they can't get it right. Wednesdays are a no-go for the swim crowd after seven o'clock once school starts."

"So since when did they let you close up shop alone? I thought you had to be older and 'more mature' to handle all this big responsibility?"

"Yeah, don't ya love it? I'm too young and innocent to clean the pool and lock the place up all by myself, but I'm okay to save a drowning victim." He gave a scornful laugh. "And you wonder why I have issues with rules? Anyway, Amber was supposed to close up, but when her ride came early and mine didn't come at all, I convinced her that I could handle the big challenge. It'll be our little secret from the insurance company. I just love sedition!" Troy doesn't have the most sophisticated vocabulary, but he's a walking thesaurus when it comes to terms for rebellion. He dropped the net down to touch the bottom, leaned on the long pole of the skimmer, and looked at me.

I stared back in silence. We were out of small talk, but we were still desperate to avoid the unavoidable. I didn't know about Troy, but for me, it felt like saying it aloud would make it real . . . and I sure didn't want that. Finally, he cracked. He looked down at the cement deck of the pool as if there were something terribly interesting there, even though we both knew there wasn't.

"No more sign of him. But he was here, Jack. He was here, and I really don't think he was watching me."

"Troy," I said forcefully. "If he was here and he was watching someone, we both know it was you."

"No, Jack, seriously. I can't explain why, but I think he was watching Chase Maxfield. I'm telling you it happened super fast, but his eyes were riveted on Chase."

Sometimes my brother could be so naïve. "That's what he wanted you to think, Troy! But trust me . . . it wasn't Chase. It was *you* he was watching. And it's only a matter of time before watching you won't be enough." Listening to my own words sent the hair on the back of my neck soaring toward the stratosphere again, but we were rescued from the intensity of the conversation by an incoming text.

Where r u? Gram! I had completely forgotten about her.

"Troy, it's Gram. How close are you to finishing? She's been waiting for awhile."

"Jack, I've got at least thirty minutes left. Go get Gram and come back for me. That should work out okay."

"What are you, crazy? I'm not leaving you here alone!"

"Good grief, Jack, I'm not twelve! I was alone before you got here, and as I recall you didn't seem in too much of a rush to arrive even after I called and told you I saw him."

"I was coming straight here, Troy. I got sidetracked . . . something with Jori." I didn't want to get into exactly what had happened to Jori until we had more time. She'd convinced me that going to the police was not the best course of action given the little-known back story of the last year of my life, which meant that Troy and maybe Julie would be the only other people to hear the story of her late afternoon stalker. Gram had spent a lot of money and called in a lot of favors to keep what happened in Paradise out of the public eye. Any discussion with the police of Mr. Eden's recent activities would be nothing more than our allegations at this point. Worse yet, in order for our allegations to be taken seriously, we'd be required to bring all of our secrets out into the open. Jori was right; the slightest leak about what went on in Paradise was sure to turn all of our lives into a complete circus—and that's exactly what Gram had worked so hard to avoid.

"Whatever. The point is I can take care of myself, Jack. I'll be fine. Geez, what are you going to be gone—twenty minutes? I don't need my big brother to protect me from the boogeyman, okay?"

I hesitated; I didn't want to leave him because of guilt—my own guilt over things that had happened a year ago. Things everyone maintains I had no control over. My brother survived, he insists, because of me. But all I can see is how I could have done things differently. How I should have seen what was coming. How I didn't do enough to protect him. "Tell you what," I said casually. "I'll just help you finish up here, and we can leave together."

He walked over, grabbed my shoulders, turned me toward the gate, and began marching me toward it. "I appreciate the sentiment Obi-Wan, but Luke Skywalker is growing up now. He must learn to stand on his own two feet." He shoved me through the gate. "I'll see ya in twenty. Until then," he pulled the skimmer dramatically across the front of his body, "I will keep my trusted lightsaber within easy reach."

I turned and put my hands on his shoulders. "Luke. May the Force be with you!"

He swatted me upside the head and turned back toward the pool. "Luke!" I croaked in a pained and dying voice. I was really getting into this. He turned back around. "Not a word about what happened today to Gram, right?"

He jumped right out of character. "Whadaya think I'm a complete doofus? Actually, Jack, I was thinking that tonight over dinner I might mention that the man who kidnapped me and tried to kill us all last year popped by the pool today to say, 'Hi.' You don't think that would unnecessarily upset her, do you?"

My sardonic younger brother could deliver a line like no one I knew. He shook his head at me in disbelief and jogged off. A minute later, I heard him rummaging around in a supply closet.

I stepped back through the gate, still reluctant to leave him, and scanned the pool area once more. A soft breeze was blowing, and lights around the pool area were coming on as dusk began its journey into night. The tidy cabanas all in a row on the south end of the pool, the deck chairs scattered here and there, and the fabulously clear water were all in place. Everything looked serene. The only movement came from Troy who was coming my way again. He was carrying a pair of giant-sized containers—each of which probably held enough chemicals to resurrect the dead. They were clearly heavy because he stopped to rest for a minute. As soon as he caught me watching him, though, he straightened his back and began a bicep work out—doing arm-curls with the jugs supplying the weight. "Hey! Just can't get enough of me, huh?" He laughed. "It happens all the time. I'm used to it by now, but just so you know, I wasn't resting back there. I was *repositioning,* Buddy-boy. Heck, I could do this in my sleep. This is how I keep these massive arms in such great shape!" Then came the trademark smile and dancing eyes that made him a favorite at parties.

"Okay. I'll try to remember that," I said and grinned at him. "I'll be back in a flash." I darted for the car and saw through the window that Jori was eagerly awaiting my return. I'd been inside longer than I'd intended, and after what she'd been through, I'm sure my lengthy absence made her nervous. As I slid behind the wheel, I still couldn't shake the idea that I was making a big mistake leaving Troy here alone, but I knew he was right. I couldn't look out for him every minute of the day. The tires of the little red sports car squealed just a bit as I pulled away from the curb, but for once that didn't bother me. The sooner we got back, the better I'd feel.

I pulled up to Sunny Days rather awkwardly. Gram was out

front, so I tried to do kind of a skid thing to impress her, and it
fizzled. "What was that?" she grimaced as I stepped out to move
into the tiniest back seat the world has ever known and give her
the driver's spot.

"That," Jori said giggling, "was Jack trying to drive like you,
Gram." She leaned back and patted my knee. "He can do the
speed thing okay when he has to, but our adorable Eagle Scout
can't make like Jeff Gordon to save his life."

"You can say that again!" Gram said. She peeled out of the
parking lot, and the back end of her car did a great impression of
a metronome; there went my tongue again. One good thing about
Gram driving—I could be sure we would get back to Troy really
fast. In fact, we arrived in what seemed like a nanosecond, and I
started pushing on the seat to get out as we skidded to a stop.

"Owww!"

"Jack? What happened?" Jori looked back at me, climbed out,
and pulled her seat forward to open the way for my escape.

"Nothing, nothing. I can tell you that I'm never getting a
tongue ring though."

We all looked up at the sound of a fairly large splash from
inside the pool area, and my adrenaline went haywire as I moved
faster than I can ever remember moving in my entire life.
"Jack? Do you want me to come . . ."

I had already crossed the road and saw that the gate was now
closed, and, I was sure, locked. The chain-link fence was pretty
high. I couldn't vault it, but I could surely climb it. I had to . . .
and fast. Something bad had happened while I was gone. I never
should have left. I knew it. I *knew* it was a mistake to leave him,
and I would never do it again. "There shouldn't be any splashing.

There's no reason for any splashing," was my mind's refrain. I hauled myself up, creating toeholds as best I could and relying more heavily on the strength of my arms than I was accustomed to, but eventually I got there. I threw one leg over and straddled the fence so I could peer out across the abandoned deck to the water. There was a body in the water! I saw the bare chest trussed in ropes, the swim trunks—a familiar shade of orange—the ankles tightly bound. He was face down in the water. He was drowning. "TROY!"

Chapter 4

He entered the elevator and checked his watch. "Good evening, Sir. Chambers?" Cora knew the answer before she asked the question. She was smart enough, though, to ask.

"Chambers."

Her fingers shot out like lightning to press the correct series of numbers. The elevator panel lit up, and she stabbed the CH button with precision. "Practice makes perfect, Cora," he had told her years ago. She remembered it well as it was one of the only complete sentences he had ever spoken to her after bringing her to his training facility. The morning he had introduced himself while she was shelving books in the museum library, he had been quite talkative. He had showered her with flattery and offered her a position immediately with a fine salary and benefits at a new facility he was opening, but he had forced her to make an on-the-spot decision, to come with him right then and there. She wasn't allowed to know exactly what the job would be, and she had to leave with him and begin training immediately or he would give the opportunity to someone else. And Cora had done something wild and impulsive then. She'd said yes.

Training began later that morning, and within hours, she understood that she would not be allowed to leave. Ever. Training had lasted several weeks, hadn't it? She was never quite sure how long it had been. She'd been placed in a very large room with elevator panels hung on the walls all around. There had been a small cot for sleeping, and someone had brought her food and drink three times a day. She remembered her first look at the panels. They were labeled *Panel 1, Panel 2, Panel 3* . . . How many had there been? More than one hundred, she was sure. A mechanical voice would call out the requested floor, and her job was to input a code as quickly as possible. The code would activate the elevator panel—lighting it up—and she would then select the correct button within a certain amount of time. She had thought it would be quite simple, but it was very, very difficult. The voice was demanding, and she had to increase her speed each time. That voice made her nervous, but she had tried, really tried to do everything correctly. And then, on the third day, she had made a mistake—pressed a 4 instead of a 5, and it had cost her. It had happened on *Panel 53.* She gasped, perhaps audibly, at the painful memory. He looked up from his watch for the briefest moment, looked in her direction. Had he heard her? Her head began to pound. Drums beat loudly in each ear. It was hot, suddenly so hot. What was taking so long? Had she punched the wrong button again? No! Please, no! She did *not* press the wrong button. She did not make mistakes. Not anymore. She always punched the right buttons.

Cora's eyes were drawn to the very top of the elevator panel, but she would not look at it. She mustn't. No, she must not think about it right now. She willed the thoughts away. There is a smile that elevator ladies are supposed to wear at all times. *Everyone knows that.* She was wearing that smile right now. She would wear that smile, and she would not look at the top of the elevator panel. At last, the door chimed, and she breathed a quiet sigh of relief when he stepped off.

"Good night, Mr. Eden." She held her voice steady and

enunciated her words flawlessly. He would not respond. He never had. Not once in twelve years. The doors closed, she pressed the correct series of numbers, the panel lit up, and she selected L for lobby. For just a moment, her eyes stole a glance at the plaque hanging at the top of the panel. It read *Panel 53*. A tear made its way to the corner of one eye, but she did not allow it to escape.

Each year, on her birthday, Cora would enter the elevator and that plaque would be gone. It was the most incredible feeling not to see it anymore! She lived for the moment each year when she could revel in its absence. But her joy was always short-lived, for there would also be a wrapped package waiting for her on the small stool she used when her legs grew tired of standing. And each year, the small slip of paper on the package read, "For Cora—Always Remember." In the box was a shiny new plaque that read *Panel 53,* and she knew, though no one told her, that she was expected to hang the new plaque in the exact same location as its predecessor. That first year, she had been surprised when an evening messenger had arrived at her apartment with a wrapped package identical to the one left for her in the elevator that morning. The slip of paper on this package read, "For Cora—Happy Birthday." Inside was the old plaque. To look at it, you could not tell that it was any different from the one she had opened earlier in the day. But she knew it was the old one. Not knowing what to do with it, she had placed it in a drawer in her bedroom bureau. That had been many years ago. Now, she had a dozen.

He stopped outside The Chambers door. It was his custom to

straighten his tie before entering, and a mirror had been hung on
the wall to accommodate this necessity. He entered, saw the back
of her strapless emerald gown, and felt a rush of confidence.
He was certain that tonight's news would delight her beyond
measure. Slowly, he was winning her trust. He reached for a
wine glass some dutiful servant had already poured, took a long
drink, and set it down on the bar. The noise brought her circling
around. Her auburn hair was framed in the faint glow set off by
candlelight, and her green eyes matched the dress perfectly.

He had no intention of becoming upset tonight as he
sometimes did. No, tonight would be different. He was certain of
that because tonight they would talk about something she cared
very much about. He seated himself on the sofa and patted the
cushion next to him. "Come and sit."

She didn't take a step toward him right away—just looked at
him and tried desperately to hide her contempt as she always
did.

He smiled tolerantly. "Darling, let's make this a special
evening. Now, I'm planning something for one of the boys.
Come now, and sit with me. I'm quite certain, Susan, that you'll
be interested in the details."

Chapter 5

I had a not-so-graceful landing coming down from the fence, but at least I was still in one piece. Reinforcements were sure to be on the way because the shout I'd put forth was bound to bring Gram and Jori on the run. I had no idea how they would find a way in, but that obviously wasn't my chief concern at the moment. I raced across the pool deck and was diving for Troy when I collided with someone in midair, and we both hit the water in a mass of arms and legs. I don't know whether he grabbed for me first, or if it was the reverse, and I'm not sure whether we were trying to attack or to escape one another. All I knew for sure at that exact moment was that I needed to save my brother, and this guy was trying to stop me. My fists went flying underwater and made contact. I surfaced, took a big gulp of air, and headed back at him. Chlorine and I have never been the best of friends, so I was opening and shutting my eyes fast, but when I saw him go up for air, I dragged him back down. A solid uppercut to my chin told me he was getting serious, but I kicked him somewhere hard—the ribs maybe? I felt something give so I knew I got him good. Wham! He came down on my head. Two more splashes arrived in the water, probably Gram and Jori trying to get to Troy. I took a quick look and caught him heading back to the surface. Was he going up for more air, or was he going after Gram . . . or maybe Jori? I dropped to the bottom of the pool and sprung off it like a rocket, catapulting onto his back. Next, I locked my hands around his throat from behind. He tried to buck me off, but I stayed with him. When Jori arrived under the water and witnessed my death grip, she motioned for me to let him go. My eyes felt like they were on fire; I sealed them shut as I shook my head "no." Didn't she see that sympathy was not what this guy needed? He started to struggle, and I pressed harder on his throat—uttering a kind of Neanderthal grunt of triumph so she'd realize I was the hero in all this. And that's when my girlfriend karate chopped at a spot on my neck that sent pain cascading to areas of the body I didn't know existed. I instantly released my enemy, and we all came up for air.

I hit the surface determined to ignore the pain. I was ready to go at him again, but Jori was between us—pushing us apart. "STOP IT! Both of you! Stop it now!" My eyes widened in disbelief. The guy who collided with me diving into the pool, the one fighting with me in the water this whole time, the person I'd just been trying to choke the life out of . . . was my brother!

"TROY! What were you . . . ?"

"JACK, you called for ME, right?

Jori was exasperated. "You two are impossible!" She started climbing out of the pool.

Troy looked at her, then at me; I shrugged, and he continued. "Okay, so I'm in the pump room, and I hear this splash. Next thing I know, you're screaming my name so loud they probably heard you on Mars. I race out to the deck and see a guy in the water. Seeing as how I'm a lifeguard, I size up the situation immediately and say to myself, 'This guy is drowning.'"

I interrupted. "Now see, Troy, I'm *not* a lifeguard, but the ropes all over him and the thrashing of his body were just huge and big clues for me on the whole drowning issue."

"Those were a big help for me, too, but," he never slowed his pace, "how am I gonna save him when you're goin' all WWF in the water with me?"

"Well, I thought you were him!"

"Him, who?"

"Him, the bad guy, Troy. Him, Mr. Eden. Or him, one of Mr. Eden's playmates. I don't know. I obviously didn't know it was you."

"Well I figured out it was *you* pretty quick, but you wouldn't open your eyes long enough to . . ."

"That chlorine stings."

"And then you kicked me so hard, Jack, I had to start defending myself again."

"Oh, yeah, I got you in the ribs there, pretty good. Sorry about that, Man."

"It *wasn't* the ribs, Jack. And if Julie and I have odd-looking children some day, you remember it all stemmed from this."

We could have gone on like that for quite some time because we usually do, but a loud shout broke into our banter.

"NO! No, don't! Somebody help! Get this crazy lady away from me! She's gonna kill me!"

"Young man, stop all that hollering. No one is going to kill you for heaven's sake; I just saved your life—me and my Jungafloats! I'm sorry they're pink. I understand that doesn't go so well with your manly physique and all, but it was the only color left on the Home Shopping Network. It's a good thing I bought them when I did, too, because I couldn't have gotten you upright in the water all on my own without them."

"GRAM!" We yelled in unison and swam over to where Chase

Maxfield was lying on the cement deck of the pool being tended to by the matriarch of our family. The ropes that had bound him were sliced and thrown off to the side like serpents with severed heads. Gram's makeup bag was open with some of the contents strewn about. She was wearing a white lab coat with the words "The Dr. Is In" sewn onto one pocket. There was a large band wrapped around her head with a small mirror attached to it that I was sure she had no idea how to use. Chase had a blood pressure cuff on one arm and an old-fashioned thermometer had just been placed in his mouth.

Gram gestured toward the thermometer. "I didn't have a digital so we made do with this old girl. But don't move your tongue around too much," she warned Chase, "or you'll activate the switchblade trigger."

"Ahhh . . . Whhaaaa?" Chase's eyes were wide, and I felt sure his tongue was stationary.

She looked at Troy and me and inclined her head toward the thermometer sticking out of Chase's mouth. "It was $9.97 on the Home Shopping Network just last week. Only three hundred of them made in the world. Squirts violet ink that turns invisible, too. I can't wait to show Howard!" Gram elbowed Jori who had dried off as best she could and joined us. "How'd ya like my SuperStep, Sweetheart?"

"Gram, it was magnificent! Boys, just look at what your grandmother pulled out of her makeup bag to get me over that fence!" She gestured toward an enormous ladder leaning against the enclosure.

Gram looked particularly pleased. "Collapsible. Folds down to the size of a pencil case. It's also a flashlight *and* it translates

Urdu if you own the converter attachment . . . which . . . I . . . do!"
She removed the thermometer from Chase's mouth, then reached
toward the two plastic inflatable tubes that still encircled his
body and turned a tiny valve on each. In the blink of an eye, the
gigantic pink Jungafloats were the size of pennies. "Jori, Honey."
Gram motioned to her bag with her eyes, and Jori knew what to
do. She opened the bag, Gram tossed the pink pennies inside,
and the lid was quickly snapped shut. Neither Troy nor I were
ever allowed to look in Gram's makeup bag, but we were always
trying to steal a peek when the opportunity presented itself.
Those opportunities were rare now that we both had girlfriends
who adored our grandmother. Both Jori and Julie were like guard
dogs with Gram's bag. She had given each of them their own mini
versions, and though they didn't carry them all the time like she
did, they were just as protective of the contents. It was a female
conspiracy. Gram regarded the thermometer. "Okay, kiddo. Your
temp's fine. The blood pressure wasn't too bad when I first cut
you loose, so it ought to be fine now and your respirations are
back where I like to see them, too. You'll live. And I think we
can put these away now, too." She lifted a pair of defibrillator
paddles into view.

Chase's eyes widened, and I knew instantly that the paddles
had provoked his earlier cry of alarm. He looked at me and his
voice got panicky. "She was gonna use those on me, Jack. And I
was breathing! My ticker was working fine, and she almost . . ."

"I most certainly was not," Gram countered. I just wanted to
show you what they can do." She flipped a small switch on the
side and what sounded a little like the theme song to *The Brady
Bunch* came blaring out, but something wasn't quite right. "It

plays classic television theme songs in five languages." Gram informed us proudly. "That's Russian!" She and Troy began singing along in English and bobbing their heads. "That's the way . . . we became the Brady Bunch!"

Chase, who had never met Gram, regarded her as if she were less than a minute out of the asylum. "Harmless." I assured him. We stood in a tight circle talking, and it was then that I noticed his swim trunks were very similar in color to Troy's. The muscular top of him compared easily with my brother, too. They were both an *Abs of Steel* commercial come to life. It was easy to see how I had mistaken him for Troy in the water.

"Listen, Chase, maybe we should get you to a hospital for an official once over. How's that sound?" He beat back my suggestion with a red-hot poker.

"I'm not going to any hospital, Jack! Do you hear me? No way! You better drop that whole idea. Right now! You readin' me?"

An awkward silence followed. I don't know if Chase realized his response was over the top, but we all did. I can understand not wanting to drop by the ER, but the intensity of his objection was way too strong. My antennae went up immediately, and I was wishing Scooby and the gang would pull up in the Mystery Machine so Freddy or Velma could take over the questioning and get some answers.

With no one speaking, Chase seemed to get the idea that he'd been out of line in his sharp rejection of the hospital run. "The old lady said I'm fine," he muttered.

Gram was repacking her makeup bag over near the guardhouse. Good thing. Jori, Troy, and I all winced and looked nervously her way. Troy crossed his neck with his index finger as if he were beheading himself and spoke quietly. "Ixnay on the 'old lady' comment, Chase. If she hears that, you'll be wearing dentures a whole lot sooner than you're planning to."

"Whatever. I'm just saying I'm not seeing any medical people." He intended it to come across as some kind of macho bravado, but I was reading it as fear. And I didn't think it was the please-don't-put-that-needle-in-my-arm kind of fear. No. This was more the I've-got-a-secret-nobody's-supposed-to-know kind. And that was a kind of fear I understood.

Jori touched his arm gently. "Chase, who did this to you? Surely you saw or heard something?"

His anger flashed again, and he shook her hand off his arm. "Look! I don't know anything! Nothing! Would you all just stop badgering me?"

Troy and I looked at each other, and I felt sure we were of one mind at that moment. He assumed his best Shakespearean accent. "Methinks thou dost protest too much!" And then he dropped the accent and challenged Chase with his eyes. "Waaaayyy too much."

Chase reigned in his bad attitude immediately and began to explain. "Look, I came back here because . . . I left my towel."

Jori looked at me with absolute disbelief. Chase didn't catch her expression, but I could read it easily. She was thinking exactly what I was thinking—that teenagers don't notice they've left their towels at the pool, and if by some act of divine intervention they do, they still don't come back to get them immediately. So, we both thought Chase was lying even though he'd just begun the story. Now, I was screening every word out of his mouth with suspicion.

"The gate was still open, so I went straight into the locker room to see if I dropped it somewhere in there. When I couldn't find it, I headed out toward the pool deck when all of a sudden somebody throws a sack over my head, drags me back into the locker room, and knocks me out. Next thing I know, I'm all tied up and doin' the dead man's float. That's it. That's all I know."

When no one spoke, he looked at Jori.

"I . . . I'm not tryin' to be a jerk." She smiled in response; then, he turned to Troy and me. "I guess I'm just a little shook up."

My brother decided on a peace offering. "Well, hey, who wouldn't be? If we can all fit into Gram's car, we'll give you a lift home. If there's not room, Jack can run alongside."

We headed toward the gate where Gram was standing with her bag. "Let's get moving people!" she chirped. "Florence and I have a game of gin rummy later tonight, and that old crow's going down. By the way, Troy . . ." She gestured to another area of the fence I hadn't noticed earlier. There was a gaping hole in the chain link! She chewed one finger nervously as she spoke. "Sweetheart, I don't want you to get in any trouble over this. Now I'll pay for it; you know I will. It's just that I wasn't sure I wanted to jump off the top of that fence like Jori and really it would have taken too long to hoist the SuperStep over to the other side, and, well, I had this new little gadget I'd been dying to try out!" She pulled a pair of sunglasses off her head that I hadn't noticed her wearing earlier. "Now they *look* like a simple pair of sunglasses, I know, but the lenses are nearly a half inch thick, and they conceal the best stuff! These little babies actually clip nails, project a microscopic laser beam that will pick *any* lock, and, best of all, there's a tiny battery-operated circular saw-type device in the right lens that cuts through metal!" She pointed again to the entrance she had effectively cut out of the fence. "Voilà!" She elbowed Chase. "I can grate cheese with them, too!"

"Gram! How am I gonna explain this?" Troy had a good point.

"No worries, Honey. I said I'll pay for it. Besides, the current supervisor of Park and Rec who oversees this pool, among other features of our fair city, chased after me like a puppy all four years of high school." She looked at Jori and giggled. "He still calls."

Troy and I both agreed long ago that we would pretend we didn't hear any of the stories Gram tells about her past romantic encounters. There are some things grandsons don't need to know. I refocused the conversation as we crossed the street to her car. "Gram, can five of us fit in here?"

Jori started to open the car door and then stopped and pointed to the piles of dripping water around everyone but her. "It's going to be a pretty wet ride, Gram. I'm the only one who's really dried off."

"I don't worry about water, Honey. It's why I always go with leather. And to answer your question, Jack—it'll be a little tight back there, but you can fit. Florence and I had seven in here once, and that's not counting Waldo's wheelchair. What a riot! We were doing Chinese fire drills. I love those things. Did you guys know Chinese fire drills are illegal?"

Chase looked from my grandmother's tiny car to me. "Is she serious?"

"Absolutely," I said, "but you can take the front. There'll be more room up there."

We all piled in, and a lively chorus of young voices simultaneously advised Chase that he should buckle up prior to ignition.

Gram fired the engine. "What's your address, Chase? I'll

have you there as quick as a wink." She threw the gearshift into drive, but before she even hit the gas pedal, Chase dropped a bombshell.

"I can't go home."

Gram shifted back to "park," and a quiet sadness filled the car. It was the way he had said it. He sounded almost alarmed at the very thought of entering his own house, as if he were no longer welcome there. You could tell there was a story. He squirmed uneasily under Gram's gaze and recalibrated his tone. It was no longer alarmed; now, it was desperate. This was the second time I had noticed Chase seemingly adjusting the emotional delivery of his words with us, and I was taking note. Were we being manipulated? When he didn't get the response he was looking for from us, was he switching tactics and trying another angle? Or . . . was he carrying a secret more frightening than mine . . . and looking for someone to help him with it? I couldn't make up my mind. And then, he said something that helped me decide.

"It's just that there's no one there. Not anymore." He turned in his seat and looked back at me. "I was really hoping, Jack, that I could go home with you."

Chapter 6

She made her way tentatively to the couch knowing that she would have to play the game of words extremely well tonight. It was always important to say exactly what he wanted her to say, but tonight he was indicating that he would be discussing her boys—one of them at least—and that was a very rare occurrence. He was offering food to a starving castaway. She knew that if she was going to find out anything that could help them, she would have to say all the right things. She would have to feign interest in his plans and surreptitiously make suggestions that might give Jack or Troy an advantage of some kind.

She knew the man coming to see her this evening was not her husband, not any longer at least. She had begun to question, in fact, if he had ever *been* her husband. He certainly looked like Chip Barrett, at times anyway, but he rarely sounded like him. He demanded she call him Adam; it was a privilege, he explained, afforded to very few people. She did as he requested, to stay safe, to stay alive perhaps. But in her mind, she had to call him Chip, had to think of him the way he had once been—long ago—when they first met. Holding onto the memory of who her husband had been was the only way she could make it through these visits. It was the crutch that allowed her to pretend she could even stand the sight of him.

She knew they were all in terrible danger, but it was Jack she feared for the most. Sometimes, late into his visits, Chip would howl with rage against Jack. He would become violent, not with her, but on more than one occasion, he had destroyed furnishings in the dwelling where he kept her—the place he referred to as The Chambers. And then he would talk of revenge against Jack and become so wild he would seem to forget she was even in the room. At times it seemed his only goal was vengeance against her oldest son for something that had happened. Over the long months she had been imprisoned here, she had pieced together that something had been destroyed, something very important to Chip. And it was Jack he blamed for it. He always frightened her, but on the nights he spoke of Jack, he was all the more terrifying.

She took her seat next to him and steeled herself for an evening of fake pleasantry and lies. It was how she survived. It was how she was trying to help what was left of her family. And what mother wouldn't do anything to protect her sons?

"Susan, do you like the dress?"

"Yes, Adam. It's exquisite. I . . . I don't deserve anything so lovely. It's *perfect,* really." Susan Barrett had always been a quick study of people, and she learned early on that the man sitting with her on the couch responded to the word "perfect" in a very unusual way. When she used the word to describe something he had done or said, he seemed to draw both strength and comfort from it. She felt sure that if she could see inside him at those moments, a physiological response would register in his body and a biochemical response in his brain. So she used the word, purposefully, to set the tone for these evenings . . . and to protect herself. A day was coming, though, when she felt sure she would use it against him.

He smiled at her use of the word. He loved to hear it. Loved it when others said it about him or about anything he did. *Perfect.*

It was a glorious word. Here she was before him. A woman who was nearly perfect herself and who would soon be entirely without fault. He was going to make certain of that. He needed to say something to make her happy. That was his primary reason for coming tonight. He would tell her now. He reached for her hand. "I've been thinking that you're lonely, Susan. You miss your family, don't you?"

Her insides squirmed the minute he placed his hand on hers, but her poise held. She heard his words, and her mind began rapid calculations. How should she play this? What was the safe response? She hadn't had more than a sip of alcohol since she woke up in The Chambers months ago, and it was a good thing. She needed a clear head each time he came to call. It was moments like this when she felt her response could prove her undoing—destroy the trust she was trying to build in him. She reached for her necklace with her free hand, turned her head to him, and projected an acquiescent smile. "Why, Adam. I have you. How could I be lonely?" She could tell by the look on his face that he believed her. Good.

"Yes, Darling. Of course, that's true. But sometimes it's all right to need someone else. Sometimes more than two is good. I'm planning a family for us you know."

She withdrew her hand. It was foolish, but she couldn't stop herself. She stood and crossed the room pretending she needed some water. "Oh?" was all she could muster.

He began to follow her but stopped a few feet away. "Well, of course. And I'm thinking of bringing Troy here. For a visit. Would you like that?"

It was a trick. He was testing her; she was sure of it. He might be trying to see if she was still attached to her family. Still thinking of them. If she showed the slightest trace of a longing for her old life, he would know. He would know that she'd been pretending all this time, and what would he do when he found out? If he brought Troy here, what then? Would he imprison her son along with her or worse? How would he bring him here? Knowing Troy, it would have to be by force. She could not bear the thought of that! Yet if she appeared unappreciative of Chip's suggestion, he might become enraged. Her response to this question, she knew, had to be worthy of an Academy Award. She gave the appearance of complete nonchalance and took a sip of water from a glass. "Adam, it would be fine to visit with Troy, if you think it's best. Whatever makes you happy, Adam."

He came to her then and took both of her hands in his. "You like the idea? Because I do. I think it's time to bring him here."

She looked into his eyes for the briefest moment and bit her tongue as she laid her head against his suit jacket. "I think it's an absolutely *perfect* idea, Adam."

"Good then. It's all settled. I'll set to work on it as soon as possible." He released her hands, walked over to the dining table, and pulled out her chair. It was a signal that they would now eat. The meal had been delivered just a few minutes prior to his arrival as always. Music would be piped into The Chambers at precisely seven o'clock.

She had great difficulty concentrating on the conversation during dinner. Generally, she could not afford to let her mind wander even for a moment during these meals for fear she would say or do the wrong thing, but tonight was different. Despite her best efforts, she could not keep herself from thinking about Jack.

Chip had said he would bring Troy to see her, but he had made no mention of Jack. Given his expressed hatred of her elder son, this was understandable, yet she was preoccupied over it. He had mentioned family, but no mention was made of Jack at all. Was Jack no longer considered family? If so, fine. As long as he was safe, she didn't care if Chip had mentally banished him. But the failure to address Jack at all worried her. Had Chip's comments on those rage-filled nights about wanting revenge against the boy been nothing more than the ravings of a madman? Or had he meant every word . . . and now the time had come to follow through? Was her son in imminent danger? She had to know.

Growing up, her mother had often accused her of touching the stove she already knew was hot. Well, she was about to do it again. She needed an action to keep her eyes from his as she spoke the words. There was only one bite of meat left on her plate; she would just have to make it smaller. The knife and fork went to work. She kept her head down but noted he was bringing his glass to his lips. "You mentioned Troy visiting, Adam, but you didn't say anything about Jack." He froze. She kept looking down at her plate, kept her utensils moving, though there was nothing left to cut. The meat was now in several miniscule pieces spread across her plate.

His voice took on a hoarse and strained tone. It was little more than a whisper. "What did you say? What did you ask me?"

Her hands began to shake, and she moved them carefully to her lap to hide them. There was nowhere to look. She would have to raise her eyes to meet his. She must not show him she was frightened. He couldn't know that she knew she had made a mistake. She would stay relaxed just as she had appeared to be all night. He would see her serenity and realize it had been nothing more than a simple question. He would forgive her instantly. This is what she told herself as her gaze made the journey across the table.

A pair of cold gray eyes was waiting for her upon arrival. With one look, he paralyzed her. She dared not breathe. "What did you ask me?" The words came again, and his mouth barely seemed to move as he spoke them.

She pulled at a loose strand of her hair. The tears were forming, and she begged them not to fall, pleaded with her eyes to be faithful and hold them back. She wanted to look away, to run away, to look anywhere but at this man, but his gaze had transfixed her. She had to answer him. One tear fought its way free from her traitorous eyes as she spoke. "Adam, I . . . I . . . asked about Jack."

The delicate glass in his hand shattered in his powerful grip and blood flowed freely from places where the shards now protruded from his skin. And still, he did not move.

Chapter 7

I have a heart for kids who've lost a parent, but Chase Maxfield had lost both parents—something I know a little bit about. Dad—died when he was seven. Tough. Very tough. But at least I could understand it. What I couldn't understand, what none of us could understand, was Mom. All he would say was that at the end of last school year, she went away and never came back. He got really bent out of shape when we pushed for more information. So, for the time being, Gram had suggested we leave it alone. No one wanted to, but we did.

This didn't all come out on the car ride home from the pool, of course. It came out in bits and pieces over the next several weeks as we got to know Chase better, and he got to know all of us. The whole "getting acquainted" thing was enhanced by the fact that he moved into my house the same day he was attacked at the pool. Gram had insisted on taking him to his place to pick up some of his things despite his objections, and then she demanded he let her inside. We were all about to come, but she held up a hand, and I saw a look I rarely see from her. All I'll say about the look on her face is that Jori, Troy, and I all got back in the car without a word of argument. We were out there for almost an hour, and no one dared approach the front door. When it finally opened, Chase had a duffel bag slung over his shoulder. He was carrying one suitcase, and I saw an iPod in the pocket of a wrinkled shirt he'd put on; his earphones were around his neck, and he was clutching a jar in his right hand that he immediately

moved out of my line of vision when he saw that it had attracted
my attention.

"Vitamins," was his hurried explanation. Gram had followed
him out the door wearing his backpack and carrying a heaping
laundry basket. She had on a gaudy purple and turquoise hat
that must have been made in glitter heaven. It said "Happy New
Year." She did her best to lighten the mood. "See what I found
in the basement! Now where are you gonna find a little gem like
this? I mean *this* is a party hat! I love this hat! Chase said I could
have it!"

I assumed, knowing Gram, and based on Chase's request,
that he was coming home with us. A year ago, the kid had no
friends. It was clear by 8:35 this morning that everyone was at
least considering becoming his friend, but until he arrived at
school today looking like the golden boy from Hollywood, no
one, including me, had ever given him the time of day. It wasn't
that I was ever mean to kids like Chase; I was just always too
busy to notice them. Or is that what I told myself? Did I stay
busy so I didn't have to notice them? I knew this was a question
I would be coming back to later, but right now I was wondering
how we were going to get all his stuff in the car.

We all got out as they came down the steps. Troy, who is the
last person you visit when you want deep empathy, took one look
at Chase's stuff and let loose. "Gram, are you nuts? How in the
world are we gonna get all this stuff . . ."

Jori stomped his foot so hard I thought I heard a bone
crack. She motioned with her head to Chase who had stopped
approaching the car. There are some things that are very hard for
me to handle. I learned that night that one of them is watching a

guy who has more muscles than I have teeth start to cry. Jori ran to take the suitcase from him, and I grabbed his duffel and took the laundry basket from Gram. She put her arms around Chase and whispered something into his ear. After that, he got into the car without another word.

Troy had been right—when we added all of Chase's things to the car there wasn't room for everyone. Gram pointed out, though, that it was only twenty-seven blocks to our house. She drove slowly for the first time in her life that night because she didn't want Troy to be alone. She explained to him that he would be wearing Chase's backpack and carrying the laundry basket as he ran alongside the car. She made him wear her new party hat, too.

Having Chase in our house wasn't really a problem, but having Bunny Fewtajenga in our house was. Day after day throughout the opening weeks of school wherever he went, she turned up, and we couldn't very well tell him he wasn't allowed to have friends over while he was living with us. The trouble was that Bunny was clearly using him to get within optimal proximity of my brother, and Chase didn't seem to get it. Or if he did get it, he didn't care, which would be even more a cause for concern. The more I watched Bunny and Chase's phony friendship play out, the more I realized that altering his outside hadn't really changed his inside all that much. He had always been a kid who was desperate for friends, and he still was. His personality wasn't all that engaging. The confidence he tried to project when you initially met him was built upon his physical appearance, and it quickly withered when you talked with him for more than a few minutes.

I was rumbling through all of this after school one day while Chase and Bunny sat at the breakfast bar drinking milkshakes. He popped a vitamin into his mouth and began saying something about an upcoming exam in trigonometry when he saw me watching him. I had made several inquiries about Chase's vitamins, but he was always short on information. I'd heard of taking a vitamin in the morning, but he took them throughout the day, religiously, and didn't want to discuss where he got them. Bunny was craning her neck in every direction for a sighting of Troy. When she spotted me in the family room, she gushed with excitement. "So, Jack, where's your hunky brother?"

"Uhhh, I think he's off visiting the polar ice caps, Bunny. Or he could be working with the FBI in Los Angeles. He might have joined the circus. With Troy it's really hard to say."

"Or he could be right here!" Troy bounced into the kitchen exuding enough energy to put a satellite into orbit. "Who's asking?" He stepped on the trash container and the lid opened. "I gotta get rid of this gum." He leaned over to spit out the gum, and a hand shot out to catch it before the trash could swallow it up.

Bunny popped Troy's prechewed gum into her mouth with a wry smile. "Why this gum has hardly been chewed at all, Troy Barrett. Seems to me like it could use a little more work."

"Bunny!" Chase beat me to the first comment. "That's gross. It's . . ."

"It's no different than kissing someone really." She began circling Troy like a tiger with uncooked filet in its cage. "It just lasts longer. Right, Troy?"

"Uhhhh, well, I mean . . ." Troy was stammering, in part, because Julie was now standing just inside the doorway and had heard and seen it all. I sat up in my chair. This was going to be good. Julie paraded into the room with tremendous confidence, threw her arms around Troy, and kissed him—and that was some kiss! When she released him, she addressed Bunny.

"It's a lot different than kissing someone, Sweetheart." Julie tossed her a stick of gum still in the wrapper. "But I understand . . . it's all you've got. Keep chewing." For a brief moment, she glanced at Chase, and I saw that same flicker of recognition pass between them that I'd noticed on the first day of school. She quickly pulled Troy through the family room and toward the staircase. I hopped up to follow them and found Troy trying to draw her into another embrace at the top of the stairs. I wanted to ask Julie about Chase and whether there was some kind of history there, but this clearly wasn't the time because she was preoccupied with slapping my brother's hands away. "Would you stop that, Troy?"

"What? Two seconds ago you were . . ."

"That was to make a point, Silly."

"Well, can't we make another point?" He sounded like a kid who'd missed his turn at bat.

"Troy, I'm being serious. Stop it. This isn't the time. I just had to teach Little Bunny Foo Foo a lesson."

"Jules, that's not nice. Her name's Fewtajenga. We've been over that before. She's just a little too friendly, that's all."

"FRIENDLY! Troy, she is chewing your gum! That's not friendly. That's . . . that's . . . well, I don't know what it is, but it's a lot more than friendly."

I started laughing. "You two are hysterical! You know that, I hope."

"Oh, and Jack, you're going to tell me that if some guy came along and was chasing after Jori that you wouldn't react the same way?" Julie challenged.

"Jori and I are in a different place in our relationship. I'm not threatened by anyone." It was a total lie, but it sounded great.

"Jules, you've got nothing to worry about." Troy touched her cheek.

"Well, it's just that she's so . . . and every time you're around she's always . . . and if she *ever* . . ."

"Jules!"

"All right, all right. I won't call her names anymore. I'll be mature, and I'll be tolerant, and I'll be nice."

"That a girl!" Troy encouraged.

She responded to his praise through clenched teeth. "I *think*."

Chase and I were on our own for dinner that night. Bunny had taken her gum and headed home following her dressing-down by Julie, who'd agreed to pizza and a movie with Troy downtown. Jori had her final planning meeting for a masquerade party the Student Council was sponsoring, and there was no way she was going to miss it; she'd been elected a student representative, and showing up at the planning meetings was important to her. I was set to pick her up after the meeting, and then we were heading out for ice cream. Gram and Florence were out on the town with Waldo and Wendell Emmerstine. "It's just as friends," Gram assured me. "But those boys are a couple of live wires. We're going over to the casino and then to the drive-in movie. It's *Halloween XII: Jason's in the Neighborhood!* I love a good horror flick. I had planned for everyone to dress in either black or blood red, but Florence is insisting she'll be wearing yellow. Yellow! To a horror movie! I can't do a thing with her though, Jack. It's 'the year of yellow,' and you know how old folks get."

I laughed. "Well, at least she'll be easy to spot this year! Remember when it was 'the year of earth tones'?" That year Florence wore a lot of brown, and Gram tended to lose her in large crowds. For the past decade in fact, Florence had named each year to a color scheme, and then she wore only that color all year long. Gram hated it, which is probably why Florence was never going to give it up.

"Hey, Jack, look at this!" Gram pulled a huge knife out her makeup bag. I couldn't imagine it was real, but it looked like it could carve a turkey or a person with no trouble.

"Gram, that's not . . ."

"Real? Heavens, no. But when the lights go out at the drive-in and Jason starts slicing up some of his neighbors, I'm gonna pull this baby out and go after Florence! She'll wish she was wearing adult diapers by the time I'm done with her! Ha! Ha!" She'd headed out the door with unbridled enthusiasm. What happened to grandmothers who baked cookies and played Crazy Eights?

Pretending not to see Chase popping another vitamin, I scooped some mac-and-cheese onto two plates as he rounded the corner of the kitchen. "Well, my friend, it's two lonely dudes for dinner tonight," I said. "You grab the drinks. I think there's some leftover salad in the fridge. When you add more dressing, it's usually still all right on day two!"

"Whatever you say, Jack." He filled a couple of glasses with water and carried them to the table as I sent a salad bowl sailing in his direction. "Whoa!" He caught it right at the edge.

"Nice catch." I said with a piece of lettuce still dangling from my lips. It's great eating with only guys sometimes.

"Yeah. My coordination's a lot better now than it used to be. Mom said that would happen once . . ."

We both stopped moving. Me—because he never spoke about his mother, so when he did, it was like a seismic disturbance in the earth, and him—because it had slipped out, and he didn't know what to do next.

"Once what, Chase?" He'd been with us long enough now that I felt it was acceptable to begin pushing a little, especially since he had opened the door himself.

"Errr. Nothing." He took a big bite of salad. "I don't feel much like talking."

"Look man, I understand. I mean your mom leaving and all, but sometimes you gotta unload the baggage." I spooned some mac-and-cheese and waited for a response that didn't come. "Chase, I'm not sure what's up, but let me just get the question out in the open that everyone in your universe is wondering, okay. What happened to you?"

His eyes stayed glued to his dinner, and he kept his fork in purposeful motion. "I told you what happened. Some dude threw a sack over my head and . . ."

"Chase. I don't mean at the pool. I mean this past summer. You left school in May looking like a beanpole and came back looking like a GQ model. You've been in the weight room every morning before school like clockwork; you do homework like a machine. You're compulsive beyond anything I've ever seen over these mysterious vitamins. It's like you're the most disciplined teenager who's ever been born! I've never seen anything like it."

"Yeah, well, I just got tired of the old me, you know. Who wouldn't? No friends, no life."

I stopped eating and leaned back in my chair. "Okay. I'll give you that. But how does it happen in three months? Tell me that. You said something about your mom telling you that your coordination was going to get better—she must've had something to do with this radical change. But you said she left at the end of the school year, which means she wasn't around this summer. Something's not connecting with the story, Chase."

He jumped up from the table, and I became a target. "Why don't you just stop badgering me, Jack? It's not like you ever paid any attention to me the way I was before! And now, just because I'm staying here, you want me to unload my whole life story. Who do you think you are? I don't need you feeling sorry for me, and I don't have to answer to you, either. You have a nice house and a grandmother who's unbelievable—not to mention an awesome girlfriend. My mother gave up everything to change me, and what have I got to show for it? An empty house, no family, and a girl who hangs with me only so she can get close to *your* ultra-cool brother!" He stormed into the laundry room, and I headed after him.

"Chase, wait a minute! I was just trying to say . . ."

He grabbed his jacket and threw open the back door with force. "I don't care what you were trying to say, Jack. And I don't want to hear it." He exploded into the backyard and took off running.

"CHASE!" I looked at my watch. It was almost time to

pick up Jori. If I went after him, I'd leave her stranded. Why did everything always happen at once? I took off after him and voice-commanded my phone. "Call Jori." I had no idea which way he'd gone, and I had really picked up my pace before she finally answered.

"Hey, Jack, I thought you were going to wait for me to call you."

"You ready for me to come get you?" I fired the question more abruptly than I'd intended, but I was irritated. Where was Chase? I headed off down another street.

"Well, no actually, I'm not, Mr. Personality."

"Jori! Sorry, okay? Chase just left in a big huff, and I'm racing through the neighborhood trying to find him."

"Forget it, Jack. I don't need you to come and get me. I've got a ride home already."

"What?" I stopped and leaned against a signpost to catch my breath. "Since when did you need a ride home? We're going out." Silence. "Jori?"

"Ummm, yeah. Listen, Jack. Brad's taking me home, okay. It's crazy for you to come all the way back to the school. My house is right on his way."

"Brad who?"

"Brad Glorious, Jack. He's been in school for a few days now. Don't tell me you haven't noticed him. Where have you been— under a rock?"

I didn't like her tone—at all. Of course, mine hadn't been so sunshiny when I'd answered either. I decided to try and soften the situation. "Jori, look, I don't know this Brad guy, okay, and what kind of a last name is 'Glorious'? I mean, give me a break!"

"Jack, people don't get to pick their last names. Is that comment even fair?"

"I'm sure he means well by offering you a ride, but we're supposed to be heading out for ice cream. I was looking forward to that. I'll just come get you, and we can talk some. Just tell him that you have plans—he'll get the message." Another ugly pause.

"Oh, yeah . . . the ice cream. I don't know where my head is, Jack. I completely forgot, and, well, I sort of made plans with Brad already. There's this . . ."

"WHAT?" I couldn't keep my temper under control. "What do you mean you sort of made plans with Brad? Who is this guy? Jori, what's . . ."

"Good grief, Jack! He's new in school, all right? The poor guy doesn't know anybody. I know how that feels in case you've forgotten. He offered me a ride home, and I suggested we grab a soda at Pop's Place on the way. That's it. I thought it might help him feel a little more connected."

"Well let him connect with somebody else!"

"Jack Barrett, you're acting like a selfish spoiled child!"

"And you're *not* acting like you're somebody's girl."

"Well then maybe I shouldn't be, Jack."

I let that hang there for a minute. "Jori, what are you saying?"

"I'm saying that I think we need a break, Jack. I think *I* need a break—from you."

"*What?* One little argument and suddenly you're . . ."

"I've been thinking about it all summer. A lot lately. You've got some real insecurities, Jack—and this conversation is even more evidence."

"Insecure? What are you talking about? Okay, so I got a little rattled that this guy is trying to take you home. Whatever. But I'm not . . ."

"Jack, we'll talk later. Okay? Brad's in the car waiting. I really have to go." *Click.* That was it. She was gone. And I couldn't shake the feeling that it might be for good.

Chapter 8

Susan Barrett trembled behind her bedroom door. She could not lock it; there were no locks on any of the doors in The Chambers except for the one that kept her imprisoned behind its ornate walls. She had instinctively made her way to the bedroom when Chip had overturned the dining room table and begun bellowing with rage about his desire to destroy Jack. She had fled here for protection in the past, and he had left her alone. The same was true tonight. She heard the splintering of wood and the shattering of glass as he vented his anger toward her older son, but he never approached the door to her room. For nearly an hour, he had unleashed his fury throughout The Chambers, and then a stillness had descended upon the dwelling that completely unnerved her. This was the time she always feared most. *Was he gone?*

The door to The Chambers slid open and closed without even so much as a hiss of compressed air, so it was impossible to tell by sound when someone entered or exited. Forty-five minutes of silence convinced her wobbly legs that he had gone, and she carefully opened her bedroom door to a scene of absolute devastation. He had destroyed nearly everything in sight. She was no more than a few steps outside the bedroom before it became impossible to walk without reaching for a wall or a pillar to steady herself across the uneven floor now littered with debris. A lone mirror was the only item she could see that had been left in one piece. It hung in its place on the wall—the only surviving witness to a massacre. She stole a look, and as she did so, his image stepped into view behind her. She gasped and turned to face him.

They regarded one another silently for a moment, and then he spoke. "Constance will have someone see to the mess immediately."

She ignored the comment and somehow found the courage to address him. "You're going to kill him. Aren't you?" One look at this room answered her question, but she wanted to make him say it. If there was the slightest trace of her husband, of Jack's father, left inside of this madman, she felt sure that his response to this question would reveal it.

He regarded her with a look of curiosity and shook his head slowly. He spoke then as if he were explaining the simplest concept to a bewildered child for the second time. "Oh, no. No, Darling, I want Jack to suffer. Terribly. I want him to suffer until his confidence is shattered and until he's riddled with guilt and until he wishes he were dead." His face contorted into a grimace that made her want to strike him, but she knew better than to move. He could be unpredictable and very, very dangerous—especially when conversation concerning Jack was underway. He continued his explanation with boastful pride. "And when Jack finally reaches the point of total despair, do you know what I'm planning to do, Susan? I'm going to offer him a way out. I'm going to help make Jack's life better than it's ever been. I'm going to make one of his dreams come true."

She cocked her head in disbelief, and his grin grew wider and more terrifying. "When things get bad enough, Darling, people take help from just about anyone."

Cora sensed immediately that something was wrong. Very wrong. It happened sometimes—a bad night in The Chambers—but this was different. His tie was askew, his hair mussed. And was that blood on his hands? She did her best to keep her eyes away from him. If he caught her glancing at him, there would be no end of trouble. Following a visit to The Chambers, he generally went to his living quarters on the top floor, which was known as The Lodge, but at times, he surprised her and requested the lobby. Given his less than ideal physical condition at the moment, she gambled on his living quarters. "Lodge, Sir?"

He checked his watch. "Lodge," was his clipped response. A special code was required to take the elevator to The Lodge, and no one other than Cora and Mr. Eden himself were privy to that code. Her fingers sailed over the correct series of buttons and the lift ascended. Though the elevator doors opened directly into his living quarters, Cora had never dared to move even a step out of position to glance inside. Her view each time the doors opened was always the same: the back of a dark red leather sofa, a large mahogany desk on some type of raised platform, and a wall of windows behind it. It was the same view tonight, but events played out differently from the past. An undisguised eagerness to enter The Lodge led him to launch himself through the doors as they were still opening, and as he did so, a key card fell from his pocket. Cora spotted it just as the doors closed, and she should have called out to him. But she didn't. Instead she allowed the doors to close, and she picked up the card and began turning it over in her hand. She assumed it opened the door to The Chambers, but she couldn't be certain. What lay behind that door was a mystery, and Cora doubted it was anything mundane.

She didn't know why it felt important to possess this card, didn't know why she wanted to keep it, but she did.

As the elevator began its descent, doubts crept forward in her mind. Why had she not called out to her boss? How could she be considering keeping this card? There were rules to be followed and terrible consequences for those who broke them. Her eyes stole a glance at the elevator plaque: *Panel 53,* and she winced with shame. She considered the card again. To keep it would be an act of rebellion, and she had never been a rebellious person. Cora was a dutiful worker as were all of Mr. Eden's employees. No one broke the rules. Everyone did exactly what should be done exactly when it should be done, and that's what made working for Mr. Eden so wonderful. And there was nothing more wonderful than working for Mr. Eden, was there? Her eyes sought the plaque again, and for just a moment, she glared at it with a fierce hatred she had never allowed herself to reveal. The emotion was banished nearly a second after it registered; however, to Cora's surprise, she pocketed the key card. She felt certain, too, that eventually she would use it.

He jammed the speakerphone button with his index finger and simultaneously pressed speed dial with another. Bill Simpson's irritated voice responded at midring. "Adam? It's late. What is it?"

"I want a report! Now! The Barrett boy has to be taken down. NOW! Do you hear me!" He was screeching and extremely agitated.

Bill sighed. These calls were becoming more frequent, and the late night ones consistently focused on Jack. He had to talk

Adam down each time, and it could sometimes take more than an hour. Tonight, Bill hoped things would be different because he had good news to deliver.

"Adam, you have to be patient. These things take time. Everything on my end is moving along very well. You'll be pleased to know that Project Sleeping Beauty launched tonight."

"Really?" Suddenly he felt almost deliriously happy. "That's wonderful! It's the best news you could have given me, Bill. Yes. I needed to hear that. And the Emissary? Is progress being made there as well?"

"We're chipping away, Adam. Slowly but surely. And on your end? We discussed a visit."

"Yes, Bill, I'm on that. The Emissary's last report mentioned a masquerade party coming up at the school, and you know masquerade parties are just full of surprises. I've decided the visit will take place early in the morning—on the day of the party. It's less than a week away so the timing is absolutely . . . *perfect.*

Chapter 9

"That Florence Petrillo! If I never see that old walrus again, it'll be too soon!" Gram was the first one back at the ranch, and she burst inside like a tidal wave coming ashore. "She showed up to meet me for lunch looking like a giant sunflower. You should have seen the stares we were getting! I have to put on dark glasses just to be around the woman with all the yellow she's wearing these days, but do you want to know what she said, Jack?" She wasn't looking for an answer to that question, so I didn't bother to respond. "Well, I'll tell you what she said! She said that I wasn't . . . wait a minute. What's wrong? Something's wrong—I can always tell." She pulled up a chair. Apparently, Florence's traitorous deeds could be put on hold, which was actually a little bit comforting.

"It's just something with Jori. Nothing really. She was trying to be nice to this new guy, and I might have felt a little jealous."

Gram leaned in toward me. "And . . ."

I sighed. "And I might have acted like a jerk."

"And . . ." Gram always goes for the full-court press.

"And she might have said we need a break from each other and hung up on me."

"Ouch. Aaaahhh, young love, I know it well, Jackie-boy." She pinched my cheek. "Trust me, Sweetheart—she'll come around. They don't make many like you, Kiddo."

"I don't think I want to talk about it right now, Gram."

"All righty then. Let it never be said that this girl can't take a hint." She punched my arm and headed for the stairs. "Take her flowers tomorrow and an apology. Write her a poem."

"A poem? Gram, I don't write poems."

She poked her head over the banister. "Do it. Girls love that stuff. I'm going upstairs to call Florence."

Poetry, huh? I reached for a pen on the counter, went to work on an innocent napkin, and read aloud as I wrote: "Roses are red, violets are blue, your eyes are pretty and your hair's okay, too." I wondered if she would like it. What I really wondered was whether or not she would talk to me tomorrow or ever again. I decided to text her. "Where r u?" No response. "Can we talk?" Nothing. It was early; maybe she was still at Pop's—with Brad. I jumped up, grabbed the car keys, and ran . . . right into Troy, who'd apparently just slipped into the house with Julie and I hadn't even heard the door. "Geez! You two should be cat burglars if nothing else works out career-wise," I tried pushing past them, but Troy stepped squarely in my path.

"Whoa there, Buddy-boy! Where's the fire?" Julie was holding his hand, and when I saw that, I suddenly felt very single.

"Uhh, sorry. I'm just goin' out, that's all." I'd never been good at hiding the truth from anyone, but I was terrible at hiding it from Troy. What was worse, in this case, was that he already knew. In fact, he had more information than I did.

"To Pop's?"

"Maybe. Yeah. Okay, yeah, I might head over there."

Julie put her hand on my arm. "Don't go over there, Jack." Her eyes told it all.

"Why?" I heard my own voice crack. "Why shouldn't I go over to Pop's?" My volume was rising. "Hey! Everyone goes to Pop's, right? You two were obviously there." I turned and let Julie's hand fall from my arm as I attempted to sidestep my brother. He caught my shoulders and brought me to a halt, stepping in front of me again.

"You're not going over there right now, Jack."

I shoved him. Hard. He caught himself and stayed in front of me with a stubborn resolve on his face that we all knew well.

"Jack!" Julie's voice said it all. She couldn't believe what I had just done . . . and neither could I. I had never been purposefully aggressive with my brother before. Not like that. I knew I might regret it later, but right now I didn't care.

"I'm the older brother here, Troy. You don't tell me where I can and can't go."

"Well, tonight I do, and you're not goin' there. At least not by yourself."

"Why, Troy, I didn't know you cared!" A hateful sarcasm that I didn't recognize was spilling out of me. "Do you think I need my little brother to protect me in case somebody tries to beat me up? Is that it? You don't think I can take care of myself?"

"Jack, where are you coming up with that? I just . . ."

I bolted forward, and he met me with equal power bringing the two of us into a kind of awkward and unintended hug.

He spoke quietly into my ear—hoping Julie wouldn't hear him. "You're not going to prove anything by going over there, Jack. You know she's there . . . with some guy. Okay? We saw them, and I know by the way you're acting that it's no secret to you." His voice carried farther than he intended, and as we separated from our maligned brotherly embrace, Julie made it clear she was not siding with the boys' team.

"Troy Barrett, that's my sister you're talking about, and she can certainly sit with a guy at Pop's anytime she chooses. The way you two are talking about this you'd think she was running away with him for the rest of her life. You know, you could give her the benefit of the doubt before jumping to conclusions, Jack."

I reminded myself that Julie hadn't heard her sister on the phone with me, and I didn't want to retell the story right now. "I just need to talk to her. That's all."

Troy's eyes were intense, his voice terse. "It just looked to me like a lot more could be getting started across that table than some friendly conversation."

Julie smacked his head. "TROY!"

"Owww! I'm just sayin'!"

My brother's last comment had exploded on impact, and I turned away from them and headed back up the stairs to my room. A whisper came then, intended for no ears but mine. It traveled all the way from my toes so that it was barely audible by the time it reached my throat and made its way out. "What's happening to my life?"

Chase returned an hour or so after Troy and Julie's big revelation about Jori. He tried to patch things up, but I was in no mood for a big reconciliation. I just told him it was no biggie—and stayed in my room sulking. My phone rested in my hands all night, but I didn't hear from her. She was stonewalling me; I knew it. At school the next day, she was a phantom. I was constantly hearing from everyone that I had "just missed her"; in fact, it was starting to feel like there was a schoolwide conspiracy to keep us apart until we literally rounded a corner at the same time. Finally, we were face to face.

"Hey!" I beamed.

"Jack. Hey." She kept moving toward her locker, which wasn't much farther. It was casual movement; she wasn't exactly trying to get away from me.

I leaned against the locker next to hers, so I could face her as she switched out her books. "Jori, listen. About last night . . . I was really stupid on the phone. I'm sorry. I just . . ."

She closed the locker and looked at me with eyes that still set my world on fire. Then, she touched the side of my face with the palm of her hand. "Jack, you're a really sweet guy, but you've got some issues that need work. Okay? I'm sorry, but someone needs to say it. Your brother and your grandmother aren't going to do it, so I will. I know you don't want to hear this, but in a lot of ways you haven't dealt with any of the stuff that happened to your family." The hallway had pretty much emptied. The bell rang, but she didn't leave. A good sign.

"Jori! What are you talking about? I'm fine! That's in the past—ancient history." And then a thought struck me. "This is because of what happened in the parking garage, isn't it? Mr. Eden showed up and freaked you out, and now you're trying to distance yourself because . . . look, Jori, I can take care of this. I can protect you!"

"You can't protect me, Jack. And that's only part of the problem. Now, please. I just need some space."

"But what about the masquerade party? Don't you want to go? You've been going to those planning meetings for over a month. I mean, surely you want to be there."

She brightened a little. "It's actually going to have a superhero theme. Did you see the posters?"

"Yeah, they look great. Let's go together, Jori. Things are going to be okay. Trust me."

"I . . . umm . . . I need to think about it, okay?" She made a move to leave, and I jumped in front of her.

"Jori, it's in four days!" I pulled my napkin poem out of my back pocket. I hadn't had time to get the flowers yet, and the apology hadn't done much good.

"Look, Jack. I'm probably going to the masquerade party with Brad, just as friends. Is that what you're waiting to hear? It feels like you're determined to make me say it, so there. I've said it." She touched my arm gently. "And I really hope you'll find someone to come with, too. It would be good for you to do more things socially, Jack." She leaned up to kiss my cheek, and I stood like a statue as she headed off down the hall.

What was going on? She was talking to me like I was some kind of social outcast. What did she mean "do more things socially"? I was fine socially! This was *my* school. She was the newbie here, not me. I knew practically everyone at this school! And I didn't have any unresolved family issues. Did I? I looked at the napkin in my hand, crumpled it up, shoved it in the nearest trash can, and stomped off in the opposite direction. I'd go to that party all right—but not with another girl. I'd go alone—how's that for social confidence? I'd go alone . . . and I'd be watching her every minute.

With Chase studying at the library, dinner was like old times:

just Gram, Troy, and me. Julie had been invited, but she had a chemistry quiz to study for, which might have been the full truth or might have been a half-truth, with the other half being that she wanted to steer clear of any potentially uncomfortable dinner conversation. This whole thing had to be really awkward for her since the four of us had spent nearly the entire summer together. The only comment she did make, and that was via Troy, was that Jori said the two of us "needed a break." It sounded even worse coming from somebody else—like the whole world knew about it, which made it all the more real.

Gram had made dinner, a rarity. It was steak and eggs, which is what dinner frequently looked like when Gram actually cooked instead of ordering Chinese. Troy had just completed adding the missing ingredient to his meal, which meant that you could no longer see the steak—or the eggs. To the untrained eye, it would appear that my brother was about to dine on a plate full of ketchup. I worked hard to avoid glancing in his direction whenever we had this particular meal.

It was about halfway through the dinner hour when the doorbell rang. Gram sprang from her seat and headed for the door, then raced back to the table and grinned at us. "Boys—with a masquerade party coming up—I knew we'd need a seamstress and perhaps an engineer. And there's only one woman to call when you need a needle, some thread, and an ounce or two of magic. It's time for a family reunion! Let's get the door now." The bell rang again, and it somehow managed to sound impatient. Gram rushed away as Troy and I exchanged curious glances and followed.

The front door was opened with great excitement just as we

arrived beside her, and Gram cried out in delight, "Millie!"

"Katy! Well, hello there, Sweetcakes! No worries, no worries. Favorite Aunt Millie is here to save the day!"

"FAM!" I called out and rushed to her. FAM stood for "Favorite Aunt Millie," which every person in the entire extended family was required to call her—except for Gram and me. Gram called her Millie since they were sisters, and I was allowed to shorten Favorite Aunt Millie to FAM. No one else was allowed to do that though, including Troy. Whenever anyone in the family asked why I was allowed to shorten her title, her response was a candid, "Jack's my favorite." She said it like she was joking, but I had always secretly hoped it was true. Everybody ought to be somebody's favorite, I think. It's like getting a booster shot of self-esteem.

"Oh, no!" Troy made to turn and run, but he was too late as always; FAM's faithful sidekick, her dog Mr. Whizzer, had nailed him. Mr. Whizzer was without a doubt the biggest, ugliest bulldog that had ever been born. He had been prophetically named Mr. Whizzer upon his arrival in her home—where he set to work "whizzing" on just about everything. He was missing his right front leg from a rafting accident with FAM in South America, though he was remarkably fast at times, and he had lost his tongue to a hyena during a trip to Africa. I have learned that dogs with no tongues are very messy eaters.

Mr. Whizzer also had an unusual affinity for Troy; it was an almost magnetic attraction that happened the moment they first met and had provided a fabulous source of entertainment over the years. Whenever the dog first saw Troy after a lengthy separation or whenever Mr. Whizzer was visiting us and became overly excited, he raced to my brother, hiked his leg, and showered Troy's shoes in urine. This customary greeting between the two of them was already underway and, sadly, Troy was barefoot.

FAM finally released me from a bear hug that threatened to collapse at least one lung. My aunt was a big woman—three times Gram's size. Everything about her was big, including her voice, and she made no apologies for it. She was kind of like Gram on steroids. "Hey there, Troy-boy! I see Whiz found ya. Ha! Ha! That dog took a shine to you years ago, and he just can't help himself." She bounded into the family room and pulled Troy into a rib-crushing hug. If she knew his feet were dripping with dog urine, she didn't seem to mind. Of course, she was wearing the trademark black boots that went with her army fatigues, so she could easily have failed to notice. FAM had been the first female general in the U.S. Air Defense Artillery, and though she was retired now, she wore her fatigues like most people wear their jeans. She had an extensive background in engineering and electronics and was forever creating "gadgets and gizmos" as she liked to call them that Gram, in particular, had thought up.

"Hey, Favorite Aunt Millie! How's . . . my . . . favorite Aunt Millie?" These greetings always came out rather awkwardly as did most conversations family members had with FAM. Her self-appointed title complicated discussions, but she wasn't about to relent.

"Couldn't be better, Troy-boy, couldn't be better." He hated the "Troy-boy" moniker, but like all things with FAM, it wasn't likely to change.

Gram and I hauled her sister's bags into the family room while Troy went off to freshen up from Mr. Whizzer's enthusiastic greeting. The dog followed him of course. FAM, seated on the sofa, reached for the side pocket of her smallest bag, unzipped it, and took out some drawings. "Now, I've been working on some costume drawings that I want you guys to see. TROY-BOY!" She nearly split my eardrums. "Get in here on the double!"

Troy came on the run with Mr. Whizzer right on his heels. "What? What's the emergency?"

"Millie's sketched costume ideas for the party. I called her right away when Jori gave me the theme. I love a good superhero party. We're having one at Sunny Days in a few weeks." Gram clapped her hands together with excitement. "And I certainly hope you are going to this party, Jack Barrett. With or without Jori. You can't stop living when times get tough. Goodness knows I've learned that one."

There was plenty I wanted to say in response to that, but before I could even begin explaining that I had every intention of showing up at this party, FAM jumped in.

"All right fellas, now here's what we've got. Troy, you're the Green Arrow! What better superhero for a nephew who's had . . . how many years have you been doing that bow and arrow stuff, Troy-boy?"

"Ten. Ten years, Favorite Aunt Millie, but I don't know about . . ."

FAM thundered on, completely undaunted by Troy's obvious lack of excitement. "The Emerald Archer, they call him that sometimes, too, has a great mask, and this'll be easy to do. We just drop you into some tight green leather, and you'll be done."

Troy was standing behind the couch looking over FAM's shoulders at the drawing. "Tight green leather?" He didn't sound so convinced.

FAM tossed her head back to look up at him. "Troy-boy, you'll look like a total stud by the time I'm done with you. Sweetheart, Green Arrow's a hottie! And he's got a slick chick running with him, the Black Canary. Katy told me about that little Julie of yours, and I've got something cooked up for her along those lines."

The "stud" line snagged him. "Well, I definitely wouldn't want to turn down the green leather after you've gone to all the trouble, Favorite Aunt Millie. It sounds great. I'll give Jules a call and see if she can come over and check this out."

"That would be good because I'll need measurements." FAM called after him, but he was already halfway up the stairs to grab his phone. My brother is the most transparent being on the planet. Now that he saw the potential to be the hottest guy at the dance, he was completely on board with FAM and her green leather.

I had noticed Gram whispering something to her sister while Troy had been talking, and just after that, my aunt grabbed a set of drawings that were clipped together and moved them to the back of her stack of papers. She thought I wasn't looking, but I saw it. "And for you, Jack, we have . . . Captain America! I like the idea of you in red, white, and blue. We'll come up with a shield, too. Cap has to have his shield."

I made no comment, but my thought was that the Captain America drawing had been for Chase. Gram wouldn't have left him out when she set this all up with her sister. The drawings that had been moved to the back of FAM's pad were what interested me. I suspected those pages contained my true costume and that it had something to do with Jori. Why else would Gram have been whispering? I was a little angry with her for a minute—if in fact she was spreading my personal business to FAM—but at the same time I told myself she was doing what grandmothers do, trying to spare me any more heartache. I came to sit next to FAM on the sofa and reached for the pad. I pulled out the drawings at the back without saying a word, and nobody stopped me. The sketches were all of Superman and Lois Lane. FAM had spent more time on these than any of the others, drawing them from several angles over three separate pages. The names Jack and Jori were scrawled underneath every picture.

Chapter 10

Three figures stepped from the car. They were dressed indiscriminately in black, and their faces were veiled. The leader's eyes were glued to Troy. The boy had been running for nearly an hour—as he had each morning this week. He was tiring; it was almost time. They waited for the coach to make his routine check of the track. He would then head down to the lounge to put the coffee on and grab a cup for himself. He'd be back in fifteen minutes, and that was fine—because fifteen minutes was more than they would need. They made their way to the door that would lead them into a hallway and at last to the boys' locker room. They had seen Troy enter through this door each day. And they'd followed, stealthily, to determine his routine. The leader motioned for a guard to remain positioned at the inside entrance to the locker room to be sure that no one would interrupt them. It was early; the school was barely alive. There would be no problems.

Instead of finishing the last lap at a relaxed pace, Troy assaulted the track, giving it everything he had. Eventually, he dropped to the ground next to his duffel and panted with exhaustion. After a few minutes, his heart rate slowed and his respirations became normal. He grabbed his bag, picked up his bow and the quiver of arrows, and headed for the locker room. There was a preliminary meeting of the wrestling team after school, so he hadn't planned a trip home before the party. He and Julie would meet at Pop's Place, in costume, just for kicks. They'd grab a bite before the party and then head over to the gym.

The outside doors of Davenport High were locked up like a penitentiary this early in the morning, but coaches had power. As long as a coach was on site to keep an eye on things inside the building, the one exterior door nearest the gym could be unlocked early. So, the coaches ran kind of a "pair and share" deal to help each other's teams. Even before the school year officially began, Coach Kaiser and his football team had been conditioning on the south lawn at the far end of the building each morning. Coach Schmidt, Troy's wrestling coach and on-again, off-again favorite teacher, served as door monitor, hall monitor—basically football-player-in-the-building monitor each morning. During wrestling season, when his team was doing heavy conditioning, the soccer coach would become the monitor. The system had worked pretty well, and Mrs. Howlett, the principal, had given it her blessing until the coaches or their players made her regret it.

Coach Kaiser and company had been on a huge winning streak, leading him to do something he had never done. He announced early in the week that if the team kept winning and didn't let up on their morning workouts, they could sleep in on Friday. The news had spread like wildfire throughout the school seeing as how Coach Kaiser had a reputation for just about everything but kindness. No practice for the football team, however, did not mean no workout for Davenport High's star wrestler. Coach Schmidt was quick to point out that there was good news for Troy, too. There'd be no waiting in line for a shower this morning.

Troy had thought a peaceful locker room would be an all right change of pace. He was used to sharing it with twenty or thirty loud football players who were always snapping wet towels at each other and making wisecracks about wrestlers to see if they could get Troy worked up. To his surprise, the deadly quiet that met him as soon as he entered the building irritated him. Like most of the school, he was pumped about this masquerade party, and some locker-room banter would be just the right touch about now. He would have enjoyed a venting session about how the entire upcoming school day was a nearly insurmountable hurdle getting in the way of the P.M. festivities. Student Council came up with a lot of ideas that never took off, but that was not going to be the case tonight. This party was all the buzz.

Now, if you were going as some lame superhero—rumor had it that Leroy Leininger was going as Underdog—not a night to look forward to. But if you were going as the Green Arrow? Well, let's just say Favorite Aunt Millie sure knew her way around green leather. When he'd tried his costume on last night, they all agreed he made quite a dashing Emerald Archer and, being Troy, he fully agreed. He especially liked the green leather bands that encircled each of his biceps because they drew attention to his impressive arm muscles. Julie, never one to gush, couldn't keep from admitting that her boyfriend was quite likely to be the talk of the party. Of course, Mr. Whizzer had ruined the mood somewhat by hiking his leg on Troy's green boots, but Gram borrowed some magic concoction from Florence that took care of both the stain and the odor. Troy chuckled remembering his grandmother's lament that it had been Florence who had provided what was needed to save the day.

"I swear I had some of that in my bag. Florence probably swiped it when I wasn't looking. You know, I think she's getting Alzheimer's." Gram's tone had been spot-on Hollywood gossip

columnist at that moment, and then she'd spoken in a highly
confidential tone, "You've got to watch the old girl every minute!
It's a good thing she's always had a lot of *young* friends. We look
out for her, poor thing." She had been explaining all of this to
FAM who looked saddened to hear that Florence was in such
poor condition. Jack, apparently feeling a twinge of outrage for
Florence who was not there to testify to her state of mind, had
started to defend her when Gram reminded him that she owed
him eighty bucks. He had then joined in, nodding pitifully, as if
all hope for Florence's sanity had indeed been lost.

Troy was still laughing at the vivid memory as he headed down
the dark hallway to the locker room. He flipped the light switch
the minute he entered, but the room remained dark. The only light
came from a few glazed windows high on the wall. He shrugged
and headed for his locker where he kicked off his shoes and peeled
off his sweat-soaked socks. As he pulled his shirt off, he heard a
noise, as if someone had dropped something on the tiled floor of the
shower room. "Yo! Somebody there?" he called into the grayness.
Another sound reached his ears, then, like a shoe sliding across a
solid surface. Miffed that somebody had somehow slipped past
Coach Schmidt and was trying to spook him, Troy headed toward
the shower room to see who it was. "If one of you dudes is . . ."

WHAM! From behind, a tremendous force shoved him straight
into the cement block wall of the shower room. He turned his
head in time to avoid having his teeth broken by the force of the
blow, but it felt as though his cheekbone might be bruised for the
rest of his life. Hands, large and strong, yanked his arms behind
his back, and he heard latches clicking as he was manacled in
three different places up and down his arms.

"What the . . ." Troy started to speak, but things were happening too fast. Now, he was spun around, and before he could even orient himself, a solid blow crossed his legs behind the knees bringing him down hard. His ankles were then grabbed tightly and pulled out and up while his head slid the rest of the way down the wall and slammed painfully against the floor. Click. Snap. Click. The sound of more latches, and Troy felt his legs and ankles tightly secured. He tried to speak, but he was feeling so confused words were not finding their way out.

Suddenly, he was grabbed roughly and hoisted up against the wall. His teeth began to chatter, and he knew that if fear had a temperature, it would be ice cold. A gloved hand pressed hard against his mouth, shoving his head against the wall with a thud. Troy groaned and his mouth was quickly filled with cloth and taped shut. He was fighting to stay conscious and trying to focus on the figure holding him, but there was a black cloth—like a veil—covering the face. And suddenly there was light in Troy's eyes. Light coming closer. And there was someone else in the room holding the light. It appeared to be some kind of video camera. Someone was filming an *attack* on him! But why? The figure holding him grasped his neck and held him in position on the wall like some type of mounted trophy. He was literally being held in position by one hand. The strength—it was incredible; it was inhuman.

His captor turned toward the light of the video camera and began calling the name of Troy's older brother, "Jaaaaaccckkk! Oh, Jaaaaacccckkk? It's early on Friday morning, Jack. Do you know where your loved ones are?" A devilishly, cruel laugh split the air and reverberated around the empty shower room, and

Troy's blood ran cold. He couldn't breathe. "You thought you could protect him, Jack. But you couldn't. You didn't. You've failed, Jack . . . again. And now I have him, and you couldn't in your wildest dreams imagine what I'm going to do with him . . . before I kill him." The voice cackled with glee, and the camera moved in greedily, seizing the moment in a close-up frame, then backing off again. The sound of the voice was helping Troy's thoughts to become more lucid. He recognized the eerie tonal combination of warmth and scorn that identified Mr. Eden as his captor. He tried to struggle, to kick out with his bound legs, to cry out, but every attempt was useless.

Next, his captor moved to stand directly next to Troy and motioned the cameraman to move in for another close-up shot. "You're never going to see your brother again, Jack, and do you know why? It's because you're a miserable failure. You've lost your mother and your brother. Better keep a real close eye on Grandma, Jack. Her days have gotta be numbered, too; nobody lives forever—right? Except me. And then there's your little girlfriend. Rumor has it she's raised the bar on what she's looking for—and guess who didn't make the cut? But then who could blame her, Jack? You're not quite smart enough, not quite strong enough, not quite good-looking enough, not quite anything enough, are you? You're average, Jack, average at best—and that's on your good days."

Troy struggled mightily against his bonds as soon as the cruel taunts directed at his brother began, and though breaking free didn't appear to be an option, Troy Barrett wasn't wired for accepting defeat without putting up a fight. He summoned every last ounce of strength he had—putting those famous abdominal muscles to work in a surprise attack as his legs came up unexpectedly hard and fast. The cameraman was on the floor before he even knew what hit him.

Troy's captor squeezed his neck with more power, cutting off the boy's air for just a moment, and a frighteningly calm voice hissed into his ear like a snake preparing to strike. "I'd hate to kill you before the time is right, Troy, but it can be easily arranged if necessary."

Once recovered and repositioned, the cameraman signaled the leader that the monologue could continue. "Jack, this has gone on much longer than I'd intended, but it's been so long since we've talked. I guess I didn't realize how much there was to say. Drop me a line sometime and let me know how you like being an only child."

Clearly, the ending line had been orchestrated in advance because the camera was shut down at that exact moment. Troy's captor then ripped away the veil and turned to face him, and the boy's eyes grew wide with terror. Though it had been the voice of Adam Eden projecting from his captor, it was not the face of Adam Eden staring at him right now. While one hand still pinned him to the wall at the neck, the other reached up with an index finger and traced a line down the side of his face.

"Why, Troy, Darling. You look as if you've seen a ghost." And suddenly, impossibly, the voice was no longer anything at all like Mr. Eden's. It was soft, feminine, and very, very familiar. Troy's captor released his neck, and he would have dropped to the floor like a rag doll had he not been caught in the nick of time and hoisted over his captor's shoulder. "There's nothing to worry about, Troy. Mommy's going to take care of everything."

Chapter 11

Chase and I were getting dressed for the masquerade party, or more realistically, I was getting dressed. He had insisted on going as Tarzan, who doesn't qualify as a superhero in my book, but FAM had gone along with it. I also wouldn't count the loincloth he was wearing and the thin strap of material crossing his chest as being dressed—a fact I had brought up on more than one occasion to Gram and to FAM and to Chase—none of whom would listen to reason. He put on the obligatory mask that's required for a masquerade party, but when your body looks like Chase Maxfield's and you're dressed like Tarzan, the idea that a mask will create the slightest sense of mystery regarding your identity is just plain stupid.

My fierce determination to attend this party was waning because every time I'd run into Jori this week she was with Mr. Glorious himself. I'd only seen them talking, nothing more, but tonight could be different. No matter what she had said about going as friends, I didn't believe it. I couldn't believe it, and she was fooling herself if she did. And why was I so desperate to see her tonight? Because I wanted to see how "friends" dress when they go to a superhero masquerade party together. They'd have to come as Batman and Robin right? Friends. Or maybe they could come as a couple of the X-men. She could dress as Storm and he could come as Nightcrawler—that would be perfect in my book. I'd love to see Brad with a tail.

Chase picked up my Captain America shield and began taking

some pretty hysterical poses with it in front of the mirror. "Man, Jack, Tarzan could really have used one of these, huh? I bet Jane woulda loved it!" We both started laughing, and he tossed me the shield.

"You know what, Chase? You're really an okay guy. You march to the beat of your own drum, granted, 'cause like I said Tarzan is not a superhero, but hey—you're bucking the system a little. I get that. And let's face it, I couldn't fill out the Tarzan duds the way you do, either."

"Yes, you could." He said it a little too fast. He was too eager to say it, in fact, and my Chase antennae, which had been retired for a few weeks, were suddenly all fired up again. I kept my tone casual, trying my best to avoid sounding as suspicious as I was.

"Really? How? Are you finally going to tell me how you got so buff so fast?" I was sitting on my bed, pulling on my superhero boots nice and slow.

"Listen, Jack." He plopped down on the floor and looked up at me with these puppy-dog, I-really-want-you-to-be-my-friend eyes. "I'm ready to tell you everything because I think you could use some help, too."

"WHAT?" I jumped up and suddenly angry words were firing from my lips like machine gun artillery. "What do you mean, I could use some help? I don't *need* any help, okay?" I stomped over to the mirror and looked at myself. "I may not be Tarzan, but the Captain America suit here is pretty nicely filled out." I flexed. "Very nicely filled out."

"Well, sure, Jack. But I mean they can help with your teeth, your hair . . ."

"THERE'S NOTHING WRONG WITH MY TEETH! Chase,

who do you think you're talking to? It's not like I'm some kind of walking disaster! Geez! I'm not . . . *you!*" I froze. Had I just said that? What was happening to me? How could I say something like that . . . to anyone . . . least of all to a kid who, though he looked great on the outside, was still pretty messed up on the inside? But he was trying to say that *I* was messed up—that I didn't have it all together. Who was he to imply that?

He stood and walked over to where I was now reviewing my teeth in the mirror. "Jack, it's okay to need a little help. That's what I've learned."

"Chase, I'm fine with the way I look, okay?"

"But it's more than just the outside; they can help with your insides, too. The way you walk and think. How do you think I got to be so disciplined? And soon, Mom says that . . ." He stopped. Something about his mom was about to slip out again.

My mind was flying through a thousand possible responses that might keep him from shutting down when my phone sang out the familiar bars of a tune I thought it would never play again: "I've Got You Under My Skin." I dove for the phone, knocking the lamp right off my nightstand. "Jori?"

There was tons of static and what I call "crackle" coming through the line. I couldn't make out anything and then the call dropped, but before I could dial back, my phone went off again. The interference was just as strong, but this time, I heard three words before the line went dead.

"Jack, help! I'm . . ." It was Jori's voice.

All thoughts of Chase, his mother, and our bizarre conversation were abandoned. I flew out of the room with him trailing behind me in utter confusion. If he hadn't jumped into the car when he did, I would have left him in the dust. Where was she? Already at the dance? Had he hurt her—this Brad character?

"JACK! You're driving like a lunatic. What's going on?"

"That was Jori, Chase! She's in danger. How much do you know about this Brad Glorious or whatever his name is?"

"Not much. He hasn't been around long. I overheard Brenda Miller telling Kelly Pringle that he was me but with a functional personality."

Ouch. How could he repeat this kinda stuff to anyone—even me? I declined to comment. "Well, he's not gonna have much of a personality when I get finished with him because he may not be breathing." I took a corner on two wheels. So this was what it was like to be Gram.

"Whoooaaaa! Jack, you can't very well help Jori from a hospital. Let's calm down here."

I tossed him my phone. "Speed dial number one. Call her!"

I took another corner much like the first because the school was just a few blocks ahead. That was the first place I knew to start. My conversation with Chase had made us late, so I had to assume she was on the school grounds somewhere.

"She's not answering, Jack."

"DIAL HER AGAIN! And keep it up, Chase. Keep trying, okay? Just do it. She called me. She said, 'Help!' I've gotta find her." Poor kid, I'd been yelling at him pretty steadily for the past thirty minutes, and he was stickin' by me. What did that say about friendship?

"It's no use, Jack. There's no answer. I . . ."

The brakes squealed, and I was outside the car and then inside the gym in the blink of an eye. Chase could make do on his own—I had a real life superhero gig to perform. I got plenty of female attention as I entered the gym, including an enthusiastic greeting from a dynamite-looking Hawkgirl, but I brushed her away. My head turned in robotic fashion this way and that. I spotted Green Arrow and Black Canary, a.k.a. Troy and Julie, and a masked Supergirl figure who looked a lot like Bunny Fewtajenga all standing in line near the photo booth. I raced through the crowd, craning my neck for Jori, but headed in their direction. A truly clueless Batgirl, who was most likely Clementine Ludwig, handed me a glass of Kryptonite punch that I foisted on Julie as soon as I reached them.

I decided I was right about Bunny masquerading as Supergirl because before I was even within earshot, I could hear her halfway across the gym. Now that I was standing with them, the look on Julie's face told me there was invisible steam coming out of her ears. She was probably remembering her promise to be "mature and tolerant and nice" where Bunny was concerned and regretting having ever made it.

"My brother collects comics, you know." Supergirl had both hands on one of my brother's arms and appeared to be trying to work loose one of the green leather bands that highlighted his impressive arm muscles. "He showed me this one issue where the handsome Green Arrow has left Star City because he's heard that Superman's beautiful cousin Supergirl is in danger in Metropolis."

"Oh, really?" Julie's voice was exuding some serious sarcasm. "The Emerald Archer leaves Star City without Black Canary by his side? That seems rather unusual."

Bunny regarded Julie for a nanosecond. "Yeah, well, she got hit by a bus."

Julie moved forward, and I held her back. "Remember your promise."

"Anyway," Bunny continued. "Just as Green Arrow is lifting Supergirl out of the debris from the falling building . . . oh, look at that! This armband came apart. You don't mind if I keep it, do you, Troy?"

"Aaahhhh, well, uhhhhh, actually, it probably . . . that is . . ."

Julie pulled herself from my grasp. "How is it that Supergirl could be buried under debris? She's invulnerable."

Bunny turned her attention away from Troy for a moment in clear frustration and blurted at Julie. "There were green Kryptonite particles in the debris. Don't you know *anything?* Supergirl's helpless when surrounded by Kryptonite." She turned back to my brother. "Isn't that amazing, Troy? One kind of green threatens her, and another kind of green saves her." She glanced back at Julie. "You don't mind if we act it out do you?" And with no further warning, Bunny jumped into my brother's arms. He caught her—but clearly didn't know what to do with her.

"Whoa! Hey, uhhh, hey there, Bunny, I uhhh, I mean Supergirl. Yeah. Well. This is awkward."

Julie didn't seem to find it awkward in the least. She knew exactly what to do. "Oh, listen, I am *all* for drama, Sweetie. You've got your green hero there, but you forgot about your green *threat*—that awful Kryptonite. Fortunately, I think I can help you out." And in one smooth motion, Julie emptied her entire glass of Kryptonite Punch all over Bunny. Troy then dropped her on instinct, and though she didn't have far to fall, her landing was far from graceful.

"Ahhhh! Ooohhhh! Ahhhh!" Bunny began squealing and hysterically tossing ice out of her lap.

Julie leaned down and grinned. "That Kryptonite is nasty stuff, huh?" She reached for the green leather band Bunny had taken from Troy's arm and wrenched it from her grasp. "Oh, and by the way, Supergirl, you gotta watch out for the Black Canary—she can be a *real* witch."

I motioned the two of them away from Bunny, and they followed my lead. "Julie—have you seen your sister? Is she here anywhere?"

"Jack," she spoke softly, "you've got to let this go. I wish I could explain what's going on with Jori, but I can't. Whenever I try to bring it up, she just . . ."

"You don't understand, Julie! She called me. Just a few minutes ago. She asked me for help. Something's wrong, you guys! I've gotta find her."

Troy nodded in agreement. He wasn't going to lecture me to let her go; he was going to help me. "Jack, I haven't seen her, but the place is packed. We could split up and start asking around if you think . . ."

"Hey guys and gals!" The Flash, who sounded a lot like Ricky Beckman, was the announcer for the evening and as soon as he picked up the microphone, the music had died away. "I thought we'd take a minute to recognize the great team who put this party together. Of course, it's *your* job to figure out who they *really* are. Heading up our committee was The Invisible Girl who brought along her date, the super-stretchable Mr. Fantastic!" The spotlights found Emily Watson and Scott Thurow, and everyone cheered wildly. "Next up, Wonder Woman accompanied by her well-known flame, Major Steve Trevor." Sarah Sidon and Brett Vandemeier waved to the crowd. He tipped his hat, and they were rewarded with uproarious applause. "And just arriving, probably fresh from breaking her latest story, it looks like intrepid reporter Lois Lane and a really super catch—the Man of Steel himself, Superman!" The crowd went absolutely wild as Jori and Brad were captured in spotlights just inside the entrance of the gym.

I had three thoughts. First, the world has a very cruel way about itself at times. How could they end up in those costumes, the very ones FAM had planned for Jori and me? Second, Jori appeared nervous from what I could tell. I was sure she was searching for me in the crowd, wondering when I was going to show up. Third, I was going to take Brad Glorious down in front of this entire gym, and I didn't care about the consequences. The live band had just finished their setup—replacing the piped-in music with some deafening rock. I hoisted my shield, which was made of some pretty serious metal. No time like the present. I sped away from Troy before he could stop me, and I had Brad Glorious in my sights in an instant. He had an arm around Jori's waist and was leading her toward the dance floor, and that's all I needed to see. I stepped up my speed and went on autopilot.

BAM! Brad Glorious hit the ground like he'd been run over by a semi, and I quickly decided that a shield is a very handy item to have at your disposal. Surprisingly, Brad was on his feet sooner than I'd expected.

"What are you—some kinda nut?" He was looking at me like I was a deranged psycho, which, from his perspective, was a probable explanation.

I took a step forward and put a right hook into Superman's jaw with what I considered to be super speed. He never saw it coming, and he was back on the floor again . . . much to my satisfaction. "You don't look so *super* right now, Mr. Glorious. And I'm just getting warmed up." The crowd around us parted, but the music was blaring so loudly that no one was getting a chaperone without a good hunt.

Jori grabbed my arm as Brad was getting up. "Jack! Stop it. What's wrong with you? Leave him alone!"

"What's wrong with *me?*" I pulled my Captain America mask off and wiped my face, which was now drenched in sweat. "You called me . . . for help. I'm here to get you away from this guy, Jori."

"Eeeeyyyyyaaa!" Brad came at me on the run while I was distracted. He lowered his right shoulder and used it like a weapon—catching me straight in the chest, and I was suddenly in flight. He didn't throw me a few feet; he threw me across the gym. My body must have taken down half a dozen girls and their dates before I crashed through the punch table and finally into the wall. I reasoned very quickly that my torpedoed classmates and the punch table had slowed my velocity enough to keep me in one piece, but I doubted seriously if anyone who actually saw Brad nail me had been able to follow just how far my flight path had taken me. It was simply too crowded, too loud, and too dark for anyone to have witnessed it from start to finish. I didn't have to reason through the other thought racing through my mind, though, because it was a fact, plain and simple. Brad Glorious wasn't human, and with all the Mr. Eden sightings of late, I had a pretty good idea what he was. The question was, had Jori figured it out? Is that why she had called me, and if so, why was she acting this way now? Was it because he was standing there, and she was terrified of him? Or was she trying to protect me in some way?

Whatever the case, she must have still cared about me because she was the first one to the scene of my collision, and I was relieved to see that she was alone. Without him standing over her, she'd be free to talk for at least a few seconds, and that's all it would take.

I grunted and raised myself from the floor. She hadn't even offered a hand, which seemed all wrong. When our eyes met, she was looking at me with a mixture of disgust and pity. Then, she started to cry. "You're taking drugs, aren't you, Jack?"

"WHAT? No, of course not! I would never. . . . Jori, you know me. I'm not some loser who takes drugs! I came rushing over here because you called . . ."

"I don't know what you're talking about, Jack. I never called you."

"But, Jori. It was your ring tone." She was brushing away tears, so I came close and tried to pull her toward me. She resisted. "Jori, what's the matter? What's he done to you? I understand if you're afraid, but I'll take care of things. Listen, I don't think he's even real. I think . . ."

"Ohhh, he's real all right, Jack. I can vouch for that. The fact that he packs just as much power as Troy might surprise you, but it doesn't surprise me."

Okay, what was with the Troy comparison? I was the one who put the guy on the floor. She's talking about Troy packing the power and Brad packing the power—well, what about me? Was I suddenly a ninety-eight-pound weakling in her eyes? "Jori, something's wrong with this whole situation. Can't you see that . . ."

"What I can see, Jack, is that Brad's been nothing but a perfect gentleman to me. I'd say you could take a few lessons from him, in fact. And people do lose their phones. I lost mine last weekend. So you see it wasn't me calling, and after the scene you've created here tonight, I probably won't be calling again. Get some help, Jack. You're a mess!" She stalked away as two men in blue arrived, and they weren't playing dress up. A police presence was part of life in all our area high schools—during the school day and certainly at night events. I didn't recognize these two, though, and wondered if that would turn out to be a good thing or a bad thing.

"Are you Jack Barrett?" a burly officer asked. It was clear he was allergic to teenagers by the look on his face. I decided to think of him as Officer Friendly in an effort to keep my dwindling spirits up. I was sure to be escorted straight to Dean Miller's office—the typical destination for first-time offenders.

"Yup! That would be me." I'd heard mostly good things about Dean Miller so I wasn't too nervous, but I was looking around for Troy or Julie just in case.

A taller, lankier officer, who seemed much nicer, took me by the arm. "You're going to have to come with us, Son. Several witnesses say you started an altercation here with another boy and that it was unprovoked. Is that right?" They were leading me through the crowd, back the way I had come.

"You could say that," I said. "Actually, it was very provoked from my point of view, but I have a sneaking suspicion you won't agree. By the way, has anyone seen my brother?"

"We'll sort it out down at the station," Officer Friendly said with a sigh.

"The station!" Now I was panicked. "Don't I go to Dean Miller? I mean this is the first time I've ever even . . ."

"Dean Miller isn't *in* on Friday nights, Rambo, which means

you deal with me." He pulled my hands behind my back and
cuffed me—never making eye contact. "Sorry. It's policy," he
said in a tone that implied he wasn't sorry and made me seriously
wonder about the policy. "Let's go, Kid."

Being escorted out of one of the hottest high school parties
of all time by the cops was putting a damper on an already very
out-of-control week for me. Thankfully, Troy showed up just as
they were bending my head down to put me in the squad car.

"Jack! What . . ."

"Troy, just call Gram and have her get down to the station
right away," my tone was nastier than I intended. They closed the
car door before I could say anything else, and we sped off into
the night.

My time down at the station improved somewhat rapidly when
Officer Friendly went on break, and his partner discovered I had
no record. I was uncuffed, given a bottle of water, and allowed
to wait for Gram in a room that wasn't filled to overflowing with
people who looked like they'd all been featured on *America's Most
Wanted*. To my surprise, Troy beat Gram to the station, and they
actually let him in to see me. He said three girls asked him out.

"They were all in handcuffs," he said, "so I just said, 'Hey!
Look me up when you're not in jail sometime.'"

I couldn't believe how uncomfortable it was for the two of
us. I was ashamed and reluctant to tell the story; he was trying
to show support but probably knew that anything he said or did
would result in me snapping at him. So we sat . . . and sat . . . and
sat. Finally, he broke the ice.

"Julie stayed at the dance. She . . . uhhhh, she wanted to come, but I told her I thought, you know, that you'd rather it just be me." I took in the floorboards and nodded my head at him. "Yeah. Yeah, that was good." Long awkward pause. I decided to do my part by contributing a little more to the conversation and looked up for a brief minute. "Chase know I'm here?"

"I didn't see him. Maybe. He might know. I think he would have found a way to get over here if he did, so probably not."

I clapped my hands together and kept my head down. "Yeah. Well, he'll know soon enough. Everyone will. I can just see the headlines now: Psycho teen wrecks high school dance!"

"Oh, come off it, Jack. Give yourself a break! We've had a lot going on."

I jerked my head up. "*We?* What do you mean, *we?*"

He seemed a little offended by that. "Look, Jack. Everything that's happened . . . before . . . and lately . . . I've been dealing with it, too."

I jumped up, slammed my hands against the wall and turned on him. "Well, pardon me for not noticing how tough life's been on you, Troy. It must be hard living the life of a superhero without needing the costume!"

"What?"

"Your life is perfect, Troy, or as close to it as anyone gets. I may be older, but I've always been in your shadow, and we both know it. You've got the charm, the looks, the popularity . . . and I'm a train wreck!"

"Jack, we handle things differently, okay. I never realized you had all these insecurities. I mean everybody can use a little improvement. It's nothing to feel bad about."

This was unbelievable! He was practically agreeing with me, and that just fueled my furnace. "Well, maybe you should sign me up for charm school little brother or make me your workout apprentice or put me on some kind of reality show for pitiful older brothers!"

"Jack! I didn't say anything was that bad, okay."

That bad! What was going on here? This was all wrong. I'd lost Jori. I was in a police station for assault on a guy I didn't even know and who I didn't think was human. And now my brother was at the very least hinting that I was slightly defective!

Officer Friendly, apparently back from break, popped in with a baneful grimace. "You're free ta go, Kid. Get outta here—and take *her* and that mutt with ya!"

FAM was right on Officer Friendly's heels, and it was clear that the two of them were not destined for romance. "In the unit I ran over in Afghanistan, Buckaroo, you'd never have made it. We left guys like you pushing pencils at a desk back in the U S of A," she snarled.

"What a terrible loss that I never served under your command." Officer Friendly remarked. "Somehow I seem to have survived it." Mr. Whizzer growled menacingly at the officer, lifted his leg, and let loose. Before things could get any more out of hand, FAM motioned us quickly towards the door, and we made a speedy exit.

"FAM, why isn't Gram here?" Though I was dreading facing her, I was a little put off that she hadn't come to the station. I also thought it very odd that FAM seemed to be ignoring my question. What was up with that? We piled into the car, Mr. Whizzer taking the front passenger's seat, and Troy and I climbing in the back.

"Favorite Aunt Millie?" It was Troy's turn. "Where's Gram?" He asked it slowly—in that way that says "I know I'm not going to like your answer but tell me anyway."

I looked into what I could see of the rearview mirror. FAM was biting her lip, hard. "Boys, your grandmother is in the hospital. Florence is with her. It's too soon to tell, but they think she may have been poisoned."

Chapter 12

Troy Barrett blinked and tried to rouse himself from his drug-induced state. He had no idea what they'd pumped into him, but the effects were wearing off. He forced his eyes open and came to the quick realization that he was lying on the floor in somebody's office. The lights were very low, and there appeared to be a large mahogany desk in front of him that was all too familiar. It reminded him of . . . his head snapped up immediately and an adrenaline rush beat back any residual effects of the drug. He was now fully awake. The manacles that had been used to secure him back in the locker room were still in place, but he engineered himself into an awkward sitting position so that he could see more of the room. "Talk about literally déjà vu," he thought. This was an exact replica of Mr. Eden's office from Paradise. A lot of things had happened in that office—bad things—violent things between Troy and his father. Troy had never told anyone the specific details of what went on in that office. It was the way he protected Jack from feeling any more guilt than he already did. And Gram? He didn't think she'd be able to handle the real truth. Though he was in bad shape when they found him, they'd assumed that some of Mr. Eden's goons handled the rough stuff, and Troy had left them with that assumption. No reason for them to know what a father was capable of doing to his own son.

And it had all happened here. In this very room—or one exactly like it. And here he was again. Troy Barrett wasn't afraid of much of anything; he never had been. It just wasn't in his wiring. He'd challenged anything that had ever dared to scare him. The first time he and some friends had walked through the Haunted Mansion in Davenport, he'd only been in fifth grade. Some spook tried to grab him, and Troy tripped the guy. The minute the pretend ghoul hit the ground, Troy had become the scary one, pulling on a mask and using his own collapsible knife to repeatedly stab at his victim. Troy's friends ran screaming, and the guy quit his job as soon as he got away. Troy just didn't do scared. But right now, he was staring at the big leather desk chair and thanking God that it was empty. And he was trembling.

Cora poured hot water into her teacup absentmindedly this morning, and so it overflowed, flooding the table and raining down onto the floor. She stopped pouring when she realized it, of course, but took no other action. She regarded the mess curiously. One rarely saw such things in this facility. There were very few real people inside this "hotel"; most were androids, and those who were real had been thoroughly indoctrinated. They all went for what Mr. Eden referred to as biweekly "tune ups," which helped reinforce their training. Cora had been going for many years, and her training was screaming to her brain that she must put a stop to this flowing water immediately. She should clean it up—making all evidence of the accident disappear, but she didn't make a move. Instead, she turned the key card over and over again in her pocket as she rose from the table, gathered her purse, and headed toward the door of her apartment. She looked back, just as the door was closing, and caught a glimpse of a thin stream of water still pouring over the side of the table. Then, she smiled with satisfaction. She found it interesting how one secret act of rebellion had unintentionally led to another.

A trim security guard raced through the stairwells at top speed—having already been informed that the elevators would be too slow. Though climbing from the lobby to the twelfth floor took time, Mr. Eden's secretary had been clear about the need for speed, and so Guy, as he was known by his pals, had moved like a track star leaping four and five steps at a time and using his strong arms to catapult himself off the railings. He clocked himself at thirty-two seconds. "Not bad for a twelve-story run," he thought as he lunged down the hallway toward the man in the dark trench coat and hat. One of Mr. Eden's hands was extended, waiting for the key card. His other arm was bent so that he could read his watch. He was irritated over having misplaced his key card, and his impatience had grown immensely while waiting for someone to bring him a replacement. Of course, no one had any idea he had misplaced it. He had simply reported to Constance that he had altered his plan for the day and couldn't be bothered to return to The Lodge to get the key. He couldn't have anyone knowing that he couldn't find something. That would never do. It would undermine his authority and influence.

He adjusted his tie slightly and reminded himself that excellent leaders shouldn't ever make mistakes. And in the rare instance that they did, they should never admit it. There was no denying he was disturbed by the loss of his key card. How could this have happened? Perhaps it was his preoccupation with the Barrett boy.

Yes, that explained it. It was all Jack Barrett's fault, and someone would have to be punished for that.

Guy knew he would be timed—Constance had been clear about that when she radioed him. He slid the key into Mr. Eden's hand in silence and bent over to catch his breath. Sweat was literally falling off any exposed skin. "How'd I do, Sir?" he asked, his quivering legs begging him to find a chair. Without warning, he felt a device press up against his neck and an intense electrical charge put his body on fire. He screamed in agony and crumpled to the ground where he made no further sound.

"You're late." Mr. Eden's whisper was barely audible. He stepped over the man's body as if it were a candy wrapper on the street, moved down the hallway to the far end, and pressed the button to call a small service elevator. When it arrived, he stepped inside, and the doors immediately closed. When he slid the key card into position, the interior panels of the elevator shifted up, down, this way and that and were quickly replaced with a rich wood grain trimmed in gold. He stepped first right and then left as the floor beneath him "rolled" away revealing a rich marble surface. The elevator made its short journey, and at the conclusion, a mechanical voice spoke. "Welcome, Mr. Eden, to the thirteenth floor."

The thirteenth floor didn't exist in any hotel that he knew of—except this one. There were very few living people actually working here, and most had no idea this floor even existed. Perhaps that was what was upsetting him the most about the missing key card. He couldn't have anyone discovering what was really going on inside this building. It was life changing. Literally. And it all happened . . . on the thirteenth floor.

He stepped off the elevator to face an impressive set of large double doors. The surgical unit was contained behind them, but it wasn't time to go there. Not yet. Instead, he traveled a short distance down the hallway and slid his key into the appropriate slot beside a finely appointed door. Nobody would ever have guessed that behind such a glorious and impressive door lay a gray cell that contained no windows and no furnishings except a cot and a chair. The McAllister girl's back was to him as he entered. Curious. What was she . . .

"Jack, Help! I'm . . ."

"In a whole lot of trouble." Mr. Eden finished the sentence but only Jori could hear him. His move to intercept had been rapid and deadly silent. He was crushing her phone in one powerful hand while his other encircled her throat.

"You have been a very bad guest, Miss McAllister." Without notice, he released his grip on her and shoved her toward the chair. "Sit." It was a command. Jori didn't move. "Sit, or I'll kill Jack." She didn't flinch.

"You'll kill him anyway . . . if you've even got him. But you're not going to have the satisfaction of using threats against him to turn me into some kind of puppet. Jack wouldn't want that."

His arm shot out in fury as he grabbed a fistful of her hair and twisted it painfully, forcing her to her knees. "JACK IS NOT IN CONTROL HERE! I AM!" His threateningly calm demeanor had vanished instantly, and the madman who dwelled just underneath had surfaced. He picked up the chair and threw it into the wall with such force that pieces of it flew in all directions. Jori stifled a scream; she didn't want to give him the satisfaction of knowing he was frightening her. "I MAKE THE RULES HERE!" He picked up a large piece of splintered wood and raised it over her. "NOT JACK! DO YOU HEAR ME? NOT JACK!"

"Yes." Her voice was soft, soothing. "Yes, I hear you." The only thing she could think to do was to speak calmly, and it seemed to be working. He lowered his makeshift weapon. And then suddenly, with no warning, he dropped the piece of wood and seemed in total control again. He spoke as if he was unaware of what had just happened, and Jori was left to wonder which side of him was more frightening.

"Miss McAllister, you mustn't contact outsiders during your stay with us. Any communication outside of our facility is subject to my explicit approval, and in your case, I summarily disapprove of everyone we both have in common."

"You should save yourself the long speech next time and just say 'no phone calls.'" She'd responded with more sarcasm than she intended. Her outrage at being kept here and her terror over what he might be planning were in a conflicted battle that made controlling her emotions much more difficult than normal.

He reached for her arm and pulled her up—pulled her very close and grabbed her face harshly. "You've got spirit, my dear. And that's a good thing, because before my plans are finished, you're going to be relying on it to survive." He thrust her across the room, and she caught herself on the edge of the cot.

"Yeah, well, I don't plan on a lengthy stay. Sorry to disappoint you, Chief."

He smiled menacingly, and his ultrawhite teeth seemed to glow eerily in the dim lighting. "Oh, I hadn't planned on you staying long either, Miss McAllister. No, you'll be leaving here most certainly. Your departure should actually begin fairly soon." He slid the key card into the slot, and the door opened in silence as always. He stepped through and looked back in at her, speaking just as the door sealed her inside. "You just won't be leaving us all in one piece."

Chapter 13

The three of us headed straight to the hospital, but FAM got sidelined trying to get Mr. Whizzer inside. A nurse who looked as though she was a former member of the Russian mafia wasn't buying FAM's story that she was partially blind, and Whizzer was her guide dog. Troy stayed to help do some convincing, and I headed straight to Gram's room. She wasn't in the ICU, which I took as a good sign. She was also very easy to find on the seventh floor because as soon as I got off the elevator, I could hear the commotion that indicated Florence Petrillo was in the vicinity. Florence has a flair for the dramatic having been in our local Davenport theater group for years. She'd always played lesser roles, but they morphed into Academy Award performances in her retellings. I found her dressed in some kind of sparkling yellow gown with a feathery boa around her neck. She had on bright yellow shoes and a blond wig not at all appropriate for someone her age. She looked like a stick of butter come to life.

"Mrs. Petrillo, please stop doing that! I'm getting motion sickness," cried an indignant nurse.

Florence was speaking in her customary overly dramatic voice and clinging to the lapels of the nurse's collar, throwing the woman from side to side.

"Do something, Doctor! You have to *do* something. Katy Barrett is like a sister to me. Do you hear? A much *older* sister, but a sister nonetheless. I can't go on without her. I shan't go on. Oh, what is to become of me?"

The nurse peeled Florence's hands off her collar. "Mrs. Petrillo, for the fourth time, I am NOT a doctor. I am the supervisor of the floor!"

"And I, good woman, have likely saved my best friend's life with my quick thinking and a secret antidote I keep on hand at all times. It's made from various plants and spices with which I am acquainted. This entire story is quite sensational; someone should call the press, don't you think? I am prepared for an interview and might be persuaded to do some autographing if the hour does not grow too late."

"Mrs. Petrillo, I really must tell you that this emotionally charged behavior is serving no purpose other than to . . ."

Florence stepped back and was instantly composed. "In the theatre, where I was brought up and made quite a name for myself I must say, I was cast as Lady Macbeth on more than one occasion. Now there's a role that calls for emotionally charged behavior. Standing before you, my good woman, is simply one friend grieving the loss of her mentor. Ahhhh! Yes, as her *young* apprentice, I learned much. I learned . . ."

"Mrs. Petrillo, is Gram conscious?"

"Jack, oh, Jack, Darling! She grabbed my shoulders and stood back to look at me. Oh, you are quite a handsome Captain America, Jack Barrett. My granddaughter Mia is just your type. Perhaps I've mentioned her before? Did I ever . . ."

"Mrs. Petrillo! Gram?"

She thrust my head onto her shoulder. "There, there, Dear Boy. Florence is here, Darling. Such a tragedy. I can't believe it's finally happening. She's lived a long life though, Jack. A very long life. We had such grand times together."

I extricated myself as quickly as possible from her death grip. "Mrs. Petrillo, good grief, she's not dead! I really need to talk to the nurse for a few minutes. Why don't you go down and comfort Troy? He's down on the first floor with FAM, and he was asking for you. He's pretty broken up." She brightened at that. "Why of course, Darling. Why didn't you say so? Florence to the rescue. Why did I ever tell you about the time I played Florence Nightingale in . . ."

I pointed toward the elevators and escorted her there personally. "Yes, Mrs. Petrillo, and it's one of my favorite stories. Troy loves that one, too. In fact, just the other day he was saying how much he'd like to hear you tell it again. And wouldn't this be the perfect time? Well, sure it would! It would distract him from his grief. See you later!" The elevator doors closed before she could respond, and I turned and ran back to the nurse, who couldn't tell me much. They were running lots of tests, but the ER doctor's guess was that some kind of poison had entered her system—though they couldn't say how or even what it was just yet.

"She's resting now. The good news is that unless something unexpected turns up in the tests, we think she'll be fine in a day or so," the nurse explained. "Whatever it was, she didn't get much of it into her system before her friend gave her something to counteract it. Mrs. Petrillo has refused to tell the doctor what her secret 'antidote' actually is, but it sure seemed to do the trick. She also called 911, thankfully. It would be best if you didn't disturb your grandmother right now. The doctor gave her a sedative to help her rest."

I opened my mouth to object, but she was ready for me. She pointed to her platinum badge that read Floor Supervisor and gestured toward the elevators. "Tomorrow is the time for visitors, and we'll see you then." She turned on her heel and headed back down the hall, adding an afterthought that unintentionally cut me to the bone. "If she'd been home alone, it would be a very different story, Young Man. You're lucky her friend found her."

"Yeah. Lucky is right," I said wandering slowly in the opposite direction. With the possible Mr. Eden sightings in the area, why had I left her home with no one but FAM? FAM could be one scary lady, true, but she didn't know Mr. Eden. Not the way I did. And then it hit me, really hit me. Gram could have been killed—just like Mom. What was *wrong* with me? I was making one bad decision after another.

I sat down in an abandoned wheelchair and tried to process it all. It didn't matter what the tests showed, really. I knew who was behind this, and I knew he wasn't going to stop until he'd achieved his goal. And that was the question, wasn't it? What *was* his goal? Was it to make me suffer? If so, why not attack Gram right off the bat? What was he . . .

"Jack?" A hand gripped my shoulder.

I looked up at Chase. "Hey, Chase. I guess you heard about my hasty departure from the party, huh?"

Two very young nurses strolled slowly by and gave Chase a careful once-over. I reached for a gown on the linen cart next to me and tossed it at him. "Put some clothes on, would ya, Tarzan?"

He tossed the gown back onto the cart and searched for some scrubs. "Listen, Jack. I'm sorry about your grandmother. I came as soon as Julie told me."

Apparently, Troy had called Julie to give her an update. I

wondered if she'd told Jori. I wondered if Jori would come. I wondered if . . . "Listen, Chase, I . . . excuse me a minute, will ya." I headed down the hallway and dove into a maintenance closet for a moment of privacy, but it was not meant to be. Chase followed me. He opened the door and stepped past some mops.

"Look, Jack. I'm your friend, okay. A lot's been happening to you, I get that, but maybe you need to confide in someone. Your family's been terrific to me. I just want to be that kind of a buddy to you."

A wave of exhaustion swept over me, and I braced my back against the wall and slid toward the floor. "I don't know, Man. I just can't understand. I mean everything is *so* wrong! And it seems like no matter what I do . . . I just can't seem to make things right."

He moved a bucket to make space and joined me on the floor. "I understand, Jack. I've been there, too. I've had those same feelings. But I'm a lot better now—and in a few months, I'll be totally better."

He was going to start up again with his Chase mumbo-jumbo, I could tell, and I wasn't in the mood. "Chase, I really can't . . ."

"No, Jack. Listen. I'm going to have the kind of personality that belongs with this body. It's going to be awesome."

I looked up at him like he was nuts. "What are you talking about, Chase? Listen to yourself! I'll grant you that your outside is some kind of three-month miracle, but people don't get new personalities. What—are you planning to pick one up at Wal-Mart?" I laughed as I said it.

"Jack, listen, I'm serious about this. There's this place—I have these friends, and they can do amazing things for you. They can *change* you. Make you the way you want to be—on the outside *and* on the inside. That's what happened to me, Jack. They changed me. And they can do the same for you." His smile was so genuine. Too bad he was looking at me like I was some kind of pitiful freak.

I grabbed the front of the scrub shirt he'd pulled on and brought us both to our feet. "There is NOTHING," I slammed him into the wall, "WRONG," another slam, "WITH ME!"

Without warning, he grabbed my costume and reversed the situation. "I let you shove me into that wall, Jack. I could've stopped you. The old me couldn't have done anything about it, but the new me could. I just didn't want to. But now I'm through. You don't want to be better than you are, Jack, fine! I only wanted to help you because from where I stand, you don't have much left to lose. I used to be a loser, Jack, but I'm doing something about it. You. You're just denying it."

By the time I left the closet, Troy and FAM were ready to put out an APB. They'd succeeded in getting upstairs by pretending to leave and then doubling back. Then they apparently entered a different set of doors where a weak-willed and not-too-terribly-bright nurse bought the story about Mr. Whizzer being a guide dog, but then they ran into Miss Platinum Name Badge herself, and she sent them packing just like me. Troy had been all set to argue, but FAM stepped in before things escalated and, surprisingly, she agreed that the nurse was probably right. Sometimes I think FAM goes along with things if she knows she's outranked—but only because that doesn't happen very often. So, they'd followed the nurse's suggestion and spent nearly half an hour hunting for me. In the end, I convinced them to go home and let me figure out a way to stay the night with Gram. I didn't tell them the truth—that I was afraid to leave her alone after what had already happened. Nurse Platinum, as I had now dubbed her, departed at 11:30 P.M., and at 11:31 P.M., I was making nicey-nice with a young girl just out of nursing school who apparently had a thing for Captain America. Voilà! I could stay with Gram, and she offered to take Gram's room for the night so there would be no worries about me getting tossed out. So, my guilt and I spent the night in a very uncomfortable chair where I dozed on and off and faced my demons.

Was I a loser? And if so, had I just recently become one, or had I always been one and just pretended it wasn't true? I considered my brother. Now there was a winner—hands down. Within minutes of meeting him, everyone was captivated. Chase had been trying to exude some of that charisma on the first day of school, but it hadn't worked. It just wasn't natural. But it was going to be natural—very soon. That's what he'd said, and I could tell he meant it. The question was, did I believe it?

I heard Jori's voice in my head again. She was disgusted when she had said it. "Get some help, Jack. You're a mess!" And Troy. We'd argued at the police station, and he said something about me being insecure and that I shouldn't feel bad if I wanted to improve myself a little.

"Hmmm." Gram stirred slightly in her bed. I looked at her sleeping so peacefully and thought about what life would be like without her. A question slid into my head like the snake entering the Garden of Eden. Would she be in this bed if I were a different person? I'd scoffed at Chase's wild stories but had never really taken the time to investigate them. I'd been übersuspicious of him but kept finding excuses not to look for answers to my questions. Was it because I identified with him on some level and just didn't want to admit it? Whatever this "place" was, they'd obviously helped improve his exterior, and he seemed completely confident they were going to alter some of his homegrown geekiness very soon. Why was I so down on him for that?

Geez, there were all kinds of self-help clinics advertising everywhere you looked. Plastic surgeons were fixing faces, and orthos were fixing smiles. Doctors were giving hair to bald men and using Botox to create wrinkle-free skin for women. Practically everybody was having "work done." We'd made progress as a society, and we were able to make ourselves better, happier. Right? Well, what was so wrong with wanting to better yourself?

If I were different, would Jori have let Brad take her to the dance? I was still nursing the theory that he was one of Mr. Eden's androids, but it really made no difference. What mattered was that she chose him over me, despite who or what he was. And then the thought I'd been beating back for months finally settled in my head. If I were different, would my mother still be alive?

Sitting there, in that dark hospital room at three in the morning, I finally began wrestling with the question I'd been avoiding ever since Mr. Eden first entered our lives. Was I responsible for my mother's death? It was the one issue I avoided talking about with anyone because I knew it would get back to Gram and worry her.

I walked into the small bathroom and placed my arms on either side of the sink for balance as I peered into the mirror. "Who are you anyway?" I let my eyes fall to the sink and examine the tiny drops of water resting in the ceramic basin. I shook my head, thinking about how messed up my family was and how it could all have been different . . . if *I* were different. I forced my eyes back to the mirror and stared hard at my reflection, speaking with a ferocity that seemed to be bubbling out of me lately from a place I couldn't identify. "I'll tell you who you are—you're who you've always been: You're Mr. Compliant, Mr. Good Guy, Mr. Follow the Rules and Don't Make Waves. You're Mr. Keep the Peace at Any Cost, and you know what that gets you, Buddy? A DEAD MOTHER!"

I don't remember throwing my fist into the glass or even feeling the shards ripping open some of the knuckles on both hands. I don't even know for sure that I woke Gram although I can't imagine anyone sleeping through my unplanned eruption. I tore out of her room and down the hall before anyone could stop me, ramming through a stairwell door and running down several flights. When I reached the ground floor, I broke out into the night air and went tearing through the streets with no destination in mind, and the whole time I was running, I was thinking back over the events that led us to Paradise and asking myself again and again: "Why hadn't I left Davenport and gone looking for my mom when she didn't come home? Why had I believed my father's lies about where she was?" I had suspected he was lying the entire time, but I hadn't challenged him. No, I hadn't challenged him because I didn't do that kind of thing. It wasn't in my nature. I should have knocked him to the ground and demanded he tell us where she was. I should have taken the car and gone looking for her myself—without asking for permission.

I should have done something . . . instead of doing nothing. And if I were somebody different, I would have. Maybe I *would* ask Chase about his friends. Maybe I should do something, before anybody else I loved got hurt.

Chapter 14

Though Mr. Eden had not been to his office all day, Constance had entered it several times per his direction. Troy could not see everything she was doing, but it seemed to him that her entrances were manufactured; in other words, she was coming into the room to check on him without making it look like that's what she was there for. She appeared to pay no attention to him whatsoever, and he didn't like that. Troy Barrett was not used to being ignored.

He grunted in frustration as the door opened for the third time that morning. What was with this chick? She had walked past him all morning as if finding half-dressed prisoners tied up and gagged on the office floor was part of the daily routine. Of course, given who was in charge, he reminded himself, that might be the norm around here.

"Mmffffff! Mmffffff!" Troy was making as much noise as the cloth in his mouth would allow and fighting against the restraints with every ounce of his strength. Of course, she knew he was there, but he wanted to force her to look at him. When she didn't so much as turn her head in his direction, he made up his mind to create some interaction. She might not help him, but she was not going to walk out of this room and ignore him again. As she rounded the corner of the desk, Troy pivoted his body in a circle, swinging his bound legs around so that they crashed into her with a fair amount of power. She cried out in surprise and tumbled to the floor. Silence. She stared at him with wide eyes and opened her mouth to speak just as a shadowy figure entered the doorway.

"That will be all, Constance. You are finished for today." Mr. Eden stepped past her briskly without offering to help her up and immediately turned his back on both of them—staring out the tall arched windows of his office. Constance seemed more than a little hurried in her departure, and Troy could understand why. He'd have very much liked to follow her.

As the door closed quietly, Mr. Eden turned and grinned at his prisoner. He imagined Jack watching the video of his brother's capture and reveled in what it would do to the older Barrett boy. Jack was sure to feel responsible, and that was the plan. Exactly. It would be one more cog in the wheel that would ultimately bring Jack Barrett to the doors of this facility. And that would be the end of him.

Troy braced himself as Mr. Eden made his way around the desk. The boy expected a beating to begin immediately and was shocked when his captor reached down and pulled the tape from his mouth. Troy spat the cloth out into Mr. Eden's face, but there was no reaction. The dark figure simply pulled out a key and began unlocking the restraints, never saying a word. Troy rose and began rubbing his sore wrists—all the while staying very alert. He knew, in a way the rest of his friends and family couldn't quite understand, just how dangerous this man could be.

"Most people send invitations when they want to see family," Troy spouted. "Kidnapping's not so much the way to go—though it does seem to be the only way you can ever get the two of us together, so maybe I shouldn't be so hard on you."

Mr. Eden didn't flinch, just regarded Troy carefully. He opened a cupboard, removed a carafe, and poured a glass of water—setting it within Troy's reach. His mouth was incredibly dry. He didn't know how much time had passed since they'd grabbed him, but he'd been given nothing to eat or drink since he'd been taken. He grasped the glass gratefully for a moment, brought it to his parched lips . . . and suddenly threw the contents along with the glass across the room where it toppled a vase of expensive-looking flowers and sent a framed art print to the floor. A large crack appeared in the center of the glass, and the two of them watched as it spread to the far corners of the print. Seconds later, the glass shattered and fell from the frame, and Troy smiled with satisfaction. "Oops! Cheap frame, huh?"

Adam Eden regarded Troy calmly. The younger Barrett brother always produced an unsettling feeling in Adam. The boy was as close to perfect as Adam had found, and Adam Eden had an appetite for perfection that could swallow Troy Barrett whole. In addition to near perfect reflexes and enviable muscle tone, the boy's mind was keen; he was quick-witted and clever, though Adam would never admit that to anyone. And he admired Troy's spirit tremendously. He had wanted that spirit, wanted desperately to possess it at one point in time. But he wanted it caged, tempered, before it was re-created in his own "son," and that had proven too difficult to accomplish at the time. The reminder of failure produced a throbbing in his head.

"So, what are you staring at, Big Guy? Oh, I get it! I must be better lookin' without all the blood and bruising, and you're just appreciating what a handsome devil I was before you beat me up last time. You're not feeling a little guilty about our last father-son squabble, are you?" Troy eyed the door and took one careful step toward it while he antagonized his captor. If there was one thing Troy had learned the hard way, it was that Mr. Eden wasn't used to being resisted. And Troy had pretty much always been king of the resistance movement where his father was concerned—no matter what identity he was showcasing.

Adam massaged his temples but never took his eyes off Troy. "Aaaaahhh, the rebellious Barrett boy. If your mouth came with a permanent gag in it, your presence would almost be tolerable."

"Yeah! Well if your brain came with a permanent *mind* in it, I could say the same for you." Troy had intended to take only one more cautious step toward the door, but his impulsive nature was telling him to make a run for it immediately. That one step quickly became five as he raced for the door. His peripheral vision told him Mr. Eden wasn't moving to intercept; he appeared, in fact, to be calmly watching. Whatever. Troy yanked the door open, and a figure barred his path. Before he could make another move, the figure before him made three deliberate, almost mechanical motions. First, a hand shot out to grab the front of his neck and raise him aloft. Next, the same hand pulled him slightly forward and down so he was staring his enemy in the face. Finally, the hand shot him backwards through the air with incredible power. Troy had the momentary thought that this could be a great new ride at Disney, and then he hit the wall and crumpled to the floor with the wind knocked out of him.

"Eve One, a pleasure as always."

The woman stepped from the shadowed doorway and crossed the room to greet Adam Eden with a slight kiss on the cheek. "Adam, you're amazing. The boy responded exactly as you predicted."

"He's impetuous and impulsive, Darling. It can get you in a great deal of trouble. I think cold and calculating is so much more effective." He walked over to where Troy was lying and beginning to rouse. "And enjoyable. Wouldn't you agree? Have a seat, Eve One. It's time for a little family gathering."

Troy turned his head from side to side as his fuzzy brain came slowly into focus. He massaged his neck and tried to stand once but faltered. On the second try, he made it upright and leaned against the wall for support. His vision was blurry for a moment, but he could make out Mr. Eden standing behind some kind of fancy chair, and seated in it was the person who'd apparently just used Troy as a shot put. Then, he remembered. It was a woman—he'd seen her face when she'd pulled him up close before hurtling him through space. Clarity arrived simultaneously in both brain and vision.

There she was, that woman. The same one who'd attacked him in the shower room at school and who'd just tossed him across this room like a stuffed toy. The two of them looked like they were posing for some kind of macabre portrait: Psycho Mom and Dastardly Daddy. She was sitting calmly in the chair with her hands folded neatly in her lap like the doting wife, and Mr. Eden was standing behind her with his hands on her shoulders like the proud husband. She was wearing jeans, a pale mint turtleneck, and an ivory cardigan sweater Troy recognized. Every strand of her auburn hair was in place and her startling emerald eyes mirrored his. Just as they always had.

A thousand wisecracks were begging to roll off his tongue as he looked at the two of them sitting there, smiling at him with unmatched serenity. But somehow, in uncharacteristic fashion,

Troy allowed his heart to dictate his speech. Hope marched from
his lips in a single word. "Mom?"

Julie McAllister's phone had vibrated three times during
English, but she was not about to pull it out in Mrs. Schott's class.
She'd worked too hard to get into one of the only two sections
of multigrade honors English that were taught by Davenport's
legendary faculty member. Julie told herself that her petition for
entrance had been based entirely on her desire to sit under the
expert tutelage of Mrs. Schott; the fact that Troy would be in the
same class had absolutely nothing to do with her interest in the
course. Ab-so-lute-ly nothing. She pulled the armband from his
Green Arrow costume out of her backpack and spun it around
on her finger. She'd told him she'd lost it, and she had—in her
backpack. There'd be no living with him if he found out she'd
kept it. She looked at his empty desk with curiosity and a trace
of longing that annoyed her. No boy had ever impacted her this
way; it was infuriating and glorious all at the same time. The
phone again. Was it Troy? She'd been hoping he would call since
she hadn't seen him all weekend. The McAllisters had left early
Saturday morning for a family wedding, and by the time they
had arrived home Sunday night, it was too late to pop in at the
Barretts'. He hadn't responded to her texts all weekend, but that
was not all that abnormal for Troy, who lost his phone multiple
times a week and had a habit of getting distracted by any number
of things that led him to forget what day it might even be. She
had to ignore the phone, but it'd be a whole lot easier if it stopped
vibrating. Pulling out your cell in class and getting caught was

a one-way ticket out of Mrs. Schott's classroom—permanently. The woman didn't mess around.

"All right, Ladies and Gentlemen," Mrs. Schott spoke with her trademark energy and passion. "I warned you last week that we were going to be turning a critical eye toward Shakespeare's *Romeo and Juliet* starting today. In addition, I've decided on a challenge for the two honors classes. You'll both be producing the play for the other English classes and the faculty. The strength of audience response will figure into your grade for the quarter. Significantly." She peered out over her tiny bifocals, and everyone sat up a bit straighter.

"Oh, Mrs. Schoott!" Julie steeled herself as Bunny Fewtajenga's shrill voice echoed forth. How did fate seat Little Bunny Foo Foo right next to her? "I'd be more than happy to play Juliet!"

Mrs. Schott loved unbridled enthusiasm, even from Bunny. "Why, Bunny, I'm impressed with your initiative. Do we have any other volunteers to . . ."

Harvey Pilk thrust his hand into the air and literally shrieked with excitement, "I'll be the boyfriend! I'll be the boyfriend!"

"Good grief, Harvey! His name is Romeo for Pete's sake—not 'the boyfriend'!" Bunny chomped her gum so loudly most of the class could hear it. "And you've gotta *look* the part, which you entirely do not. Right, Mrs. Schott?"

Julie felt bad for the teacher, who suddenly looked very uncomfortable. "Well, Harvey . . . well, I was actually trying to ask if there were any more interested volunteers for the role of . . ."

"I mean," interrupted Bunny, "no offense Harvey, but we need someone with rugged good looks to play Romeo. Someone with a strong, commanding presence who can bring a tragic hero to life."

"And it wouldn't hurt if he were drop-dead gorgeous, Mrs. Schott!" hollered Dee Dee Wentworth, one of Bunny's A-list pals.

"Dee Dee's right, Mrs. Schott. If this is going to be part of our grade, it needs to be spectacular, and to be really great, the cast needs . . . *chemistry,*" Bunny added.

Julie rolled her eyes. She was glad Troy wasn't in the room to hear all this ridiculous banter about . . . Suddenly, Julie caught her own breath. She saw a devious look among three of Bunny's gaggle of girlfriends and knew instantly what they were engineering: a hostile takeover—of her boyfriend.

"Mrs. Schott, if we want this to be *believable,* Troy Barrett's the only choice for Romeo. He could sure make a believer out of me." Trudy Grady winked at Bunny and cackled.

"But he isn't even here!" Julie broke in before she realized it. These girls were clearly trying to commandeer Troy for some late-night rehearsals, and she wasn't about to let them get away with it.

Bunny looked her square in the eye. "His absence makes the day far less visually appealing, Sweetheart, but it doesn't mean we can't cast the play."

Mrs. Schott had been teaching a long time. A very long time. And while she tried to stay out of what she referred to as schoolyard squabbles among her students, she did not tolerate bullying of any type. And that included girl bullies. The McAllister girl was new and while any savvy high school teacher could pick up on what was going on right now, Mrs. Schott was the kind of savvy high school teacher who would do something about it.

"Students, I agree that we can begin casting today. At least we should get the leads out of the way, but I prefer a more democratic system. The hats, please." Rajiv Patel and Sandra Cox grabbed

Mrs. Shott's third-period "hats." The teacher had both guy and girl headgear for each of her class periods and inside were the names of the students sorted by gender. She used them for all manner of decision making, and now she ceremoniously removed a slip of paper from a man's top hat. "Romeo will be played by . . . well, how about that. Trudy, the stars must have agreed with you! Troy Barrett will be our Romeo!"

The class went wild and as the volume rose, Bunny leaned across the aisle to Julie and spoke. "Ancient civilization never had it that good, huh, McAllister?"

"And now . . . for his Juliet!" Mrs. Schott winked at the class and began rummaging her hand around in a Roaring Twenties flapper hat as the students became even more boisterous with anticipation.

Julie held her breath. Bunny and her entourage were all leaning forward in their seats as Mrs. Schott pulled her hand from the hat and considered the paper. She smiled broadly. "Well, it seems that our play will be rather true-to-life, everyone. It's no secret around here that Mr. Barrett finds Miss McAllister to be a rather fetching young lady, and now he shall be enjoying her company on stage as well! Julie McAllister is our Juliet."

"WHAT?!" Bunny's voice was contrite. "I want to see that paper!" The room fell quiet immediately, and though Mrs. Schott was barely 5'3" she seemed to grow very quickly. As she headed from her desk down the aisle toward Bunny, most eyes were riveted on the teacher; as far as Julie could tell, no one else noted that the piece of paper Mrs. Schott tossed back toward the hat had missed its target. It floated gently to the floor, landing just underneath the front part the teacher's desk.

Mrs. Schott's voice had taken on the kind of teacher tone that only gets used when someone's really in trouble, and Bunny was *really* in trouble. "Just exactly *what* are you insinuating, Miss Fewtajenga? Please, now that you have succeeded in garnering everyone's attention, let's be quite specific regarding the meaning of your little outburst."

"I . . . I . . . I . . ." Bunny was practically speechless.

Mrs. Schott, however, was just getting warmed up. "I have taught English in this very room for more than thirty years with excellence and integrity, my dear, and if you would like to suggest otherwise, then I surely hope you have an army ready to stand behind you. And when I say an *army* Miss Fewtajenga, I mean a very large group of people with a lot more stamina than a few flibbertigibbet girlfriends who'll likely leave you standing in the rain when they discover you don't have an umbrella."

Bunny was shrinking back in her seat as if Mrs. Schott was a slasher villain from the movies who'd just come to finish her off. The teacher was leaning in toward her victim, and she wasn't slowing down. "I have a *host* of individuals to call to my defense, Miss Fewtajenga, if you are considering questioning my honesty. I taught our current mayor and all five of his children. I taught the fire marshal, the police commissioner, the head neurosurgeon at Davenport Medical, every member of the last five school boards, and the lady who owns the Dairy Queen. I'll ring any one of them you want to talk to about your very serious allegations regarding my virtues." Mrs. Schott's nose was now less than an inch from Bunny's, and the entire class was out of their seats and surrounding the two of them. The teacher's voice became a low and challenging whisper. "Who you got?"

The bell rang. Mrs. Schott withdrew and stalked back to her

desk in righteous indignation. Julie felt sure that no classroom on the face of Earth had ever emptied more quickly. She was the last to leave, stopping first to pick up the paper under the desk. "Mrs. Schott, my name never quite made it back to the hat. You dropped it and . . ." Julie hadn't realized how thin the paper was. For the second time that day, it slipped from a hand, but this time it fell open on the teacher's desk. They both stared at it in silence; it was impossible not to see Dee Dee Wentworth's name clearly scrawled on the paper.

"Mrs. Schott?" Julie was stunned. She picked the paper up and handed it to the teacher.

"Hmmmm? What's the issue, Miss McAllister?"

"Mrs. Schott, it's . . . it's not my name. It's Dee Dee's name."

Mrs. Schott adjusted her glasses and appeared to study the paper for a moment. "Isn't that odd? It looks like *McAllister* to me. I swear I'm going to beat the man who sold me these bifocals over the head with my thesaurus. Well, what's done is done. That'll be all for today, Miss McAllister. Be on your way. I'm much too busy for idle chitchat."

Julie placed her hand with its smooth ivory skin on top of the wrinkled hand that had been reaching out to students for over three decades. "Mrs. Schott . . ."

The teacher's eyes looked over the top of her glasses for a moment with compassion—communicating that no accident had taken place. She wondered where it was written that school always had to be so hard on new students, and she reminded herself it was one reason she was still teaching. "It's okay, Honey. You won't be a new face forever. It just takes time." She withdrew her hand as Julie headed for the door.

"Miss McAllister?" Julie turned at the sound of the teacher's voice and was surprised to see Mrs. Schott's face turn beat red with what looked like embarrassment. "If he looks half as good as Romeo as he did as Green Arrow, we're all in for treat, aren't we? I . . . uhhhh . . . I was chaperoning at the masquerade party and bumped into him." Mrs. Schott pretended to fan herself as if she were overheating, then drew herself up in her chair forthrightly. "That'll be all Miss McAllister."

Julie left the room laughing; so even Mrs. Schott was not immune to the charms of Troy Barrett. She smiled and twisted a piece of her hair, a habit she hated but was losing the battle to correct. Had any girl ever felt about a boy the way she did about Troy? She imagined him for a moment in his Green Arrow costume and a shiver ran through her. Of course, she would never in a million years have told Mr. Ego-central just exactly how incredible she *really* thought he looked in that get-up. But in the privacy of her own mind, Julie McAllister entertained the idea that a girl purposefully putting herself in harm's way might just be worth the risk if she knew in advance that Troy Barrett was the hero coming to her rescue—clad in green leather, of course. He was, in many ways, a crooked arrow, and she was as straight an arrow as they came, but somehow, they both always seemed to hit the target at the exact same point. And she liked it that way. Very much.

The phone again. A call—not a text—which meant it was not Troy. She didn't recognize the number.

"Hello?"

"Julie, it's Marty."

"Oh! Hey, Marty. Wow. It sure took you a long time to get back to me."

"Sorry, Kid, we've been moving our office the last couple months. It's a mess with phones, Internet, lost mail, messages everywhere. You name it, and it's chaos around here. Anyway, I just found the message from your call a few weeks ago. Better late than never right? I checked the file on Chase Maxfield. He hasn't been back to the Friend's Network since sometime last spring. You were the last one he talked to, Julie."

"Okay, Marty. Thanks. That helps. It's just that with me here now—in the same school with him—it can't be like it used to be, and I keep wondering what he's thinking."

"Have you asked him about it?"

"No. No, I haven't brought it up, and he doesn't seem to want to, but it's weird, Marty. He's different. Really different. And we're like silent strangers in crowded rooms. It's so awkward for both of us. But this helps, Marty, really. Before I made any quick decisions, I wanted to see if he'd returned to the Network. Now that I know he hasn't, I can figure out what to do."

"I hope he's not in some kinda trouble, Julie. Is that it? Is Chase in trouble?"

"I don't know, Marty . . . and that's the problem. I just don't know."

Chapter 15

When I got home it was very late. Troy and Chase had obviously tried to wait up, but they were both currently sound asleep with limbs dangling haphazardly from the family room furniture. Mr. Whizzer, rounding out this little Hallmark scene, was resting on the fireplace hearth, snoring peacefully. My eyes lingered on FAM's best friend for a moment, and a nagging thought came creeping slowly forward from the recesses of my brain. Before it could make itself fully known, though, my attention was drawn to FAM. The sound of her boots, now functioning as mini-rockers, beckoned my eyes in her direction. She was standing with her arms folded and staring me down coldly. Clearly, I was about to cross into enemy territory, and I quickly decided it would be best if I spoke first.

"I guess the hospital called, huh?"

She motioned me through the French doors and into the den. "Conference, now!" She had never used that tone with me before. I figured she'd call forth all of her military training during the upcoming interrogation, but she surprised me. She sat down across from me on a large ottoman and spoke calmly. "What on Earth is going on with you, Jack? First, you attack a boy at the dance, and I'm picking you up at the police station. Then you convince me to let you stay with Katy but up and leave her halfway into the night. And the mirror? The report is you shattered it and took off running like some kind of delinquent! So, I'm asking you to lay it on the line, Soldier. What's behind all this? This isn't who you are, Honey."

It was late. So much had happened in the past few weeks—some of it she probably knew by now, maybe all of it. It had been so long since anybody asked me to talk, really talk, and FAM was safe. She was safe in a hundred ways that were hard to explain to people who didn't know her, but I knew I could tell her everything. Tell her what a mess I was, and how everything would be different if I had done things differently. I could tell her how I had suspected Mom was in trouble last year, but I'd done nothing about it. And how I'd been burying the guilt, but now I was ready to accept the responsibility for her death. I could even tell her about Chase's suggestion and see what she thought about me talking with these "friends" of his and maybe getting some help.

And I was about to do it, about to spill the whole thing to her, every bottled up piece of me . . . but then I glanced through the glass panes of the French doors and caught sight of Mr. Whizzer again. My eyes lingered on the dog just long enough to allow the unfinished thought from a moment ago, the one FAM's very presence had interrupted, to finally make itself known. And that thought didn't come tiptoeing quietly out from behind the curtain of my brain like some shy little idea that wasn't quite sure of itself; no, it arrived like a powerful position statement crashing onto center stage with deliberate confidence so that all at once I knew that something was wrong. Very wrong. I just wasn't sure what it was. Yet. My eyes shifted from the dog to Troy. Why did I suddenly feel like I'd just finished an entire case of Red Bull? I got up and opened one of the doors, scanning the family room for . . . I didn't know what.

"Jack?" FAM's voice was concerned as she approached me from behind.

Mr. Whizzer let out a soft moan and readjusted himself on the hearth, and that's when everything snapped into place. "Why is he so far away from Troy?" I didn't even realize I'd spoken out loud until I heard my own voice.

"Jack, what are you talking . . ."

"FAM!" My volume increased the way it does when you know you've made an important discovery, and somebody else isn't quite there yet. "Why is Whizzer so far away from Troy?" I posed the question, but already knew the answer. In fact, my thoughts were suddenly moving so fast I couldn't keep them in check. Mr. Whizzer at the police station—he should have been waterfalling Troy's leg because he hadn't seen him all day—but there had been nothing. Mr. Whizzer getting into the car with us to go to the hospital—he should have been leaping for Troy's lap, yet he had sat up front with FAM. And now, here the dog was sleeping across the room from my brother when he should have been within a hair's breadth of him.

"FAM, it's not Troy!" I said it with conviction because I knew I was right.

"What? Jack . . . it's been a long night. You're . . ."

I flung open the doors and marched into the family room. "WHAT ARE YOU?" I yelled at the top of my lungs, grabbing his shirt and pulling him to his feet. "WHERE'S MY BROTHER? WHAT HAVE YOU DONE WITH HIM?"

Chase was quickly roused from his slumber and staring wide-eyed at me. At this point, he looked convinced that I was in need of a jacket with straps tied in back because from his perspective, I was now asking my brother, who was standing right in front of me, to identify his whereabouts. Seeing as how Chase was in no way up to speed with my family's recent past, which included Mr. Eden's hobby of replacing real people with new and improved models, the only logical conclusion he could draw was that I was basically nuts. "Jack, Dude, how about letting your brother go and just relaxing. Okay? Let's just sit down and talk."

"Jack?" FAM's hands were on my shoulders. Her tone suggested I had her attention, and she wanted to hear more.

Troy, or whatever he was, sneered slightly at me, but no one else could see it. I imagined he was evaluating the situation. Should he play dumb and see if they would straightjacket me, or expose himself and see what our next move would be? To my surprise, he chose the latter. He grabbed my arm with the inhuman strength I had come to associate with Mr. Eden's androids and pulled me extra close so he could speak directly into my ear. "Don't congratulate yourself, Big Shot. Because if I'm here, it means your brother's in a whole lot of trouble. You lose again, Jack! Here's a little love note from Daddy." He pulled a DVD from underneath his shirt—and I had the briefest opportunity to wonder if androids have some kind of storage compartments where we have organs—before he shoved it into my stomach, threw me across the room like a bean bag, and fled.

Mr. Whizzer began growling and barking wildly, but he was thoroughly confused, and our guest was long gone before the dog could be of any great assistance. "Ouch!" I couldn't help but comment on the pain as there was currently a long-handled fireplace utensil pressing into my back. FAM helped me up, and Chase went to close and lock the front door, which had been left open by my runaway sibling. They were both anticipating an explanation that I was not looking forward to providing. "That," I sighed, "was an android with very poor manners."

"A WHAT? You don't mean android like sci-fi android do you?

Being a nerdy science geek, even though he no longer looked like one, I knew Chase would pick up on this fairly quickly. "The simple answer, Chase, is yes, that is exactly what I mean. And they're not like the ones in the old movies that can't use contractions or move really slowly. And FAM . . ."

"I'm on board, Jack. You don't think my sister kept the entire last year of her life a secret from me, do you? I know everything, or at least everything she told me. But how in the world did you know it wasn't Troy?"

"I never would have guessed, FAM. Mr. Eden's obviously improved them, but he didn't *smell* like Troy—and Mr. Whizzer knew it. He ignored the new Troy, and it just hit me like a load of bricks a few minutes ago when I saw them sleeping so far apart."

"Whoa! Awesome job, detective Barrett. But why do you think it took you so long to notice?"

"Chase!" FAM was shocked.

"What? I didn't mean anything. It's just that the longer Troy's gone, the more danger he's probably in, right? I mean I don't know who this Eden guy is, but if you're telling me that he kidnapped Troy and replaced him with an android, then things obviously aren't good. I just wondered if there was something else going on, you know, with Jack. Something to keep him from noticing that his brother was missing."

FAM was about to really let loose. "Look, Kid. This is my

nephew you're talking about. Now he was the only one who . . ."

"STOP IT!" I hadn't meant it to come out as a shout. "Chase is right, FAM. I was totally preoccupied with my love life, and if I hadn't been—I would have noticed right away. Every minute that was lost is one more minute Troy's been in danger."

"Jack, that's ridiculous!" FAM shot back.

I headed for the stairs. "No, FAM, it's not. It's the truth! And since we can't call the police, and we don't know where Mr. Eden and Company are—I'm going to my room to get some rest. I'm sure we're all going to need it."

Chase came to the bottom of the stairs and looked up. "Jack, I'm sorry, Man. I was a little raw there. Maybe we should try to contact this Eden guy or something. You think?"

"Trust me, Chase. We'll be hearing from him soon. You can count on it. Now both of you just leave me alone for a while. Please."

I had no intention of resting. I just didn't want any interruptions while I watched the DVD Troy's double had given me. I'd hidden it in my back pocket as I recovered from my less than graceful landing, and now I wanted a private viewing.

The minute the image of my brother in captivity came into focus on the computer screen, I couldn't hold it together. I was flashing back to the beaten state we'd found him in a year ago and telling myself that it had all started just like this. And then there was Mr. Eden's chilling voice, speaking the truth about me into the privacy of my room. It was ripping my insides open.

"You thought you could protect him, Jack. But you couldn't. You didn't. You've failed, Jack . . . again. And now I have him, and you couldn't in your wildest dreams imagine what I'm going to do with him . . . before I kill him."

I threw myself down on the bed and put my hands to my ears, but the sound came through anyway. There was no escaping the intensity of Mr. Eden's voice or his message of unadulterated hatred for me.

"You're never going to see your brother again, Jack, and do you know why? It's because you're a miserable failure."

I kept staring at the image of Troy, struggling to get free, struggling to cry out for help. He was calling for me. I knew it. I closed my eyes, trying to block it all out, but that sadistic voice trailed on, and I heard every word.

"You've lost your mother and your brother. Better keep a real close eye on Grandma, Jack. Her days have gotta be numbered, too; nobody lives forever—right? Except me. And then there's your little girlfriend. Rumor has it she's raised the bar on what she's looking for—and guess who didn't make the cut? But then who could blame her, Jack? You're not quite smart enough, not quite strong enough, not quite good-looking enough, not quite anything enough, are you? You're average, Jack, average at best—and that's on your good days."

Someone knocked, and I sat up quickly to find Chase already in my room. He was knocking on the top of my dresser.

"How much did you see?" I questioned.

"Enough. Jack, I'm just here to say I'll do whatever I can to help you. This guy's seriously mental. Shouldn't we call the police?"

"No. There's too much involved, and I don't have time to go into the back story. Just trust me, Chase. Dealing with Mr. Eden is something *I* have to handle. Now . . ." I couldn't believe what was about to come out of my mouth, but the DVD had pushed me over the edge. Looking back, I understand that it was all part of Mr. Eden's plan—to shatter my confidence, to achieve the ultimate revenge by destroying me from the inside, but at that particular moment, he was nearing the climax of his success. He had me exactly where he wanted me—panicked and so desperate for help that I'd seriously entertain ideas that would normally never even make it onto my radar. "Chase, that place you told me about . . . can they make, *improvements,* in people fast? I mean I don't have a whole summer like you did."

"I . . . I don't know, but I could find out. I mean . . ."

"Chase, I'm not trying to be better looking or anything. There isn't time for that, and I don't want you to think this is about Jori because it's not. Not really. It's about Troy. I need to be stronger, a lot stronger. And smarter. Can they do anything about that? I don't even care if it's temporary. Do they give you guys shots or something? Pills?"

"Jack, you might be getting a little carried away. This isn't some kind of . . ."

"Chase, he murdered my mother, okay! Do you get that? And now he's put my grandmother in the hospital. He nearly killed my brother the last time, and he's just told me that he's planning to finish the job. What do you expect me to do? Nothing? I've tried that before, and it's not a road I'm walking down again. I have to stop him. Me. And the guy I am isn't up to the task, so we gotta do something. We gotta fix me somehow! I'm beginning to think you were heaven-sent because if you weren't here giving me some kind of alternative, I wouldn't have any hope left at all. Now, where is this place?"

"It's on the outskirts of Vegas. It's not really in what you'd call the high-traffic area, Jack."

"I'm good with that, so pack a bag, Buddy. There's no time to waste. Troy's been saving money for as many years as I've been spending it which means I'm perpetually broke, and he's always flush. And he always keeps a stash of cash in the dog treat jar in the pantry."

"Jack, you don't have a dog."

"Right. Which is why it's a brilliant hiding place for the money. Now let's head to the airport and figure out flights on the way. I want to be on the first flight out in the morning, so we're leaving now."

"But, Jack, I should call and see if . . ."

"Chase! There's no time. You'll call them on the way. We have to get out of here before FAM tries to stop me. If I can get there and convince them to do something to help me, maybe I'll have a shot at saving Troy."

"Jack, are you sure? I mean . . ."

"What is it with you, Chase? You've been hot on this place from the get-go, and now that I'm finally ready to check it out, you're hesitating? This is my best shot. If they can't do anything to help me, then we'll regroup with FAM back here." I put a firm hand on his shoulder. "I need to do this, Chase. I'm no good to anyone the way I am. Now let's go."

Chapter 16

Troy knew that the woman standing before him wasn't really his mother—or if she was, then she'd been brainwashed because she'd never be sitting with this psycho nut if she had any idea how dangerous he could be.

"Hello, Troy. Come give your mother a kiss."

He didn't move, nor did he speak. It was a tough decision for Troy, but he wanted to see what they would do.

Mr. Eden sighed and shook his head. "Always difficult. Even to the end. All right, she's not your mother." The woman smiled and moved her head in a sultry, snakelike fashion. "Her name is Eve One, but you need to do as she's asked."

"Why?"

"Because I said so."

"And you think I find that sufficient motivation to do *anything?*"

"Give Eve One a kiss, or I'll get my hands on your little girlfriend Julie and wring her neck." Mr. Eden gestured toward Eve One—indicating the expectation that his directions were to be followed.

Troy's eyes spit fire, and he remained stationary.

"Oh, yes. I know about *Julie McAllister,* Mr. Barrett. My grip reaches anywhere it needs to. Now, OBEY ME!"

Reluctantly, Troy moved toward them, leaned over quickly, and kissed Eve One on the cheek. She grinned with satisfaction, and Mr. Eden spoke with triumph. "There, now that wasn't so hard, was it?"

"I'd rather eat dynamite than do it again," Troy retorted.

"And I could arrange for that, Mr. Barrett. I really could." They stared each other down in silence for a quiet moment. "Aaaahh, but right now, it's time for you to have a visit with your real mother. She's still alive, you know."

Troy regarded him casually and arched one eyebrow—a trick he'd picked up from his mom by the time he was seven. He told himself Mr. Eden was lying, but somewhere in his heart hope began to flutter.

"Yes, she's still alive. And it's time for you to see for yourself, but I think I should be your escort. She and Eve One haven't met, and I can't imagine they'd get on well at this stage of the game."

"I'm guessing not," Troy retorted sarcastically. He was trying to keep a tight reign on his emotions, but the battle was being lost. For once, he needed Mr. Eden to be telling the truth.

Kathryn Barrett was seated in her favorite camel-colored wing back chair. She was noticeably pale but had insisted on being released from the hospital late that morning, threatening to buy it and fire everyone if they didn't let her out. The suspicion was that something had been mixed into the powdered sugar on some cookies she bought from a woman selling them door to door. She'd taken only one bite of a cookie before heading over to Florence's, so the damage had been quite minimal, but the crowd in her living room right now, which consisted of her sister, Florence, and Julie, was still concerned.

"Those hospitals always worry too much over details!" she

complained. "I'm fine! Now we all know it was likely one of Mr. Eden's goons selling those cookies, so we just throw out the whole batch and move forward. By the way, Florence, what was that awful liquid you dumped down my throat when you saw I was in trouble?"

Florence tossed her head dramatically to the side and laid the back of one hand against her forehead. "Well, Kathryn, when I realized your life was in imminent danger, I had to take action."

"It was a tainted cookie, Florence, not a grenade!" Gram countered. "I probably would have needed to eat a dozen before they really got me. Whatever they put on them messed up my breathing for a few minutes, but I was far from death, I assure you."

"Untrue!" Florence protested. "Entirely untrue! You were scarcely breathing after the smallest bite! Had I not sprung to action when I did and administered some Icy True-Blue Punch, you would be dearly departed, Old Friend. You would have done the same for me, I know, though perhaps not as quickly. I'm not sure you're as spry as you once were, Katy."

"Florence Petrillo, you take that back right now! Why I could run circles around you backwards. And how dare you try to save my life with some store-bought kids' drink mix!"

"GIRLS!" FAM put a stop to the bickering with one loud outburst, and Mr. Whizzer gave a sharp bark as well.

Julie shifted uncomfortably on the sofa and wiped her eyes again. As soon as she'd arrived, FAM had explained that Troy and Jack were in serious danger. The question they needed answered was whether Chase might have had something to do with it. Julie had immediately begun spilling everything she knew about Chase Maxfield, but she couldn't keep her mind off of Troy. "How long has Troy been missing? How could I not have realized he'd been replaced with an android?"

"Sweetheart, none of us knew it wasn't Troy, and blame won't do us one bit of good." Gram reached over to the sofa and patted Julie's hand as FAM, unable to stay seated, stormed about the room.

"We don't know for sure how long Troy-boy's been missing and we don't know where they are, but I found a DVD with a video on it in Jack's room that . . ." FAM faltered, and Florence, clad in so much yellow she could easily be mistaken for the sun come to Earth and wearing a blond wig at least eight inches high on her head, took over.

"Well, I will say that the video makes it clear our Troy is in the gravest of peril. I will also say that this Mr. Eden could use a few hours with my old voice coach; the man sounds absolutely ghastly!"

"Julie, Honey, we need your help," Gram's eyes were cloudy. "Is Chase trustworthy, or is he leading Jack into danger?" Gram wrung her hands in frustration.

"I don't know, Gram. In the past, I would have said that Chase was very trustworthy. But now, I just don't know if we can be sure. I wish I had said something sooner, but there's an oath at the Friend's Network to protect the kids who come there. I've never broken it before, and I just . . ."

FAM's thunderous voice took charge. "What's done is done! No going back—forward motion is all we have, BC."

Julie smiled. FAM had a way of making everyone feel better. She had been calling Julie "BC" for Black Canary ever since she delivered the costume along with Troy's Green Arrow gear the day before the party. Julie was more fond of FAM than the nickname, but you didn't tell a woman like FAM she couldn't give you a nickname if she wanted to.

FAM paced toward the fireplace, then back to the center of the room, and then over toward the entrance to the dining room with Mr. Whizzer following her every step of the way. "So let me get this straight. You volunteered at this Friend's Network in your old town, and Chase's mother drove him all the way there every week to see you?"

"Right." Julie brightened as she explained the network in more detail. "It's a really wonderful program that reaches out to kids who are, you know, finding school to be a tough place socially. They go to the network in another city to stay somewhat anonymous and basically get hooked up with a friend they can talk to once or twice a week. There's a lot of data on the number of kids who claim the network saved them from some pretty scary decisions."

"And you, Julie, were Chase's friend through this network, yes? I find myself racked with emotion over the entire affair. This is all so moving. It's worthy of the theater!" Florence reached for her throat. "It reminds me of the time I played in *Beaches*. You've seen the movie haven't you? What am I saying? Of course, you have. Everyone has seen that movie—about the woman dying of cancer and leaving behind her best friend." She stole a quick glance at Gram. "The critics loved me in it on the stage."

Gram couldn't resist. "Florence, you played the part of 'Woman 2' in a supermarket scene for all of three minutes."

"Katy Barrett, no one ever selected broccoli with more dramatic flourish than I!"

FAM popped in. "I'm sure that's true, Flo, but back to business. So you were Chase's pal in this network, BC, right?"

"Right. I mean I worked with him for nearly two years, but it was tough. The network tries to stress to these kids that they are okay the way they are, but Chase always wanted to talk about changing himself. He idolized the most popular guys in school and wanted desperately to become one of them."

Florence interjected. "Ahhhh, wanting to be someone else. He sounds like a theater man to me. Perhaps if he were to study with an acting coach?"

FAM shook her head. "I'm not going anywhere near that one." She turned her attention back to Julie. "Did you ever make any headway with him?"

"I thought I had at one point and then something happened at school. He got roughed up by a bunch of guys and refused to see me that week. His mom said he was too ashamed of the way he looked."

Gram came out of her chair. "The mother. You've met his mother?"

"Well, yeah, but just during drop off and pick up—except the day he wouldn't come, of course. She came and stayed nearly an hour. She was so broken up about what had happened to Chase." Julie rested her chin in her cupped hand recalling the memory. "It was the strangest conversation. Just before she left, a kind of calm came over her. She told me that she'd been thinking about taking matters into her own hands and that she'd been contacted by a place that claimed they could help Chase make an amazing transformation. Her eyes got this ferocity to them when she stood to go, as though she'd finally made a decision she'd been thinking about for a long time. I never saw Chase again until the first day of school this year, and the network oath says that we always protect the anonymity of a friend. Chase hasn't acknowledged me, so I haven't said anything to anyone . . . until now."

Florence rushed to Julie's side and hugged her briefly. "There, there, Poor Darling. Florence knows just how this feels. You should have seen me in *Friendships, Secrets, and Lies*. I'm still getting fan mail even after all these years."

Gram walked to the sofa and put an arm around Julie. "Sweetheart, please tell me that you charted your sessions at the network, and please tell me that Chase's mother mentioned the name of the place that was going to help him."

FAM pounded a fist into her open hand. "Because that's where Chase and Jack are headed. Jack left a note that said as much, but of course no information on where they were actually going."

Gram continued. "He won't answer his cell because he doesn't want us to follow, but, Julie, there is something very, very wrong about all of this. And if Mr. Eden is behind it, there's no telling how much danger the boys are in."

"The network did require us to chart reflections on all of our meetings. I can't remember for sure, but maybe Chase's mother did mention the name of the place."

Florence extended a hand to pull Julie up off the sofa. "Well, where are these musings of your mind, Darling? We've not a minute to lose."

"They'd be in the logs at the network office. If the information's there, I could find it pretty quickly. I'll need a ride though, and they've just moved so I'm not sure . . ."

"Have no fear, Florence to the rescue!" The elderly woman began dragging Julie to the door. "I'll get you there on my

Harley, which is twice as fast as Katy's, but I'll have to take it
a bit slow today because of all this hair!" She gestured toward
her tremendously tall wig. "I just felt the need for some height
today; it sends a message to the world," she said with pride.

Gram was on her feet. "It certainly does do that, Dear. It tells
the world you're trying to bring back hairstyles from the '70s,
but I won't say a word." She patted Florence's shoulders. "People
your age can get away with that type of thing. And by the way,
Florence Petrillo, I've bested you in seven motorcycle races, so
you stop all this storytelling. Why your Harley has eaten more
dirt from my . . ."

Florence was marching Julie toward her motorcycle and
drowning out Gram by telling a story about the time she played
Maria in *West Side Story*. It was at this point that FAM assumed
her best take-charge voice. "Katy, I'm assuming you want to
keep law enforcement out of this?"

"Oh, Lord, yes, Millie. Can you imagine the looks we'd get if
we tried to explain any of this to the police? Besides, even if they
did believe us, it would turn into a media nightmare that would
destroy any sense of normalcy we have left. And these days that's
not much! No, I don't want police."

"Well, assuming we're going to get a location, we're going to
need reinforcements, specialized equipment, and transportation. I
can go to work on the equipment if I know who I'm equipping."

"I'll give you a list of names, Millie. We'll have plenty of help,
but we'll need to protect their identities; I'd hate to have Mr.
Eden able to track them down if he survives this."

"Never a worry, Sis. You give me names and sizes, and I'll
handle disguises as well as equipment. That's my department."

Gram rose and gave her sister a hug. "You're such a dear. I'll get you everything you need, and I've got a wonderful pilot who'll take us wherever we need to go; transportation is not a worry."

Bill Simpson had spent most of the morning on the phone again today. Adam was leaving loose ends all over the place, and Bill was growing tired of cleaning them up. So much time was being spent on this new facility in Nevada that the international site was falling far behind schedule, and Adam's preoccupation with Katy's grandson Jack was seriously undermining the Master Plan. Bill shook his head. What was he thinking? Master Plan! Now Adam had *him* calling it that—as if Bill had wanted any part of this. The only thing he'd ever wanted—was out.

When Chip Barrett asked him to lunch nine years ago, Bill had been suspicious. Amos and Katy's son had never been high on his list of favorite people; Chip had hurt his parents, many times in many ways, and Bill's fierce loyalty required him to be cautious. He'd agreed to the lunch meeting reluctantly, and it had turned ugly. Bill had left before even finishing his salad. What Chip was asking was outrageous!

"Chip, you're out of your mind!" Bill's voice had become so intense he'd momentarily drawn the attention of the other restaurant patrons. "You want to unload stock in your own parents' company? That'll destroy them emotionally . . . and it could hurt the company financially. How can you think, even for a moment, that I would help you do that?"

"Bill!" Chip reached across the table, roughly grabbed the

cuff of Bill's suit jacket and hissed the next sentence. "I need money. I need a lot of it, and I need my identity protected. You're the only one who can do that. Now I don't have to take it all at once, but over the next several years I want the stock sold and little by little . . ."

"I won't do it, Chip! No way, and I can't understand for the life of me what would ever make you think I would." Bill had never been one for conflict; this was unfamiliar territory for him, but his sense of duty to Amos and Katy was endowing him with a momentary fighting spirit. He just wasn't sure how long it would last.

No response. Chip's eyes seemed to cloud over for a moment, and his anger dissipated as quickly as it had erupted. It was unusual—almost chilling. He continued speaking as if Bill's refusal was entirely meaningless. "I'm going to be investing in land, Bill, and a building venture will eventually follow. I just need this all handled very quietly and . . ."

"Chip, I said, 'No!' What part of that word don't you understand? I will not allow you to do this to your parents who, in case you've forgotten, are my best friends, and I certainly won't *help* you do it!"

Chip's voice remained matter-of-fact. "Now if you were to buy the stock from me, Bill, you could protect the company's interests from falling into other hands, which I'm sure you'd want to do, seeing as how you're such a loyal friend. My parents won't know anything about this unless you involve them, and I can't imagine you'd want to do that knowing how upsetting it would be for them. Do I have that right?" He didn't wait for Bill to answer but moved ahead. "So, they'll never know, which means they can't become upset. See there, Bill, everybody wins. It's really quite simple."

Bill remembered standing abruptly at that point and tossing his napkin onto the table in disgust. "You're amazing, Chip. Everyone wins? You see, I seem to have missed out on your unique point of view because I can't see how my betrayal of your parents is going to make me feel like a winner. And I have neither the time nor the stomach to listen to you elaborate on the details. Don't contact me about this again. Ever." Bill had stormed out in a huff, but as he crossed the street and glanced back through the restaurant window, his pace had slowed. Chip remained seated and appeared to be finishing his lunch in a relaxed and casual manner. He was laughing and chatting with a waitress as if he hadn't a care in the world; he did not exhibit the affect of a man who only moments before had been the recipient of news he should have found very upsetting. And it had bothered Bill Simpson the rest of that day. His mind had returned again and again to the image of the calm and smiling Chip Barrett finishing his lunch as if all were right with the world.

Bill's only distraction from the situation had come near day's end. He'd been leaving to grab a quick bite to eat before returning to the office. End of quarter was always a busy time, and he found the quiet of evening work comforting and less interruptive. Lucille had given him a fateful message as he headed out the door late that afternoon, and it had set in motion a chain of events that had summarily destroyed his life. The message made perfect sense now, but at the time, it was simply peculiar. "Oh, Mr. Simpson, before you go, I meant to tell you that a Mr. *Eden* phoned around four o'clock. I told him you were in, but he didn't seem to want to talk. He insisted on leaving a message. It was so crazy this afternoon with end of quarter reports coming due that I just . . . oh, where did I write that down?" Lucille was hurriedly rifling through her papers in an attempt to find the message.

"Eden?" Bill had scratched his head. "Can't recall anyone by that name, but then . . ."

"Oh, here it is, Sir! I jotted it down on the back of this spreadsheet and just didn't get it transferred. He simply said to tell you that he'd be seeing you later this evening."

Bill had walked out of the office rather puzzled. He decided to disregard the message, thinking it was likely some kind of prank. He rarely made evening appointments, and he was quite sure he hadn't forgotten one with a man he'd never even met.

And then Mr. Eden had shown up at his office door late that stormy night. Bill shuddered at the memory. When the figure clad in the dark coat and hat introduced himself as Adam Eden, Bill had no idea, at first, that it was Chip Barrett. It was only as Adam's discussion of his desire to create what he called a "unique community" moved forward that Bill got his first clear look at the face hiding behind the turned-up coat collar and the wide brimmed hat. It had been all Bill could do to remain calm. Chip was clearly not sane, and Bill had never been in the presence of someone in such an unbalanced mental state.

Though Adam Eden *was* Chip Barrett, Adam's voice, his posture . . . his very presence was altogether different from Chip's. In Bill's mind it was Adam, not Chip, who had forced him to make the decision that had so dramatically changed his life. For all Bill Simpson's big words about faithfulness and loyalty, for all his denials to help Chip Barrett unload his stock, it was remarkable how weak-willed he had become when Adam showed him the photograph.

The man in the long, dark coat stood and slid the first of two photographs across Bill's desk, stepping back into a corner of the office as he spoke. "I believe this is your older sister, Mr. Simpson. Your only living relative—am I right about that?"

Bill stared at the photo, his heart nearly skipping a beat. It was a very old picture, one he hadn't seen in years. It had been taken at his sister's senior prom. When no one had asked her to the dance, she had cried for days. And then Bill had told her he would be pleased to be her escort, and she had cried even harder as she accepted her brother's offer. Unexpected acts of kindness had always had that effect on her. She was a girl who'd only survived high school based on the charitable acts of others. A smile from a classmate or a request from someone to borrow her pencil were cause for celebration in her life. Hopelessly plain, not particularly bright, and with a personality that could best be described as bland, his sister had one standout feature: she was "nice." Bill had learned at a fairly young age, watching the world respond to his sister, that when "nice" was all you could bring to the table, you'd generally be eating alone. And he'd decided, all on his own, that for the rest of his life he'd do what he could to make up for the world's callous disregard for his sister and others like her.

"How did you get this photograph?" Bill's voice was suddenly as dry as parchment.

"That should not be your primary concern, Mr. Simpson. I wonder though," he held something now by the corner between his pinched right thumb and index finger, "if this more recent photograph of her, taken just yesterday in fact, would be of even greater interest to you."

Bill quickly rose from his chair without making a sound. He couldn't mask his disbelief. "That's not possible. She's . . ."

"Missing? Yes, it's been a few years, hasn't it? No leads on her disappearance, such a shame. Of course, the police are bumbling idiots, so it should come as no great surprise that they've botched the entire investigation."

"What? How do you know so much? How can you . . . Wait! Are you saying you've *found* her?" Bill was still trying to take it all in. "Do you know where she is?"

Adam had moved purposefully in Bill's direction then and gently pushed him back into his chair while simultaneously placing the newer photo of his missing sister before him on the desk. The sight of her was like fresh water to a castaway. She was alone in the photo, and she appeared to be standing in a very small room. "Where is she?" Bill was embarrassed at the almost childlike tone of his voice, but this was his sister. She was all he had left in the world, and this man was saying she was still alive.

And then, the Adam Eden who had so gently reseated him became an evil monster before his eyes. "I didn't *find* her, you idiot! I *took* her; I suppose I actually *hired* her, truth be told, for the type of job that suits someone with her limited abilities. Not that anyone other than you would have missed her anyway. You're quite a pair of wallflowers, *Bill*—you and your sister. Such simple-minded folk are easy prey for the up-and-coming like me. I arranged her disappearance in case you found a spine for the first time in your life and didn't agree to the arrangements my partner presented. We had intended to make our proposal to you quite some time ago, but things became complicated. Sorry your sister ended up disappearing so much earlier than was truly necessary. These things happen."

"Your partner? I don't know what you're talking about, but if you have my sister . . ."

"Barrett, you imbecile! Chip Barrett is my partner, for the moment at least. He's not much, but at least he's a step above you!" He swept both of the photos from the desk.

Bill wanted to rise and go for the man's throat. He wanted to force him to release his sister or to tell where she was being kept. He wanted to do so many things, but the pictures had melted him. He'd been out of character already today, acting as he did with Chip in the restaurant. Bill Simpson was a peaceful man, warm and kind. The battle he'd fought earlier today had taken most of the fight out of him, and these photographs had finished the job.

"Tomorrow, *Bill,*" Adam had spat the name as if the sound of it had soured in his mouth, "you are going to call Chip Barrett and tell him you've reconsidered your position regarding this afternoon's conversation. You're going to buy as much stock as he needs to sell, *Bill,* every year for the next several years. And you're not going to tell a soul. With you doing the purchasing, the Barretts' business will stay protected. And with you keeping your mouth shut, they'll never need to know what their son has done. More importantly, with you doing everything I say, your sister will stay safe. I've already given her a job and a place to live. She's quite comfortable; I assure you. So you see, Bill, everyone really does win when I'm happy. And as long as you keep me happy, your sister *Cora* will be just fine.

Chapter 17

I hated sneaking out of the house on FAM, but there was no way I could let her in on this. Besides, someone needed to keep watch over Gram until she was released from the hospital, and with FAM there, I knew everything would be fine.

"Jack, I got something here!" Chase was using his phone to search the Web for tickets while I drove us to the airport. "Here-to-There Airlines has tickets to Vegas for $69.99!"

"Never heard of 'em, but I like the price." I yanked my wallet from my back pocket and flipped him a credit card. "Make it happen."

"You've got plastic?"

"Gram arranged it for emergencies three years ago. I've only used it once to buy some, uhhh, Girl Scout cookies, so let's hope it's still good."

"The Girl Scouts take credit cards?"

"Well, no, actually they don't, but I didn't think about that when I gave her my card number and . . . let's just say you can't always fall for those innocent little girls in uniform." He was just staring at me, clearly waiting for more of the story than I was intending to reveal. It had taken me three months to get my account straightened out and to convince that girl's parents to pay for all the *High School Musical* paraphernalia she'd bought online with my credit card number. "Chase, just buy the tickets!"

Five hours later, we were crammed into seats 36 A and B,

which, being in the last row of the plane, failed to recline. Our seating situation contrasted dramatically with that of the man and woman seated in 35 A and B. Ten minutes after takeoff, they were both leaning so far back that I felt the need to begin a shampoo treatment. Chase had wisely left his tray table in its original position, allowing him the luxury of moving an arm or hand. I had stupidly lowered mine and between that and the gentleman's head that was begging for a scalp massage, I was basically paralyzed, so it was a great time for conversation. "So, Chase, did you reach your friends and tell them about me?" He was supposed to call while I had been printing boarding passes.

"Uhhhh, yeah. Yeah. They know you're on the way, Jack."

"So everything's good then. They're interested in working with me?"

He wasn't looking me in the eye which was bugging me, but I decided to ignore it. Note to self: failure to make eye contact always means something. "Sure. Yeah, sure. They . . . uhhhh . . . they're already planning for your arrival. No worries, Jack. No worries."

"Okay, great!" I was psyched. If they could do for me physically at least some of what they'd done for Chase—and if they could somehow adjust me mentally—I could return home, gather FAM and other reinforcements, and find a way to locate and stop Mr. Eden once and for all. This little stopover at Chase's Vegas voodoo parlor was sure to do the trick. I rocked side to side in an effort to dislodge a hand from the vise grip of the seat and tray table combo and gain a new position. Chase should have been laughing at my antics, but he was lost in thought. I snapped my fingers. "Hey, Buddy-boy. Look! I managed to get one hand free." I waved my fingers in his face.

"Huh? Oh, hey, yeah . . . yeah . . . good move, Jack."

His face, those chiseled features that contrasted so sharply with his geeky personality, was masking something right now. If I could get him talking, maybe it would all come out. "So let's hear it, the story of how you became the new you, Chase. I'm all ears."

"You know, Jack, I'm starting to think it would better if we just waited. Once they have you, it'll be . . ."

I jumped on that comment with a sinister laugh, which I'm pretty good at replicating from the old horror shows. "Wha, ha, ha, ha, ha! Ooooohhh! Once they *have* me! Now it's starting to sound like a scary sci-fi flick . . . or a cannibal's dinner party. Is there something you're not telling me, Chase?"

He just stared at me. Didn't say a word but stared long enough that my old worries about this place and what had happened to him there were scrambling back to the surface. I shoved them back down again.

"Jack, I can't do this. It's not worth it. . . . I . . ."

"Can I get you gents somethin' from my cart? I got all kinds a stuff on this little baby. Beer, wine, and cocktails are $5.00. Ohhh, wait, you're not old enough for none of that stuff. Well, I got some Pringles potato chips or a cookie pack?" The flight attendant was behind her cart instead of in front of it, which put her behind our seats and made it kind of hard to carry on a conversation since we couldn't see her face. Worse yet, the audible chomping of her gum reminded me distinctly of the daffy real estate agent Mr. Eden had hired to keep our old house from selling.

"Hey, I'll take a cookie pack. And some milk, too. Do you have milk?" Why was I surprised that Chase was ordering milk and cookies? He just didn't get that teenagers, especially ones that look like he did these days, don't order milk and cookies. "Jack, spot me some cash, will you?"

I squirmed in my seat trying to get to my money as the flight attendant began banging and clanging the drawers in her cart with so much commotion she could have sent the plane veering off course. "Oh, sure thing, Kiddo. I got milk on here somewhere. I gotta hunt around a little, you know, 'cause working these carts is a lot more complicated than you'd ever guess." She pushed her cart forward a bit, bringing herself into view just as I passed Chase some bills. I caught a quick flash of platinum hair and turquoise-and-purple earrings in the shape of giant giraffes.

"Oh, no." I thought. "It can't possibly be." And suddenly there she was in all her glory—handing Chase his cookie pack. She extended her hand in greeting and shook his, which is completely contrary to anything I have ever seen a flight attendant do.

"Mimi Rosenfeld, flight attendant extraneous! Pleased to meetcha, Kid! It's my first official day on the job. A newbie, that's what they call me. I forgot my uniform so the pilot's not so happy, but I'm over it. You're a real looker, Kid. How old are you?"

Chase was looking at her like she had two heads. She was wearing a red smock with the name "Bree Ann" embroidered into it. Some kind of brown-and-pink-striped turtleneck was underneath the smock and was clearly working against the color scheme. Chase ignored her compliment and her question about his age. "Errr . . . your name thing says 'Bree Ann.'" That was the best Chase could do on short notice. I forgave him though.

I felt certain that there were few among the human race who participated in normal conversations with Mimi Rosenfeld.

"Yeah! Well, I figure she'll never know I borrowed it. I look more official with this on, but I can't wait to wear mine. It says 'Destiny' on it. Don't cha love that? 'Cause I'm thinkin' of changin' my name to that anyway. Mimi's too popular, ya know? Everyone knows a hundred people named Mimi, right? I hate just blendin' in all the time. I'm thinkin' if I change my name I'll stand out in a crowd more. Ya know what I mean? Okay, so here's the milk. I only got whole milk so I know that's okay, right? I know that's okay because that's the only kind I got. Ha! Ha!" It sounded like a goose was honking . . . or dying when she laughed.

I knew what was coming next, and it did. If I recognized her then . . . "Hey! I know you! You're the kid from the skate corral right? The one that asked me to skate doubles, and I had to tell ya I was too old for ya. I still think about that a lot, ya know. No, wait, that's not it. Oh, I know, I know, you're the kid from the bowling alley who wears little-kid-sized shoes on accounta that weird foot disease? How's that workin' out for ya? Ahhhhh! Never mind. I got, I got it. You're the kid with the whacked out dad who hired me to sell the house and then . . . that's you isn't it? I knew it the minute I saw ya." Mimi patted her head. "Mind like a steel collander!" she announced with pride.

"Yeah. Well, hey there, Mimi. It sure is nice to see you. Water will be just fine."

"Can do, Kid, can do. I get it, really. You don't want to talk about your nutso pop, and that's okay by me, but you know he still owes me five Gs, right? If ya see him, ya might mention that 'cause I could use a little extra spendin' money right now. This flight attendant trainin' is expensive, and I'm thinkin' of takin' the advanced classes next year. Savin' up and all." She handed me the water and mercifully headed back down the aisle when some passenger rang the call button. I wondered about the type of people who would ever purposely ask Mimi to come back to their seats.

Chase looked at me. "You know her?"

"We met once. This time will be much like last time. I will try to push it as far back into my mind as possible. Chase, what did you mean when you said you couldn't do this? What can't you do?" I was anxious to restart our conversation from before Mimi's arrival.

He closed his eyes. "Never mind. I just get weird on planes is all. I didn't want to tell you that I'm afraid to fly, but I am. I just meant that I can't do this—I can't fly. But here I am, so I guess I can. Forget about it, Jack."

He wasn't going to say any more, but I wasn't going to forget about it either. Chase was lying. I knew it, and so did he.

The minute the wheels hit the pavement, Chase started texting, and when he saw me watching him, he spoke nervously, "Just letting them know we've arrived."

"Fine," I said. Suddenly, something was different between us. I didn't understand it, but it felt like we were no longer the team I thought we were when we left. Now, it seemed like we were going to be more like stranded fliers who end up renting a car together just to get where they're going.

"We're meeting in the parking garage, level 2, section G," was the last bit of conversation as we exited the plane and made our way through the airport and out toward the garage. Every attempt I made to engage him in a discussion was completely ignored, and I was wary of starting an argument because I needed him to get me where I was going. Eventually, we arrived at a black town car with no visible markings. A man got out, rather nondescript, and pulled out two handkerchiefs as he approached us. I backed away, but Chase stood erect and allowed the man to blindfold him. He then turned around and submitted his hands, which were cuffed with expert precision. The man gently helped Chase into the back of the car. Then he moved toward me, and I took another step back.

"Whoa there, Buddy! Chase . . . Chase, Man, what's up with the whole blindfold and handcuff theme here? You didn't say anything about . . ."

"It's for protection, Jack. This facility is kind of a 'best-kept secret,' so they blindfold you as you enter and leave it. The cuffs are just a precaution to be sure you don't remove the blindfold. It's nothing, really."

I was at a crossroad. Every instinct God gave me told me that letting anybody blindfold, handcuff, and put you into an unmarked car that's taking you someplace in secret is just a very bad plan, but I needed what this place had to offer. At least I thought I did. So I submitted to the blindfold, but as I did my old friend, doubt, resurfaced. I heard the silent chauffeur pull the cuffs from his pocket, and my doubt won out. I wasn't doing this! I moved to pull at the blindfold, and he grabbed my arms with force and cinched the cuffs so tightly they bit into my wrists. He then paraded me to the other side of the car and shoved me inside with far less care than he had given to Chase. He closed both rear doors, effectively trapping us inside, and a few minutes later, the car glided forward as a terrible sense of foreboding came over me. "Chase, this is all wrong, my coming here. Suddenly, I just know it's wrong. This is a big mistake, me doing this. Isn't it?"

His voice was cold and distant in reply. "Depends on your perspective, Jack. I can't say it's such a bad thing from my point of view."

"How so?" I forced out the question with trepidation.

"Because, Jack. Your arrival at this place is going to save my mother's life."

Chapter 18

Cora was standing outside the door to The Check-Up Room as she did every other week. It was nearly time for her check-up, which took place precisely at 2:30 P.M. on her scheduled day. She would enter the room as always and take her seat in the special chair. The electrodes would be strapped to her head and body in the exact same places, and she would answer the same questions she always did. She would give the same responses that Constance would have given a few moments before. Cora didn't know a lot, but through the years, she had learned a little about how Mr. Eden ran things. There were only three people in his inner circle of employees who she knew were not androids: his assistant, Constance, who was always leaving The Check-Up Room just as Cora entered it; Cora herself; and a third mysterious person she had never seen. She knew of the existence of a third only because the facilitator had made a comment, following one of her regular check-ups, that the equipment could not be put away because there was one other yet to arrive. There were often a few humans around whenever they moved to a new location, but it seemed Mr. Eden quickly had androids created to replace them. She smiled, thinking of that nice technician—Guy—who'd come running past her in such a rush the other day. He was still human, she could tell. It was always nice to be in the company of someone more like her.

The door to The Check-Up Room opened, and Constance exited as Cora entered. Each knew who the other was, but the two women had not spoken since they met on training day several years ago because Mr. Eden did not allow idle chatter. Cora took her seat in the chair as the facilitator moved the electrodes into place. She hadn't given an incorrect response since her very first check-up, two weeks into her employment. Incorrect responses were severely punished, and Cora didn't like punishment. It was best, she had noted long ago, to choose behaviors throughout the week that mirrored your verbal responses during your check-ups. She certainly had not done that this week. She looked around worriedly, wondering if her traitorous thoughts could be seen on the outside, but the facilitator did not seem to take note.

Cora tried to embrace the mindset she had grown accustomed to over the past several years. She needed to be thinking about how she had always believed these things were true; she needed to be who she was expected to be while she answered these questions, or the machine might sense she was lying. She suspected that the controls were not set to such rigid parameters as would have been expected years ago when she was first hired, and that gave her hope that perhaps she could be successful. She made it through all of the questions with no troubles, and then the last one came. The facilitator delivered the question in the same monotone voice Cora was accustomed to hearing, but today she heard it differently.

"Is there anything more important than making Mr. Eden happy?"

And for the briefest moment, she had wanted to scream "YES! Yes, there are a thousand things more important than making him happy! And I used to know what they were, but now I can't seem to remember." The dangerous thoughts sent her reeling into panic mode, and her mind grasped at them wildly and sought to seal them away in a vault from which they could never emerge.

The facilitator gasped. A light blinked indicating that an inappropriate response was being considered; however, it did not blink a second time. Cora stole a nervous glance at his face as he studied the machine; it appeared this was a very rare occurrence. Though not specifically recorded in the guidebook, protocol would be for him to ask the question again, and he was preparing to do so when Cora spoke up.

"There is nothing more important than making Mr. Eden happy. *Everyone knows that.*" She said it with the practiced ease of a woman who'd been saying it for years because that is precisely what she'd been doing. And she'd always believed it was true—until today.

Bill Simpson sighed and put down the letter he was reading from his sister. Cora was safe; he knew that because Adam allowed them to write weekly letters to one another. Adam had also, on occasion, allowed him to view Cora on video monitors in her apartment living room, but Bill was never allowed to see her in person, and she had no idea where he was or what he had sacrificed to protect her. The letters were their lifeline to one another, and they had come to mean a great deal to both of them. Letters with fake routings and addresses. Letters filled with lies about their joy-filled and interesting lives; each letter intended to assure a beloved sibling that all was well. Bill, of course, had the disadvantage of knowing they were both lying, and that the lives they were leading were much closer to a hellish nightmare than to any of the Sunnybrook Farm-type scenes described in their correspondence. He wondered, often, if somehow Cora also knew that they were both lying.

The whole Nevada Project had come to fruition out of Adam's need to avenge himself. Though the real Chip Barrett was gone, two other Adam Edens remained. Were they clones or android copies? No one seemed to know, and Bill knew better than to ask. One worked internationally, as Bill did, but they rarely saw one another and never communicated electronically or by phone. In fact, Bill was not sure he would even know how to go about contacting "International Adam" if he needed him. It was "U.S. Adam" with whom Bill spoke regularly during phone and video conferences. The two Adam Edens never spoke of one another, and Bill had no way of knowing for sure if they even knew that one another existed, yet wouldn't they have to know with bank accounts in their names and contracts constantly being signed? His head hurt whenever he thought about it, so he tried not to. He felt certain the one in Nevada was a clone because at brief moments in time, a more subdued personality seemed to be fighting with Adam's sinister persona. Bill had seen it on occasion during video calls; in fact, it had reached the point where he could sometimes even sense it during a regular phone call. It often happened late at night or when discussions concerning Jack were particularly violent. Though he was no medical or psychiatric expert, Bill felt sure that only a clone would carry Chip's personality disorder into another body. And if that had indeed happened, then in those moments when Adam seemed at war with himself, Bill felt that Chip Barrett, barricaded somewhere inside the deepest layers of Adam's psyche, was trying to surface or, at the very least, to exert some level of control over Adam's actions. Chip had never been successful, that Bill could see, but one could always hope. Either way, the two Adam Edens kept Bill Simpson on his toes. And the one in Nevada never had Jack Barrett far from his thoughts. He was determined to break the boy, psychologically, and then physically as well.

Bill had given up trying to reason with Adam on the issue as it was clearly a lost cause. He couldn't help Jack if he'd wanted to because he didn't know specifically what Adam was planning. For that matter, he didn't know exactly what went on in the Nevada facility. He knew that it functioned as a hotel to the outside world, but they were always full so no one ever got in without a reservation. No one walked in off the streets in other words. He'd asked Adam several times about the actual services being provided in Nevada, and his response was always the same. "We're making people happy here, Bill. Very happy. We're especially making me happy, and that's all you need to know."

Bill considered for a moment what he actually did know. He knew that it was not really a hotel; it wasn't possible given the cash flow. He was responsible for managing most of Adam's finances, and this facility was generating tremendous amounts of money, which were being funneled out of the U.S. and to international accounts Bill managed on a weekly basis. He knew that the Paradise village was currently under construction in another location outside the U.S., and he knew that the Master Plan, as Adam called it, involved the original village being successfully re-created. It was where the Edens would have their "happily ever after." Exactly who the Edens were, Bill wasn't entirely sure. But comments Adam had made led him to believe that the Barretts were to become the Edens in some manner. How that would happen, Bill couldn't venture to guess. Or maybe he could, but he wasn't willing to dwell on it long enough to imagine it coming to fruition.

Bill reached for the photograph of Kathryn Barrett he kept on his desk and fingered the frame gently. As he brought it close, sunlight streaming through a side window hit the glass just right and superimposed his own reflection over the photograph beneath it. He turned his eyes away. Bill Simpson didn't like reflective surfaces; their tendency to reveal a pure image unsettled him. He was no longer the man he'd once been, and he'd long since given up hope that he could ever be that man again. He settled the frame back onto his desk and spoke in a tender voice though no one was there to hear him. "I'm sorry, Kathryn. I'm sorry old friend, for so many things." The phone rang, but Bill didn't answer. Instead, he rested his head in his hands and ignored what sounded like desperate pleas from the receiver. One poor decision, his desperate attempt to save his sister's life, had led him to sell his soul to the Devil or at least that's how he'd come to think of it. Nine years ago, when this all began, he'd never have guessed that the Devil wore a black trench coat and a wide-brimmed hat. Now, he knew differently.

Jori McAllister had lost all track of time since her watch had been taken. The windowless room in which she was imprisoned didn't offer her any help, so she had no idea what time it was when a blank-faced attendant wheeled an unexpected visitor into the room then silently left without a word of explanation.

The woman in the wheelchair looked thoughtful. She peered

at Jori with one good eye; the other eye was made of glass, and Jori forced herself from staring. She had never seen a glass eye up close but now wasn't the time to explore the situation. Her visitor was dressed in a pink bathrobe that had bits of a white gown peaking out from underneath. Her slippers had basset hound heads on top of them, and her smile was warm when she spoke. "Hello there, Young Lady. I was so excited when he told me I was going to visit with someone; I haven't had anyone to talk to for months. I can walk, actually, but I'm not so steady yet working with only the one eye, so they want me to use the wheelchair for a little while longer. Who are you here to help?"

Jori, seated on her cot, pulled her knees to her chest subconsciously. "I'm not here to *help* anyone." She was about to reveal that she was being held prisoner here but reversed course at the last second and took the conversation in a different direction. "You said 'he' told you that you were going to visit with someone. Who did you mean?"

"Why Mr. Eden, of course. He's been so good to me."

Jori felt the world spin backwards on its axis. Mr. Eden— charitable? What had he done—given this woman shelter when she returned from a tour of duty in Iraq? Paid for her eye surgery following a car crash? Every thought racing to her mind was completely unimaginable. Mr. Eden didn't help anyone other than himself. She decided she might get more information if she played along. She lowered her knees, removing the barrier between them. "Yes, he's such a good man. What has he done for you?"

"Well, it's not what he's done for me directly, but it's what he's *allowed* me to do . . . for my son. Mr. Eden believes all things are possible; he's amazing! Truly. That man can make anything happen."

Jori continued to play along. "He certainly is all about helping others. What was he able to do for your son?"

The woman smiled shyly. "Well, I hadn't planned on ever telling anyone, but with no one to talk to in all these months, I feel a little desperate to share the good news!" She leaned forward in her chair a bit—a gesture meant to indicate that she was about to take Jori into her confidence. "Mr. Eden's begun the process of helping my son become the young man he's always dreamed of being. I have before and after pictures. Wait until you see!" She reached into her robe pocket and pulled them out one at time, setting them face down on her lap. Then, she wheeled the chair closer to Jori. "There," she said, turning over one of the photos. "That's the before photo."

Jori looked at the boy. He was clearly high school age, with pale skin and flat hair. His build was wiry, and there was no mistaking that his somewhat yellow teeth were in need of braces. She imagined his life in high school could not be pretty.

The woman's eyes were filled with sadness. "He had it rough. I tried everything I could think of to help him, but nothing worked. Kids can be so cruel, you know. Ahhhh, but then Mr. Eden entered our lives, and here's my boy today!" She flipped over the other picture. "Look at my Chase now!"

Jori didn't need more than a casual glance at the hunky boy in the photo to realize that this was Chase Maxfield's mother, and suddenly a very dark thought began to form in her mind. "Mrs. . . ."

"Maxfield. Gloria Maxfield, Dear. Now look at the photo."

"Mrs. Maxfield, how did . . ."

"No questions! I don't want to hear questions! Look at him!" The woman nearly lost her balance grabbing at the photo and thrusting it into Jori's face. "You barely looked! He deserves more than that. He's a fine looking boy, now; don't you think? Why a girl like you would be a good match for a boy like my Chase the way he looks now, wouldn't you?"

Jori remained silent but gently guided the woman's hand, still clutching the photo, back toward the wheelchair.

"You would look good together, wouldn't you?" Gloria Maxfield's voice was desperate, and her leaking eyes pleaded with Jori to respond. "I gave up so much for this."

"He's a very handsome boy, Mrs. Maxfield. Any girl would be lucky to be on his arm, but I already have a knight in shining armor, and I'm desperate to get back to him."

"Yes, Chase is a very handsome boy, now. I did the right thing; it was the only way, wasn't it?" It seemed as if Mrs. Maxfield was suddenly speaking to herself—almost as though she'd forgotten Jori was in the room, and her rambling monologue took on the eerie quality of one she might have been repeating aloud for all the lonely days she had spent here. "There was no other way. Yes. Yes, I did the right thing."

"Mrs. Maxfield," Jori reached out and touched the woman's hand. "How did you lose your eye? Was there some kind of . . ."

"Accident? No, nothing like that, Miss McAllister." Mr. Eden's forceful voice broke in and completed Jori's question before she could finish. He had obviously been monitoring the entire conversation from somewhere outside of the room because he entered as if on cue. A blank-faced attendant joined him and was preparing to take Mrs. Maxfield away when Mr. Eden held up his hand and all movement ceased. "Surely you've heard people say, 'I'd give my right arm' in reference to getting something they want, Miss McAllister?"

Jori rose and regarded him coolly, nodding at his comment but remaining silent.

Mr. Eden grinned, knelt at the side of the wheelchair and spoke warmly to Chase's mother. "Well, Mrs. Maxfield's right arm wasn't needed, but I had a buyer who was desperate for her right eye. Mrs. Maxfield sold me her eye—to get what she wanted. I'm touched by the determination of this devoted mother to alter the destiny of her child." Gloria Maxfield took his hand and laid it against her cheek.

"You're such a good man. Thank you. I did the right thing, didn't I?" She was staring at Jori as she spoke.

Mr. Eden straightened from his bent position next to the wheelchair, waved his hand, and the attendant reached for the chair and guided Mrs. Maxfield out. Jori thought it interesting that despite his shadowy facial features, she knew he was scowling. His voice radiated contempt when he spoke. "I never had that kind of a mother."

She struck him in the face and moved immediately to a fighting posture. She didn't normally put her black belt training to work in this manner, but with this man, all rules went out the window. She had made up her mind that if she were ever alone with him again, an attack might be her only way out.

"I'm going to let that go." Her blow had set him back a few steps, but he rebounded—casually extended one hand and leaned against the wall in a relaxed pose. "Because that's quite possibly one of the last times you'll be using that hand."

"If you think you can scare me with a bunch of double-talk, you can think again, Chief." Jori took two lightning quick steps forward, and her leg shot out with precision timing that should have taken her opponent totally by surprise. Instead, his left hand targeted her ankle and locked on it in midair. A flick of his wrist nearly snapped the bone, and she was suddenly sprawled on the floor in a less than graceful position. Gasping from the pain, she repeatedly shoved down the groan threatening to escape her lips. She didn't think her ankle was broken, but the sprain was serious. She was sure he would do worse if she continued to test him, but she'd never been a docile girl, and she certainly wasn't going to become one in his presence.

"You've no idea how much money I could lose if you're seriously injured, Miss McAllister. That's why I'm trying to control my temper." He sighed. "Three buyers have already wired several million dollars to my international accounts in prepayment for some of your organs."

"What?" She tried to disguise her fear, but some of it was seeping through.

Mr. Eden bent down and grabbed her face. "I'm in the business of making people happy, Miss McAllister. That's what we do at this facility. We give desperate people what they want. I *facilitate* happiness by allowing people to part with their organs in order to improve the quality of life for their family members. There's a very wealthy woman in Bahrain right now, whose eyesight has been fully restored thanks to Mrs. Maxfield's generous donation. He leaned toward Jori and grinned, "And the wealthy woman in Bahrain paid me $1.2 million for Mrs. Maxfield's eye. I call it a finder's fee. I spent a pittance of that on plastic surgery and cosmetic dentistry for the Maxfield boy, then set him up with a dietician and fitness coach and began pumping him full of steroids. Voilà! He's a new creation, mother's happy, and I'm able to fund my business venture overseas."

Jori tried to pull her face loose from his grip, but he held her fast. "You're sick is what you are. You're so twisted and messed up there aren't words to describe it. You're . . ."

"Thus far, I've only sold organs, but I've been toying with the idea of transacting in limbs as well. Your lungs, kidneys, and liver have already been bid on and sold. But I'm wondering how much I might be able to get for your arms and legs. I bet they'd fetch a fine price." He released her, stood, and paced the room. "You see, I've got another village under construction, and somebody's going to have to pay the bill. It should comfort you to know that your *contributions* will be providing a sizeable donation."

She crawled backwards, dragging her wounded ankle. "You're even crazier than I thought. There's no way you can get away with that. No one would . . ."

He moved back and forth in a semicircle, pinning her against the wall like a lion targeting its prey. "People are dying every day, Miss McAllister, all over the world. They need hearts, livers, lungs—everything really. And some of those people are very, very wealthy. They'll pay anything to get what they want, and they won't question where it came from, I assure you."

She had managed to pull herself up and sit on the cot, and she shrank back as he approached her directly now.

"And then there are the unhappy people who simply need their eyesight restored or who might want your legs, Miss McAllister, simply because they are more beautiful than their own." He reached for one of Jori's legs, and she jerked to the side violently to keep him from touching her. He grabbed her wrists in one of his powerful hands and ran the index finger of his free hand across her palms. "They might want your hands because they are so much softer than their own." She spat at him and watched her saliva roll down his right cheek. He grabbed her hair in response and pulled her toward him. "Someone out there might even want your *face* Miss McAllister; I'll get back to you on that." He shoved her roughly backwards and stood to go. "They'll be coming soon to take you to the surgical unit; it's right down the hall. I just stopped in to say good-bye and to let you know I'll be filming everything when they take you apart . . . piece by piece. I'm going to show the movie to Jack while *he's* on the operating table."

Susan Barrett had received word that Adam was coming with a visitor, and her heart and mind were enemies at once. From the moment Adam had told her he was bringing Troy to see her, she had been wrestling with thoughts and feelings no mother should ever have to consider. To see Troy, here, meant he was alive and safe. She could see for herself; she could know for sure. But if he was here, she had little doubt he would have been brought here by force and that he would likely be imprisoned here as she was. How could she be pleased about that? She paced the generous rooms of The Chambers and decided it would be best to bury any emotion. Adam should see that she was pleased to see Troy, but it would be dangerous to appear overly excited. After all, Adam Eden was enough to make anyone happy—right? As long as she kept him thinking she really believed that, she felt she had the upper hand.

"Susan?" His voice interrupted her thoughts as he stood in the foyer of The Chambers.

"Adam, hello, I didn't hear . . ." she turned, saw him standing there with Troy, and all her carefully laid plans disintegrated. Her son was dressed in nothing but a pair of running shorts, yet she didn't question—she simply ran to him. No woman had ever crossed a room so quickly or held her son so tightly. Susan Barrett's delicate frame heaved and sobbed in such a torrent of emotion that no words could make their way out. And her boy clung to her in like fashion.

"MOM!" Troy cried real tears for the first time in a very long time. He knew this was his mother—the woman who had spent most of her life trying to protect him from a man who insisted Troy was never quite all that he needed to be. Troy had always been good enough for his mother just the way he was, and now he was finally with her again. He knew instantly that there would be no interrogation of her, no twenty questions about his growing up years; all the proof he'd decided would be necessary before he would trust her was tossed aside the minute they embraced.

She took the slightest step back and ran her fingers through his hair, ran her hands down the sides of his face. "Troy, oh, Troy . . ." and then she was sobbing and holding him again.

Mr. Eden tapped his fingers on the doorframe impatiently. "I believe a 'thank you' is in order, Susan. I believe I am owed that much." His voice was terse, edgy, and it fractured their reunion. She drew herself away from her son and turned to address Adam. But she couldn't bear to lose physical contact with Troy, not yet, not even for a moment, so she reached out to take his hand and gasped aloud at his chafed wrist, rubbed raw from the manacle. She stepped back farther and saw the same markings in several other places on his body where the metal bonds had imprisoned him for hours. And then, Susan Barrett spoke in a tone she'd never dared use since arriving in this place.

"*What have you done to my son?* Look at his skin! He's been bound like . . . like some kind of animal!"

"Susan, I don't care for your tone." He reached for her, and she backed away. "Don't you *touch* me. Ever! Never again." She grabbed a vase of flowers and threw it with all the force she could muster directly at him. He stepped to the side with ease, but his face grew dark and angry. His fury, however, was no match for hers. "You are a MONSTER! Do you hear me? And I hate you! I HATE YOU, and I always will."

Adam Eden leaped toward her and grabbed her arms with his powerful hands. "You will *not* speak that way to me! You will respect me, and you will admire me. You will obey me, and you *will* love me. You will . . ."

"Let her go, Dad." Troy's voice was icy and calm. Mr. Eden turned to look at him, and his eyes grew cloudy. Troy's voice was filled with steely determination. His muscles tensed for action, and he kept his eyes locked on his target. "Let her go. Now."

There was a quiet moment when no one moved. Without warning, Mr. Eden released his hold. He regarded Troy briefly, then shifted his eyes back to Susan to be certain she was clear that she was the one he was addressing when he spoke. "This isn't finished. This isn't *nearly* finished." He turned then and abruptly exited The Chambers.

Chapter 19

Chase barely spoke again for the rest of the car ride. Every conversation starter I tossed out received a clipped response, and I imagined him physically turning away as if he couldn't quite face me. If he hadn't begun acting strangely the minute we landed, I wouldn't have been so suspicious, but his behavioral about-face coupled with the whole cloak and dagger airport pick up was a pretty clear sign I was in trouble. Was this all staged? His near drowning in the pool, his moving into our house and becoming part of our inner circle—had he planned it all? Were the events of the past few months all orchestrated to bring me here? The car stopped, and so did my rambling thoughts. I wanted my senses alert.

We were escorted from the car quickly over some rough terrain. I heard the sound of a metal door open with a great deal of difficulty and nearly lost my balance as we began following a steep path down into the earth. We were inside some kind of underground tunnel, I knew, because of the absence of light. Great! Underground with blindfolds and handcuffs—my idea of a swell time. Eventually, I heard the quiet "swish" of a modern door, and we came into an area lit with artificial light; I could sense that much. Our silent driver/escort walked us around for quite a while, to be sure we had no idea where we'd come from, and I heard Chase's cuffs being removed—but not mine. By the time Chase removed his blindfold and pulled mine off, we were alone. He checked his watch, then grabbed me and shoved me down on a small bench. "Look, Jack. I have five minutes before I'm supposed to deliver you, okay, so . . ."

"Deliver me! What are you talking about, Chase? What's going on? What have you gotten me into? I thought we were friends. . . ."

"We were! We . . . are. But there isn't much time," he glanced nervously at his watch on and off as he spoke. "Listen, this *is* the place that helped change me, Jack. I was telling the truth about that, and I know they can change you, too. For sure."

"How? How do you know for sure? Before, you said that maybe, *maybe* they could help me."

"Okay, so that part wasn't true. I knew they could help you because they wanted you here all along. They're *interested* in helping you, Jack. It's a good thing, right?"

"Chase! What are you, nuts? How could they even know anything about me? And before . . ." Suddenly a shot fired in my brain. "Chase who runs this place? It's not the guy on the video with Troy is it?" My skin was crawling. "Chase is Mr. Eden behind this?"

"NO! Jack, no way. Trust me, if I'd ever met a loon like that, I'd remember it. I don't really know who's in charge. My mom handled all that stuff when we came here last June. The only guy I ever met was in a video conference call. His name was Simpson, Bill Simpson. Seemed like a really good guy."

I felt the sweat breaking out all over my body, and I heard my voice get shaky. "Chase. Chase, listen to me, very carefully. You gotta get these cuffs off me, now! NOW, Chase! Mr. Eden *is* here. He's behind all of this. Simpson is linked to Mr. Eden. Chase, please!"

I could see the uncertainty in his eyes as it played out, but he didn't move to release me. "Jack, Mr. Simpson was really nice! I'm telling you. . . ."

"Chase, LISTEN TO ME! It's not what it seems. They have Troy! He's here. And once they have me—who knows what they're gonna do. I don't know what they told you or promised you, Man, but if Mr. Eden's involved, I guarantee you're in danger, too."

"Listen, Jack. I've been through this once, and everything was fine. It's just that it's really expensive. My mom had to pay for it, and we didn't have the money. So she . . . she kind of sold one of her . . . eyes." He was staring at the ground in shame.

"WHAT?" I stood up, which was no easy task, but I had to move as an expression of my extreme panic. "Please tell me you're joking. Please tell me you don't mean *eye* as in one of the two organs in the body that provides sight, Chase."

He started to cry. "She said it was the only way. The only way to give me what I wanted. I didn't know, Jack, I swear I didn't know what she was doing until it was too late. And now I'm here for the second phase of treatment. They're going to do something to my brain and make me act cool and talk cool—all the time. It's going to be a whole new me."

My freak-o-meter was off the charts, but I was trying not to condemn him. If I came down on him, he'd stop talking, and information was a vital weapon right now. "Okay, Chase. Okay, listen, now. Think. Changing you on the outside was one thing—cosmetic dentistry, plastic surgery, fitness routine, I don't know, maybe those vitamins they gave you aren't really vitamins? But changing your *brain?*"

It was like he hadn't heard a word I'd said. "Mom was going

to sell her liver and lungs to pay for it." He looked up at me in grief beyond what I had ever seen on a human face. "I couldn't let her do it, and that's when Mr. Simpson asked if I knew you. They offered me a deal, Jack. If I could convince you to come here and get some help for yourself, then they would complete my second phase in return. My mom gets to go home with me when we're done here! She has a glass eye, but that'll be all. So, you see, no harm done. Really. It's just you didn't need any help, so I had to sort of . . . convince you. And it wasn't working at first, but then all the stuff started going wrong with Jori, and it suddenly got easier because you were so down. And then with your grandmother getting sick and Troy . . ."

"CHASE!" Finally, it all came into clear focus. "Chase, it wasn't Jori! He must have replaced her the same way he did Troy. He's got her, too. Think about it, Chase. THINK! It's like you said, when I wouldn't bite, all these things started happening to undermine my confidence. They were orchestrated! Mr. Eden made it all happen—Jori, Gram, Troy—he's put events in motion that would lead me here."

A shadowy figure, dressed in his trademark coat and hat, rounded the corner and pressed an object against Chase's neck. One quick jolt of electricity, and he went down. "Lousy watch, Kid." I could tell Mr. Eden was looking at me, but his face remained somewhat hidden as he spoke. "He never had five minutes, only three and a half." He kicked Chase's body to the side like day-old garbage and made his way to me.

"I've heard of kicking a guy when he's down, but you take it a step further and do it when he's unconscious. Does that make you feel like a big man?"

He grabbed the front of my shirt and let his right fist have a loud conversation with my face. As I hit the ground, his foot chatted up my rib cage once or twice, too. "I am your *master.*"

I could taste blood in my mouth, but with my hands cuffed behind me, there was no way to do anything but let it trickle out. I comforted myself by thinking that it probably looked cool. "Master? Not on your best day, Champ. I already took you down once, remember?"

"Oh, I remember, Jack." Another hard kick, and this time I felt a rib crack. "I remember all too well, and today you're going to pay for it." He hoisted me up and hit me again, knocking me against a wall that was now doing more of a support job than my legs. His fist was a steel beam colliding with my flesh. One more would finish me. He came again, and I pulled my head to the right as his fist went straight through the wall. He was grunting, trying to pull it loose, and I ducked around him and went running back at him using my head as a battering ram, colliding with him from behind. BAM! He hit the wall, hard. I know because my head felt it on the other side of his body. I backed up and repeated the process twice more until he collapsed with his arm still partially caught in the wall. "You know this has been just a really swell time and all, but I have to run!"

I hated leaving Chase, but one look told me he was out cold, and with my hands still cuffed, there was nothing I could do for him right now, so I took off. Thinking about what would happen once Mr. Eden regained consciousness kept me moving fast. I had to get these cuffs off, and I had to find Troy and Jori. The sight of elevator doors was my first beacon of hope. Maybe if I got on before he found me, I would buy some time. Lady Luck

was in my corner because the door opened before I even looked
for a button, and I found a familiar face as I tried to board. It was
Cora, the elevator lady from the original Paradise village.

"I heard you coming, Mr. Ed . . ." She started to speak in the
same monotone I remembered from Mr. Eden's office in Paradise,
but something seemed different when she looked at me. For just
a minute, she looked horrified by my condition. I didn't think that
could happen with an android. I had seen concern in her eyes.

"Get . . . get me . . . outta here . . . please!" Suddenly it was
hard to breathe. I grabbed my rib cage. "My name's Jack Barrett,
and I need help. Please, Cora. Help me. He's going to kill me."

She stole another glance when she heard my name; it was like
she recognized it, and then her hands began to shake as if the
very thought of making an independent decision was unnerving.
"I wouldn't know what to do to help anyone," she said, but she
quickly punched a series of buttons and a panel of floor choices
came to life. She chose a button at the far top of the panel, the
door closed, and we began to move.

"You have to get out of this elevator as soon as possible, Jack.
This is *his* elevator. You can't be in here." For a moment, she
sounded almost human, and her decision to call me by my name
was a message—even if she didn't intend it; she was considering
doing more to help me. I noticed her hand move into her pocket.
There was an object in there, and she appeared to be fingering
it nervously. Then her voice returned to the monotone, and she
began a recitation. "I'm Cora, the elevator lady. I run the elevator.
Mr. Eden likes me to run the elevator. Running the elevator is an
important task. *Everyone knows that.*"

I pivoted my body backwards so my hands could grab the

'stop' button and pull it out. "Eeeyyaaa! Wow, did that hurt!" The elevator came to an abrupt halt and something fell from above, landing face up on the floor of the elevator. It was a plaque that read *"Panel 53,"* and though it didn't mean much to me, Cora's eyes were transfixed by it. "Look, Cora, would you look at me? Please! Look what he's done to me. I need help. Haven't you ever needed someone to help you, Cora? Hasn't anyone *ever* in your whole life come to your rescue?" I sounded as desperate as I felt, and in the middle of my plea, my knees gave out, and I crashed to the floor. Another audible moan escaped as my ribs screamed in protest. The elevator car was spinning. I was fighting to stay conscious.

Her chest began to heave. "Oh, great, she's having a heart attack" was my first thought, but then a cry erupted from the tiny woman that might have reached all the way to heaven. She looked at the plaque with enough hatred to set it ablaze and ground the heel of her shoe into it. Then, she carefully made her way to the floor.

"Bill." She said it through sobs as she began wiping the blood from my face with a handkerchief she'd retrieved from her pocket. "You asked if anyone had ever come to my rescue, and the answer is 'yes.' My brother Bill was always coming to my rescue. My brother was my hero. Oh, how I love him, but I haven't seen him in years. Mr. Eden won't allow it. All I get are letters from him, and that's all he gets in return. And everything I write in mine is a lie."

"Well, Cora, my brother needs a hero right now—and it's gotta be me. Help me up. Can you?" Between the two of us, I reached a standing position. "Mr. Eden has kidnapped my brother Troy and my girlfriend. They're both somewhere in this facility, and they're in as much danger as I am. You said Mr. Eden's kept you from your brother; well, he sent me a message telling me he's planning to kill mine."

"No." She shook her head and glared at the plaque on the elevator floor. Her voice trembled. "No, he will not do that. This has to end; he must not hurt any more people." She pushed the stop button back in and, before the elevator could resume its motion, hastily pressed a series of numbered buttons. I noted the panel of floor choices didn't light up this time, but the elevator started moving upward—fast.

"Where are we going?"

"I'm taking you to the one place he'll never think to look for you; it's the one place we might find something to help stop him."

"But, he'll find us, he'll know where . . ."

She interrupted. "There are only two places in this facility that don't have monitoring cameras. One is in my elevator, and the other is in The Lodge. And The Lodge is where I need to take you."

"The Lodge?" What's . . ."

"It's where Mr. Eden lives, Jack. I'm taking you straight into the lion's den."

Chapter 20

When Florence and Julie returned to the Barrett home, Gram's makeup bag was overly full; "I'm ready for action, girls," she said smiling.

"And I," Julie responded, "found the location of Chase's extreme makeover in my notes. I suppose because his mother said it was near Vegas the name never really registered. Now, of course, I can't believe it didn't click. "They're heading to the Paradise Hotel."

Florence blanched at the name. "*Paradise* Hotel! You'd think the man could at least come up with something less trite." She began adjusting the huge mound of hair on her head. "Hasn't he, literally, done that word to death?"

"Hey, Gram! What are these?" Julie held up what appeared to be a dainty pair of lavender house slippers made from a very sturdy substance. They each had a small metal shaft coming out of the back that looked like microsized car mufflers."

"Hey, aren't those nifty?" Gram's voice was filled with excitement. "They . . . oh, no, oh don't touch that, Honey, you'll . . ."

"Aaahhhh!" Florence screamed in panic as flames shot out of one of the slippers for a brief moment and set the top of her wig ablaze. "Aaahhhh! I'm on fire! Katy, I'm on fire!" The fake hair began smoking, melting, and drooping immediately.

"Oh, Florence, calm down. Everything's under control!" Gram began rummaging in her bag while Julie dropped the slippers and raced to the kitchen.

"Don't worry, Mrs. Petrillo. I'll get some water or some flour. I'll get a blanket! I'll get . . ." Julie raced back into the room with her arms full of sundry items just in time to see Gram, now clad in a firefighter's red helmet, release the contents of a fire extinguisher, shaped like a flashlight, right onto Florence's head. The foam engulfed the smoking mass of hair that was falling down all around Gram's friend.

"Hey, Florence! Now you look just like some of those young pop artists in their wild music videos!" Gram said brightly.

Julie was shifting her weight from one foot to the other and staying very close to Gram. "Mrs. Petrillo, I am so, so sorry! I had no idea, I mean, I just didn't think that, and I heard Gram say 'no,' but by then, I had already . . . Are you terribly mad?"

Florence flung her tresses behind her back and composed herself. "My dear, I am a seasoned veteran of the stage. I live for the unexpected and have won out against it on every occasion, I assure you. Alas, I must freshen up at home before I'm off to Sunny Days to referee the sand volleyball tournament; then it's dinner with Mia and Tia."

Julie regarded Florence quizzically, then shifted her gaze to Gram.

"Florence's granddaughters," Gram explained, repacking her fire helmet. "She couldn't be more proud." She grabbed Julie's elbow and pulled her close. "And believe me when I say that."

"Well, Katy Barrett, you're a fine one to talk! You go on and on about Jack and Troy as if they were . . . well, you go on as if . . . why it's almost as if you think . . ."

A large passenger van pulled into the driveway, and the driver laid on the horn. FAM was at the wheel. She stuck her head out the window and bellowed, "Let's move it, Ladies; we've gotta pick up the rest of the team and head to the airport."

Gram patted Florence's hand. "Oh, Florence, for pity's sake it's just your Alzheimer's acting up. Don't feel bad, you'll finish that sentence eventually. But we can't stand around waiting—gotta go." Gram kissed her friend on the cheek, and she and Julie sailed toward the van.

"Why, Katy Barrett—you old vulture, you—how dare you say that I have . . . Katy! KATY!"

Troy Barrett sat with his mother on the sofa. She had offered him the only oversized sweatshirt she had—which unfortunately was pink. Once he'd ripped the arms off and cut the collar out—leaving a jagged ring around the neck—he'd decided it would do. "I'm afraid I don't have any shoes that will work for you, Darling."

"No troubles, Mom. I'd rather go barefoot than have Jack see me in ladies' shoes and a pink sweatshirt." She squeezed his hand again. They had spent the past couple of hours talking nonstop as Troy brought her up to speed on the events of the past year.

"Mom, tell me about this place. What is it? Where is it? Why are we here?"

"Sweetheart, I don't know. I don't know anything, really. He refers to this set of rooms as 'The Chambers.' It's the only place I've been since I first left our house in Davenport for my morning meeting with Mr. Eden. I was drugged within minutes of arriving at his office in Paradise, and I woke up here. An attendant brings food and drinks and takes them away, but he never speaks. I've had no one to talk to but Adam. He seems to be courting me almost, trying to convince me that I love him. I've played the game to survive, Troy. It's all been about hoping that somehow I'd find a way out."

"You call him Adam. Don't you mean, *Dad?*" Troy's voice was filled with a bitter hatred he could almost taste.

His mother shot him a look. "Troy, that man is not your father. Chip was out of control, obviously way over the edge near the end, but he wasn't always that way. And if what you're saying is true, then he was sick, very sick."

"Whatever." Troy didn't feel like an argument now that he was finally with her again. He stood and went to grab an apple from a bowl of fruit. He couldn't remember the last time he'd eaten. "The question I want answered is . . . who is he, really? Somebody died in Mr. Eden's office in Paradise. We all saw it happen. I thought it was Dad, but maybe it was an android. Maybe this is Dad, and if it is, maybe you can reason with him. Maybe there's some part of him you can still get to."

"No, Troy. I've tried. There are moments when a kind of glazed look comes into his eyes, and I've fantasized that it's your dad fighting for control, but I've never had the courage to speak his name out loud. Adam can be so frightening. I've just tried to stay alive. To get back to you boys and Katy."

"He said he was going to kill me, Mom, and he means it." Troy took a bite out of the apple and tried to resume his customary nonchalance, but the veneer had cracked during his last statement. He was scared.

Susan Barrett moved to her son and put her hands on his shoulders. "He will do no such thing. We're going to get out of here before anything happens to either of us. We're going to get back to Jack and Katy. And I'm going to meet this Julie who seems to have captured my Romeo's heart."

"Romeo." His eyes were dangerously close to waterworks. He bit his tongue hard to keep his emotions under tight control. "You haven't called me that . . . I haven't heard you say it . . . I think I'd almost forgotten how you always . . ."

"Sweetheart, you didn't forget. You tucked it away to protect yourself from any more hurt. It's a defense mechanism, and it's okay. But I've walked around these rooms talking to you and Jack for months, pretending you could hear me." She reached up and kissed his cheek. "And I've called you Romeo most of the time because it always made you smile. I've been calling you that since you were in kindergarten, and you talked that second-grade girl into letting you kiss her." His mother chuckled. "Boy, was her mother mad when she called me." She tousled his hair. "And you remember what I told her, don't you?"

He grinned. "You said that one day her daughter would have bragging rights because your boy was going to be a real-life Romeo, and she had just become his first crush."

"You got it! She hung up on me, but I was right." She stood behind him and wrapped her arms around him in a motherly bear hug. "And I'm right about one more thing. We're going to get out of here. We just need to figure out how."

Jori twisted and turned on her cot in agony. Her ankle's complaints were impossible to ignore, and she had no way of tending to it. There was also no denying her terror anymore. She knew Jack would come looking for her, but would he find her in time? Mr. Eden had made it sound like her trip to the surgical unit was scheduled soon, and she shuddered at the thought of what was to come.

Jori McAllister was an organ donor; it said so on her driver's license. But suddenly she was calling that decision into question. She tried reminding herself of how sadistically different this situation was. In this case, someone was taking her life to sell her organs—that was certainly not the same as her willful decision to donate some of them once she had died of natural causes! But Mr. Eden's words had chilled her to the core, and she felt filled now with a selfish desire to guard every part of her. She moved into a sitting position, resting her back against the wall. She was contemplating the entire situation and trying to keep her mind off the pain when two women startled her by stepping into her room as the silent door opened. They both looked exactly like Jack's mother, and they were clothed identically in pale violet dresses. Every feature of them was the same except for the color of their earrings.

"I'm Eve One." The one in the green earrings spoke with authority. "It's time for you to share a little of yourself with the world, Sweetie." The cruel sarcasm was clearly intended. "Get up."

The second woman stepped forward. "I'm Eve Two. I can't imagine how frightened you are, Little Lamb, and I know your leg is hurting terribly. I brought you something for the pain." She bent down and placed a pill in Jori's hand, then offered her a glass of water.

For the briefest second, Jori thought about swallowing the pill. What if it really was something to help the pain? But there was no way she was going to trust anyone in this place. Spitefully, she turned her hand over and let the contents fall to the ground, then dumped the water glass out as well. Eve Two moved back just in time to avoid having her shoes baptized.

Eve One stepped in close. "Do something like that again, and I'll snap the other ankle."

Jori looked up at her defiantly. "Go ahead. Let's see what your boss has to say about that. I bet I'd be worth a lot less money that way."

Eve Two began shaking her head vigorously. "Oh, no. He wouldn't like that, Eve One. You shouldn't hurt her. Please don't do that. Let's not have any disagreements. Family members should never disagree. *Everyone knows that.*" The kinder version of Jack's mother sat on Jori's cot. "This little lamb is just frightened, and that's okay."

"Yeah, well when people are planning to cut you up and sell your organs to the highest bidder, it does tend to affect the mood," Jori's edgy voice spoke aloud. "And by the way, we're *not* family." She wanted desperately to vomit on Eve Two.

"Get up you little wench, or I'm gonna force you up." Eve One wasn't kidding.

Eve Two immediately put one arm around Jori's waist as the girl tried to stand. Jori hated herself for doing it, but she had to reach toward the woman's shoulder for support. "There, you see how easy this is going to be?" Eve Two said cheerily. "We get so much done by working together. Now it's time to begin our little journey down the hall. Why don't we sing a song on the way? That would be fun, wouldn't it?" No one responded. They left the room as a trio, but only one of them was singing. Eve

Two was trying unsuccessfully to pull the others into a skipping motion as her lovely voice echoed in the hallway, "We're off to see the Wizard, the wonderful Wizard of Oz, we hear he is a whiz of a Wiz if ever a Wiz there was . . ."

Chapter 21

The Lodge was quite the place—decked out with every amenity known to man and not a speck of dust—it was a window into Mr. Eden's daily life. More important though there was evidence here that the fractured psyche of my father, Chip Barrett, still existed.

Cora found a toolbox in a back laundry area and, after attacking the chain connecting my cuffs with a variety of tools, was able to sever the link and free my hands. I rubbed at my chafed wrists while she found some duct tape, which I begged her to use on my ribs. I was sure one was broken because the pain when I breathed was unlike anything I had felt, but a few tight circles around my waist gave me the support I needed. "I don't think I want to be around when you try to take that tape off your skin, Kiddo," she said good-naturedly.

I grinned. "That's okay. I know a girl who's just right for the job, and as long as I see her again, I won't care about the tape. Right now, I need it." We agreed that Cora would search the living area while I concentrated on the bedroom. There had to be something in The Lodge that could help us locate Troy and Jori. I scoured the bedroom closet, the bathroom, and every nook and cranny of the bedroom furniture with nothing to show for the effort besides an odd fascination for the systematic order Mr. Eden had for everything from his suits—hanging on very expensive hangers and sorted by color—to his toothpaste choices—seven different brands, each in a perfectly sized bin and labeled by the day of the week. I was just about to head into the living room to check on Cora's progress when my eye caught sight of something sticking out from underneath the mattress. I wedged my hand into the space and pulled out a journal—the handwriting was my father's—and the words and thoughts recorded made it clear that this was his journal, not Mr. Eden's. I drew in a breath. My father was still buried in there; somewhere in the layers of Mr. Eden's consciousness Chip Barrett still existed. I had never considered the idea, not even for a moment, that my father might still be in there—aware of everything that Mr. Eden was doing—but powerless to stop him. I had convinced myself that my father was dead. Gone forever. I had seen him die, after all. And it was easier this way, easier to consider Mr. Eden as the lone enemy rather than entertain the idea that my father was in league with him again. Or maybe not? Maybe the alliance that brought Mr. Eden to life in the first place had been severed. Maybe we had an ally, and he just couldn't reach us.

I thought back to the darkest day of my life. Mr. Eden, devastated at having destroyed his cloned version of Troy, had leveled a weapon at what was left of my family. It was clear he had no qualms about killing us all, and I had done the only thing I could think to do . . . called out to my father. Over this past year, I had come to the decision that Dad had heard me calling him, and that he had tried to destroy Mr. Eden to protect us.

The entries in the journal were dated, and the time was recorded in the upper right corner of each one. I noted they were all very brief and many were written late at night or early in the morning. I didn't have time to read them all, but from what I could gather quickly, it seemed that my father could, on occasion, create a pause in Mr. Eden's forward motion. He would attempt to seize control of the body, and though he rarely won that struggle during the daylight hours as evidenced by the small number of daytime entries, he had been able to wrestle control of the body away from Mr. Eden and come out, sometimes, while he slept.

A photo slipped from the journal, and I reached down to retrieve it. I was shocked to find it was of me. I hadn't seen this picture in years. Dad had always carried it in his wallet, though, and he'd take it out now and then to embarrass me. That was Dad before Adam Eden had entered our world and destroyed our family. I focused on the photo in my hand and laughed, recalling how my brother and I had begged our parents for Underoos, which were a cross between sleepwear and underwear with both tops and bottoms. They were all the rage when we were little. I was probably six or seven in the picture—wearing my Superman Underoos with a blanket tied around my neck. I had saved everyone in the family in that outfit, but Grandpa Amos was my favorite family member in need. He'd pretend he was trapped in a burning building or had been taken hostage in a bank and then call for Super Jack to save the day, and I'd come running to his rescue. He'd scoop me up in his strong arms when we were done, and his warm voice would always repeat the same words. "Jack, this family's in good hands with you as the oldest. Grandpa knows you'll take care of everyone."

I pocketed the photo and flipped to the last page recorded in the journal. It was dated yesterday, and all it said was, "Jack will be here soon. He's the only hope for Susan and Troy. I have to find a way to help him."

I read it again. And again. "Susan." It said "Susan." I stuffed the journal into my back pocket and raced out of the bedroom.

"CORA!" I nearly collided with her as she came scurrying toward me. "Cora, my mother's here somewhere, isn't she? My mother's alive!"

"Why, Jack, Honey, I wouldn't know. I haven't ever seen your mother to know what she looks like. I rarely see anyone except another employee now and then. My elevator is reserved for Mr. Eden. No one rides in it without his permission. I'm supposed to lock it each time he enters or exits to keep from transporting random passengers."

"What do you mean, 'lock it?' It's just an elevator. How can . . ."

"It's *his* elevator, Jack. Normally I punch in a code to lock it each time he exits. Once it's locked, I don't move until he calls it with a special code. That keeps anyone else from ever riding in it but him or someone he chooses to be inside it."

"But I rode in it with you just now."

"Because I didn't lock it. He was in such a rush, and he said that he would be right back. I just decided to wait for him, and I should have locked it, but I didn't." She reached for a key card in her pocket, pulled it out, and began turning it over and over in her hand. "I haven't been so good at following the rules lately. Anyway, when I heard the commotion outside the elevator door, I just assumed Mr. Eden was back. That's why I opened the door. I thought it was him."

The thought struck me then of how different things might be in the world were it not for random moments of choice—like an elevator lady who doesn't follow the rules. "Cora, where could he be keeping my mother? Think! There has to be someplace where he would have put her."

"I don't know, Jack. I just don't know. I only go to my apartment really and The Check-Up Room. I don't . . ." A buzzing noise came from the elevator, which stood open and ready for their escape. Cora's hands flew into the air. "Oh, it's him. Mr. Eden's calling the elevator. I have to go; I have to go now, or he'll know. You can keep looking here, and I'll try to stall him. I'll do something to keep him from coming here."

I doubted she had any idea how she would begin to accomplish the incredible feats she was describing, but she seemed determined to help me. She stepped into the elevator and turned to find that I had followed her.

"Cora." I reached out and gently squeezed her shoulder. "Please. Where could Mr. Eden be keeping my mother? Since he didn't kill her, I'm thinking there's still some kind of romantic spark there for her. He might have her in a special place."

The elevator buzzed—and it seemed to me that the buzz was longer in duration than it had been the first time. Cora bent down and nervously reached for the plaque on the floor. She was intent on wiping off the scuff marks from her shoes as her voice took on a weepy sadness. "I don't know, Jack. I don't know. Really. He rarely speaks to me at all, and he certainly wouldn't . . . Ohhh!" The key card slipped from her hands, and as she reached for it, she appeared to have an epiphany. There was an audible intake of air as she gasped, "The Chambers. She's in The Chambers! That's where she is, Jack, I'm sure of it." She thrust the key card into my hand, "He dropped this key, and I . . . I kept it. I don't really know why. I shouldn't have; it's against the rules. But now I know why—I kept it because I was meant to give it you, to help you find your mother."

I heard certainty in her voice, and I was so desperate to believe it was all true—that my mother was alive, that Troy would be with her, that Cora could reunite us . . . and that maybe, hopefully, Jori would be there, too—I stepped fully into the elevator. "Take me there, Cora. Please."

She didn't answer me verbally. Her fingers danced over the keys, the panel lit up, and when she pressed the "CH" button, we began our descent. Then, she gave me her attention again, "Jack, he'll be wondering what took me so long. Mr. Eden isn't used to waiting for anything. We're going to need someone on the inside for awhile, and that has to be me, so I've got to make him believe the story I'm going to tell him." Cora stood a bit straighter and seemed to be steeling herself for something. "Okay, Jack, hit me."

"What?" I was looking at her like she'd grown three heads.

"Hit me in the face. C'mon, I'm old, but I'm not dead. I'm going to tell him that I was worried when he didn't come right back. I'll say I stepped off the elevator, and you attacked me and forced me to take you to the lobby. It's the only way."

"Cora, I can't hit you! I'll get off the elevator right now, and you can go straight to him. I'll find my way to The Chambers on my own."

"You're a sweet boy, but you're a little slow." She patted my arm. "Hang this up when I'm done." She gestured to the plaque, which suddenly and with no further warning became a weapon that plowed directly into her face. She hit herself so hard that she took three backwards steps and fell into the corner. Had a stool not been there waiting, she would surely have hit the floor just as the plaque did.

"CORA!" I leaped toward her even as blood spewed from

a gash just above her left eye, which was already beginning to swell. I was sure it would be black and blue within minutes. The elevator buzzed—a sustained buzz that was somehow furious.

"I'll be all right, Honey. He would do worse if he didn't believe me." The elevator came to a graceful stop, and the doors opened. "Now hang the plaque back up there and get out. The Chambers is at the far end of the hallway on your right—its all that's down here."

I stepped off the elevator and looked up and down the hallway. There didn't appear to be another exit. "Cora, where are the stairs? How do we . . ."

"There's no other way out, Jack."

"But building codes would require . . ."

"Mr. Eden makes the rules here, Jack. The Chambers is completely isolated. I'm your only way out." She leaned out of the elevator and gave my cheek a quick kiss. "The code to call the elevator is 1151; you punch those numbers in, and I promise I'll come for you."

Chapter 22

Duke Redmer was used to getting last minute calls from Katy Barrett to go flying, but this was a different story. This time the spunky lady needed a bigger plane, room for several passengers, and no questions asked. The flight was to Vegas and, as always, money was no object. He'd called in more than a few favors on this one, but you didn't tell Katy Barrett "no" with much success. He was going over the instruments one more time when the squeal of tires brought him to the door of the plane. A lime green van peeled into the parking lot, and in minutes, the passengers were headed toward the plane with Mrs. Barrett—at least he thought it was Mrs. Barrett—leading the way. She had a mask on that matched the color of the van—as did most of her outfit.

"This way everyone, step on it! We're already behind schedule because Irma lost her teeth again." Yes. It was definitely Mrs. Barrett, he decided. No one else sounded quite like her, and no one else would be parading a group of senior citizens dressed in costumes onto an airplane.

"G'day, Mrs. Barrett. Don't mean to be a sticky beak, but . . ."

Katy Barrett pushed Duke aside as she boarded the plane. "If you don't want to put your nose in it, then don't, Duke. I believe my sister told you no questions when she called you, right? So, no questions. We're just a group of friends taking a private plane to Vegas. We're dressed for a superhero costume party, but our invitations came late. We didn't have time to get real superhero outfits so we

just made do. We're . . . uhh . . . we're all using code names to get
into the spirit of it, you know. My code name is Surprise."

"Surprise, Mrs. Barrett?"

"It's all about the bag, Sweetheart. Batman had his utility belt.
I've got this little baby." She hoisted her makeup bag into view
and stepped aside as the passengers boarded. "Trust me when I
tell you, I've got some surprises in here. Okay, watch your step
there, Warrior Princess. This is my sister, Duke, and step aside;
she's a big girl."

FAM boarded the plane in an outfit that looked like Cinderella's
gown and G.I. Joe's fatigues had been stuffed in a high-speed
blender for a few go-arounds. She had a tiny tiara on her head,
which looked wildly out of place on a woman who once put
an entire team of soldiers through their paces. A machine gun
with a full round of unusual looking cartridges was slung from
her shoulder to her waist, and she barked out orders the minute
she boarded. "All right, let's be careful with that wheelchair!
Tomahawk's got a bit of a temper, there."

"Hee! Hee! You said it, Lady! Watch out there, Pilot, or I'll
scalp ya! Ha! Ha! I'm gettin' pretty good with these things,
Katy-gal!" Waldo Emmerstine raised a tomahawk playfully at
Duke while his brother Wendell shook his head in frustration
and wheeled him up the ramp.

"You ain't supposed to call her by her name, you old codger.
She's Surprise! They told us a hundred times not to use names
on the mission."

"Well, I never heard nothin' about that!" Waldo complained.

"That's because you're an old coot, and your hearing only
works when you want it to. I oughta left you behind."

"Ha! That'll be the day. Without me, you wouldn't know when

to turn around. You'd forget your own name, Wendell, if I weren't around to remind ya."

Wendell smacked his brother on top of his bald head as the disabled man pulled himself out of the wheelchair and made his way toward the first row of seats. "Stop sayin' names, dagnabbit! You're supposed to call me Laughing Kid."

Waldo looked his brother over as the siblings settled into seats next to one another. "Laughing Kid! There ain't nothin' funny about ya that I can see. Oh, wait, I forgot about your face—now there's a great weapon if I ever saw one!" Waldo exploded into gales of laughter that turned into a coughing fit—forcing Wendell to slap him on the back several times to bring his hacking under control.

Duke was still eyeing the gun across FAM's body. He looked at Katy. "Mrs. Barrett . . . er . . . I mean, Surprise—that's not, that's not a real gun she's wearing, is it? I mean regulations . . ."

Katy pointed Duke toward the cockpit. "Duke, have no fear. She has delusions of grandeur, but she's harmless. I'm sure it's fake."

He stepped inside but ducked his head back out. "You're sure?"

"Fly the plane, Sweetheart. I've got things under control. Almost. Irma, Ohhh, I mean Piranha, would you keep those teeth in your mouth, please? We don't have time to hunt them down again."

"BC!" barked FAM. "Slam those teeth back into Piranha's mouth and get her on board." FAM waved her arm in a forward motion with great energy.

"Will do, Warrior Princess!" Julie, clad in her Black Canary outfit and mask gently positioned Irma Gladfell's teeth back into her mouth and pointed her up the ramp. Irma smiled and nodded in response as she made her way toward Katy Barrett's waiting hand. Irma had been at Sunny Days for nearly four months and had never spoken. Her tendency to play with her false teeth—and to misplace them—had nearly led Howard Breen to call the health board over sanitation concerns several times, but Gram or Florence always calmed him down. Irma also had a habit of biting anyone she didn't like; Howard had needed a tetanus shot by the end of her first week at Sunny Days. Julie wasn't sure what a nearly mute woman with a dangerous pair of chompers was going to add to their arsenal, but Gram had insisted. "Irma needs to get out more; besides, everyone brings something to the table—sometimes we just stop looking too soon." That had been her final word on the matter, and everyone knew better than to argue.

"So, this is how it's going to end," Jori thought. She was strapped down to a table in what looked like a very sterile operating room. Eve Two remained at the table, talking in her disgustingly gentle Mary Poppins' voice. She reminded Jori of Glinda, the Good Witch of the North on Valium.

"Now there's nothing to worry about, Little Lamb. It'll all be over very soon. Adam says you're doing a really good thing by sharing yourself with others."

"Uhhhh!" Jori grunted and pulled at the restraints. If she could have gotten her hands around the woman's neck, she would never have let her come up for air. Of course, Jori reminded herself, Eve Two didn't need air; she was an android. "Why don't you go have your gears greased, you bucket of bolts?"

A woman clad in surgical gown and cap walked over to the

table. "Eve Two assists in surgery. She needs to remain. Every surgeon needs an assistant." The woman spoke only in short staccato sentences as she raised her surgical mask and tied it in place. Jori wasn't surprised to find that the surgeon was another replica of Jack's mother.

"Who are you, Eve Sixty-seven?" Jori's anger was battling with her fear, and from moment to moment, it wasn't clear which was winning.

"I'm Eve Three. I assist Adam by performing various surgeries. He has explained what must be done. You are to be *shared* with the needy."

"Shared! Is that what he told you? Is that what you call this? Look, if you're going to slice and dice me and then sell off my organs to rich people, let's find something else to call it 'cause *sharing* really isn't working for me."

"Eve Two, you will need to prepare yourself to assist."

"Oh, yes, Eve Three, of course." Eve Two touched Jori's cheek gently. "I'll be back in a few minutes, Little Lamb. Don't worry."

"Yeah, well, absence makes the heart grow fonder, right? Maybe you could jet off to Singapore in the back end of a cargo plane and create some real emotional turmoil for me," Jori responded.

Eve One, still clad in the pale violet dress, crossed the room. Jori heard the sharp click of her heels on the floor and instantly knew who it was. The most dangerous member of the trio of Eves scowled down at the helpless girl, grinned menacingly, and showcased a small digital video recorder in her hand—moving it back and forth in triumph. "I'll be filming this operation for your sweet Jack. Adam wants to play it on a monitor overhead while your boyfriend's having his own surgery."

Jori suddenly felt desperate in a way she had not before. She knew every member of the Barrett family was in danger with Mr. Eden loose, but the thought of this—what they were going to do to her—happening to Jack brought on a whole new kind of panic. "Listen, Eve One, listen to me, please. You don't want to do this to Jack. Go ahead with me. Start now. Right now. It's fine; I won't resist. I promise you." She was trying so hard to sound convincing, wanting with every fiber of her being to sound sincere as she made her next statement. "It . . . it . . . will *destroy* Jack to see what's happening to me . . . and," she felt the tears coming but fought them, "and that will be enough. There's no need to hurt him physically, right? I mean you'll want, that is . . . Mr. Eden will want Jack *alive*, to suffer the loss! If Jack's dead, there'll be no point in any of this."

Eve One was completely unmoved by Jori's battle with her emotions. The android scoffed. "Oh, Jack's going to suffer, Sweetie. Trust me. And he's going to stay alive, too; you needn't worry about that. But trust me, he'll wish he were dead by the time we're finished with him. Adam doesn't do anything halfway, Doll. When he wants revenge, he gets it."

The sound of Eve Three's equipment preparation a few steps away had become a frightening accompaniment to Eve One's words, and Jori put forth a sudden and violent burst of force against the restraints as she called out. "Jack! JACK!" She screamed his name, howled it in desperation several times, but it echoed around the sterile room and flew back at her.

"Sedative?" Eve Three questioned her nefarious triplet.

"Don't bother. Let her scream all she wants," Eve One replied with confidence. "It's already too late."

Chapter 23

I had conflicting emotions as the sight of a wounded Cora disappeared behind the doors of her elevator. "1151 . . . I'll remember, Cora." Letting her return to Mr. Eden while I got to play family reunion didn't seem right, but as the hum of the elevator sent her sailing away, I was left with only one choice. As I fingered the key card and headed down the hall, I thought about the door in the basement of the Paradise house—the one that actually led to a tram. How was it I was always trying to figure out what was behind mystery doors? And why did they always have to be so far underground? I shivered a little thinking about how far under the earth it felt like we were. Good thing there weren't any windows to look out of and see that there was nothing but earth all around me.

As I stood outside the entrance to the place Cora called The Chambers, a thought struck me. Did Mr. Eden know I was freaked out by basements? My father knew . . . so did that mean Mr. Eden automatically knew? Of course, it could be a coincidence that he liked to build way down into the earth, but considering the issue led to questions I'd never thought to ask before. I wondered how much access Mr. Eden had to my father's mind and memories. He obviously had some access, but did he have it all? Was there anything my father had been able to keep from him? And if so, did we have an advantage we might not realize? More important, did we have an advantage *he* might not realize?

"Okay," I said and pulled out the key card to insert it into the door. "There's nothing ceremonious about this. I need to 'just do it.' Either Mom's in there . . . or she's not." I slipped the key card gently in and out of the mechanism, and the door glided left without the slightest noise. I stepped inside a tastefully decorated room. It was empty, but I heard noise coming from another room that must have been in the back of the dwelling. A stirring at my right led my eyes to a set of double doors—the entrance to a bedroom maybe? A flash of red hair as a figure crossed the room. Then a voice, a pure voice. It wasn't mechanical or robotic or anything else that it should never be. It was the voice of my mother, and in that moment, I understood that planets may be downgraded to asteroids and countries can disappear from maps. World leaders can fall from grace and celebrity stars will come and go, but the sound of your mother's voice just doesn't change. I don't remember falling on my knees but suddenly—there I was. And I found out very quickly that eighteen-year-old boys who find out their mother is still alive can be very unpredictable.

I thought it would come out as some kind of guttural cry of anguish, rising from a place deep inside and bursting forth with the power and speed of a locomotive. But to my great surprise, it was a quiet prayer spoken from the balcony of a long-deserted cathedral. "Mom?"

She came to the door of the bedroom, and our eyes met. My mother didn't speak at first. I blinked, and she tackled me with enough speed and power to land her a five-year deal with the NFL. She was holding me, then, and sobbing and making me very glad my rib cage was surrounded with duct tape. And once she started talking, she didn't come up for air. "Jack! Oh, Jack! Thank God you're alive." She pulled us out of the embrace and looked me over, doing the mother thing with the hands through my hair and down the sides of my face, then we were back to the Incredible Hulk embrace again. "What's he done? Adam. Adam did this to you, I know he did. I'm so sorry, Jack. Are you all right? Oh, but you're alive, and you're here! Jack, you're here, we're together again. Everything's going to be all right now."

"I know, Mom. I know." She was crying so hard I found it easier to keep my own emotions in check. There was one issue, though, that I knew I had to face, and I couldn't put it off. "Mom, I'm so sorry. I should have come looking for you." I maneuvered us gently out of the ninth rib-crushing embrace and tried to hold myself in check, but without warning, a year's worth of anger and guilt came out, and I launched a verbal assault against myself—a confession of guilt before the victim. "The *minute* you didn't show up at that wrestling meet—I should've come looking for you. Why? Why didn't I come? Why did I *believe* him? He kept lying to us, and I kept telling myself you were fine. But you didn't call. I knew you should have called. You would have called. If things were fine you would have called, Mom. Right?" I started to shake then, and tears came . . . but tears of guilt are different from any other kind. They burn coming out, and you swallow some down the back part of your throat where they feel almost like a mild acid that's desperate to punish you for all your wrongs. "Everything that's happened, Mom. Whatever he's done to you . . . it's all my fault, and I'm so sorry. I should have saved you!" I shook and stared at the ground, couldn't bring myself to look in her eyes.

"Jack Edward Barrett, you look at me!" She grabbed my arms with as much strength as she possessed. "Look at me, Jack." The weight of my exposed guilt threatened to paralyze me, but slowly I managed to meet her gaze. "Darling, you *did* save me. Oh, I was gone, physically, within minutes of meeting Adam—there was nothing you could have done to change that. But, Sweetheart, you have been with me, right here," and she pointed to her heart, "saving me. Every moment from that day 'til now."

"Hey, Mom! This toothpaste sucks! Ohhh, Jack's here." Troy came walking down the hall like we were on vacation in a rented beach house. I was relieved to see that he looked okay and was about to ask about his lovely pink sweatshirt when he made a comment that took me by surprise. "'Bout time you showed up to save the day."

Mom released me, and I quickly wiped at my eyes as I stood staring at my unflappable brother. "What do you mean 'save the day'?"

Troy rolled his eyes. "Jack! It's what you do, okay? Everyone knows. You save the day, right wrongs, protect the innocent, you know . . . all that stuff. The rest of us play at superhero, Bro—you really are one."

"Troy, I'm not some kind of saint. Is that what you think?"

"No, I don't think you're a saint, geez! I saw Florence give you a fifty once when she was paying you for yard work. She counted it as a five, and you didn't say a word. Saints don't do that."

"She and Gram had been fighting for nearly three weeks, Troy. That was back pay and . . . and *interest* for all the times she delays payment because Gram has made her mad. Plus, I had a credit card bill to pay—that Girl Scout's parents were still not convinced I wasn't the one who ordered the life-sized posters of Zac Efron."

"Whatever. I'm just saying, you're the good guy, Jack. You

always have been, always will be. I look really good on the white horse, Jack, but nobody rides her to the rescue like you. I've learned to live with it. I just look in the mirror—and I feel all better! 'Scuse me, gotta go rinse." He headed back down the hall.

My mother was grinning from ear to ear. "Oh, how I've missed listening to the two of you spar. We're one step closer to home."

"He's jealous of me? Troy . . . a little . . . is that what he's saying?" I was replaying the conversation over and over again and still trying to figure out how it could be possible.

"Of course he is, Jack. What a ridiculous question. How could you not know that? Oh, he compensates marvelously, but that's what all his bravado is really about. He's had to create a larger-than-life identity, Honey, so he isn't completely overshadowed by his amazing older brother. You mean you're just now finding that out?"

I smiled then—not a haughty, arrogant smile—a sincere one. It was an "I'm-an-okay-guy-after-all" smile. And it felt good. Really good. In fact, it felt like the tower of self-doubt Mr. Eden had so painstakingly erected inside me had just crumbled. "You think I'm amazing, Mom?"

"Not just me, Honey. Everyone. Troy's right. You don't just play at being a hero; you're the real thing—heart and soul." She walked over and kissed my forehead. "And you always have been, Jack Barrett—even in your Underoos!"

"Hey, Jack!" Troy's voice called from down the hall. "Did you think to bring my Green Arrow costume? I want to show Mom!"

Chapter 24

By the time Adam Eden managed to free his arm from the wall and meticulously search the remainder of the floor, he was physically shaking with rage. Where had Jack gone? As with The Chambers, the regular elevators didn't reach this underground level known as EE, and though it had a stairway that led to the lobby, the door at the top was locked. The lone exterior door, the one through which Chase and Jack had entered the facility, was magnetically sealed and impossible to open from the inside. So, where could Jack have gone? Adam could head to The Lodge and review camera footage to track the boy, but that was more time than he wanted to spend. Every moment Jack was loose in the building was a concern. Adam punched in the code to call Cora for the third time. What was the delay? Why was he *waiting?* His head began to throb as he considered the fact that he was waiting for an elevator, as if he were a normal person. The very idea of it was preposterous. At last, the elevator arrived, and he stepped inside.

Cora stood erect, waited for his instructions, and tried to control her trembling. Fortunately, she had managed to apply enough pressure to her head to stop the free flowing blood, which she knew he would find distasteful. If his destination should be presumed, she had been trained to suggest it; however, in this case she could not know where he was going so it was acceptable to wait politely and allow him to direct her. Such situations represented the only times he ever spoke in her presence. When no word came, she gave a fleeting glance up at him. He was surveying her, scrutinizing her really. "Sir? Mr. Eden, what floor, Sir?"

"I was waiting on you, Cora. Waiting." His voice was filled with quiet intolerance and disdain, and though it was clear she had been injured, he made no mention of it. "I called you three times! I don't call *anyone* three times! I. Don't. Wait. Not for anyone, and certainly not for *you*." He spat the final word at her as if she were less than a living being.

She kept her gaze on the doors, which had closed. To look at him would be disastrous, she knew. "I'm so sorry, Sir. When I dropped you off here, you told me you would be right back. Sir, I . . . I decided to wait for you . . . to be right here the moment you called, and when I heard footsteps coming . . . Mr. Eden, Sir, I . . ."

"You opened the door without waiting for the code, didn't you, Cora? Didn't you?" He moved to stand directly in front of her with his back to the elevator doors, and he hissed the last two words at her like a snake preparing to strike. "You imbecile!" He slapped her face so hard that she fell against the back wall of the elevator and crumpled to the floor. "You let HIM in MY ELEVATOR! MY ELEVATOR! You took him somewhere, helped him escape me, DIDN'T YOU? Stand up! Get up, you old goat! NOW!"

Cora reached for her stool hoping she could use it to gain the leverage to stand, but she was shaking so much she collapsed. He reached down without warning, grabbed one of her arms and yanked her to her feet, pulling her very close and leaning down so that he could speak directly into her ear. It was a deadly whisper. "Where is he, Cora? Where did you take him?"

She had rehearsed it over and over again, and she delivered a flawless performance. "I don't know, Sir. He threw me from the elevator and took off. When I called it back, he was gone."

He forced her to the stool. "You're lying, Cora. Where is Jack Barrett?"

"Sir?" She didn't know where to go next. She hadn't expected this. He was breathing heavily as if his rage was on the verge of bursting forth again, and she didn't want that to happen. Still, she knew she was buying Jack time that he probably needed. "I'm not lying to you, Sir. You should always tell your boss the truth. *Everyone knows that.*"

She had thought the phrase would calm him, but he erupted like a volcano. "YOU'RE LYING! He wouldn't just take the elevator and go. He doesn't know where to go, nor does he know the code to make it move, so he would have asked someone. Cora. He would have asked *you.*" He turned and began beating the wall of the elevator with his fists. "WHERE IS JACK BARRETT? WHERE IS HE?"

Cora stood and spoke very calmly. "Well, Sir, after he threw me into the hall, he . . . he couldn't make the elevator move, of course. He was hysterical, and he . . . he threatened to beat me if I didn't tell him how to make it move, and . . . well, I was so shaken, Sir, that I must have mumbled the code. But he was only able to use it that once. He doesn't know the code to call the elevator back." She kept her voice steady as she lied her way through the final sentence.

He was eyeing her now, and it seemed he was trying to decide whether he believed her. She felt the need to give him something more.

"I believe, Mr. Eden, he said something about his girlfriend."

He paused for a moment, and then burst forth with exuberance. "The girl! YES! Of course, he's looking for the girl!" Suddenly his mood swung to that of a giddy, delighted child. She'd never seen him like this—like a ten-year-old who'd just opened a lemonade stand and sold his first cup. "He knows she's here, then! What did you tell him? What did you say? Did you tell him she's on the thirteenth floor?"

"Sir, I haven't seen anyone. I couldn't tell him anything." The frightening shift in personality was alarming, but her ears didn't miss his mention of the thirteenth floor as the girl's location. Cora hadn't known there was a thirteenth floor, and her elevator certainly didn't travel there. If the girl was being held against her will along with Jack's other family members, how many other people were imprisoned in this building right now?

Of course, Cora had long since abandoned the notion that the building was a real hotel. For one thing, the "No Vacancy" sign was perpetually lit, and every time she'd been to the lobby, the same people were at the front desk. Over the months, she'd begun to realize that the same people walked through the lobby at the same time each day. The same woman bought the same stick of chewing gum in the gift shop, the same man cautioned his children to quiet down while waiting in line to check in. Cora felt sure that none of them were real, but she never said anything.

Without warning, Mr. Eden cleared his throat and seemed to quickly regain his composure. All evidence of the childlike personality was gone. "Twelfth floor," was all he said.

Cora keyed the elevator, the panel brightened, and she pressed the twelfth floor button. In a matter of seconds, they arrived.

"Good day, Mr. Eden," she said as he departed. He ignored her, but she craned her neck, something she had never dared to do before, and saw him press the call button for the small service elevator located next to hers. She noted he removed a key card from his pocket with stealth. And then, just as the doors of her own elevator began to close, he caught her eye—clearly saw her looking at him for the briefest instant—and he tipped his head and stared at her. It was less than a moment, yet his gaze had a way of holding people so that she felt as if it lasted for several minutes, and in that time, she could neither breathe nor move. Instead of the peace that generally washed over Cora when the doors of her elevator closed, this time it was panic because she was left wondering. Had she discovered the way to the thirteenth floor? She wondered if he suspected that she'd betrayed him; she wondered how long it would be before he discovered that she had. And she wondered . . . if he already knew.

Adam Eden slid the key card into the appropriate slot, and the service elevator began its amazing metamorphosis. He would have preferred to have Cora delivering him to the thirteenth floor; however, he had deemed it too risky to allow her access to that area, which is why the special elevator had been created. The three Eves resided on the thirteenth floor and had access to it at all times, but two of them were androids who never left their rooms unless ordered to do so. And Eve One, well, Eve One was in a category all her own. He'd taken risks with her, but then that's what made life interesting.

"Welcome, Mr. Eden, to the thirteenth floor." The elevator

doors spilled open, and he headed straight into the surgical unit. Eves Two and Three were already in surgical gowns and masks. The android nurses who assisted in these operations would, he expected, arrive soon. They were housed on this floor in small compartments adjacent to the main operating room. He noted Eve Three preparing an injection as Eve One rushed to greet him with a kiss. "Adam, Darling! You're timing is *perfect* as always. Jack's little sweetheart has been enjoying the last few moments of her life." She showcased the video camera, but his eyes were tracking Eve Three's movements. "Adam, I'm all set to record."

"Eve Three . . . don't put her out." The android looked up instantly. "Yes, Adam."

He moved to the operating table. "Eve One, move to begin filming. Eve Two, I need the feed from that camera to go live on every screen throughout the building."

"Yes, Adam." The two spoke in unison and hurriedly began to make his wishes a reality.

Jori glared up from the table at him but chose not to speak. His devilish grin was giving her chills, but she refused to give him the satisfaction of knowing how terrified she truly was. He pulled his hat down a bit lower and spoke to her in a tone of great confidence. "Change of plans, Miss McAllister. I've momentarily lost track of your boyfriend—but when he sees you in danger, we both know what's going to happen. He's going to come racing into this room to save you," he leaned down and whispered the last part into her ear, and his hot breath made her flesh crawl. "And that will be the beginning of the end of Jack Barrett."

"He won't come! Jack's too smart to respond to a threat from you." She choked out the words, but she knew they weren't true.

He would come and very quickly—because that's who he was. Jack Barrett was a hero, and the hero always shows up.

"Adam, Darling, we're ready."

"Good. Tape her mouth."

"Gladly." Eve One responded and quickly forced a thick piece of gray tape over Jori's mouth—applying far more pressure than was necessary. "No more commentary . . . and no messages to your boyfriend either."

"Screens have opened throughout the building, Adam. Wherever Jack is—he'll see what's happening here." Eve Two clapped her hands with enthusiasm. "It's so wonderful how you can always find a way to talk to your family!"

Adam Eden winked at Jori. "Show time, Miss McAllister." He stood tall, straightened his coat and hat, and moved to stand at the head of the table on which Jori lay. "Hello, Jack! Round One goes to you, I'll give you that. Aaahhh, but here we are at Round Two. And, Jack, I have to say that I'm positioned for the win this time." He gestured down at Jori on the table and motioned for Eve Three to move into view. "We're only moments away from an operation, Jack, and this poor, unfortunate girl is, well, she's in a sad state really. I can't imagine you could ever live with yourself, Jack, if anything were to happen to her, right? Now I'm not making any promises about her safety or future well being, but I'm a man of my word. And if you show up in this room in the next ten minutes, Jack, I'm going to let you talk to her. And after that . . . well, after that, we'll just have to see, won't we?

Any elevator can take you to the lobby of this facility, Jack. So get there. Once you're in the lobby, pick up the red courtesy phone at the far end of the concierge desk. I'll give you directions at that point. And Jack. If you're even one second late . . . you won't recognize her when you finally get here."

Cora had been digging through her small purse for some antacid pills to calm her stomach when the emergency screen had unexpectedly come on in the elevator, and Mr. Eden's message to Jack had been broadcast. She could hardly believe anyone could be capable of such malevolence. Though Mr. Eden's very presence put her on edge, riding up and down in an elevator with him over the years had not provided her with an opportunity to understand who he really was. As the message came to a close, she fingered her necklace nervously. "Oh, dear. Oh . . . no . . . Jack's not going to hear the message!" And she felt certain, absolutely certain, that he wouldn't—not if he was in The Chambers. If Mr. Eden was truly trying to win the affections of Jack's mother, then the message would never have been broadcast where she could see it. And there was so little time. Cora's fingers danced as she brought the panel to life and stabbed the large L button. Within minutes, she was racing across the lobby for the red phone, praying with every step that she'd be able to execute her plan.

When she picked up the receiver, Mr. Eden spoke immediately. "Very good, Jack. You take direction well."

Cora made no response. She felt sweat breaking out across her entire scalp. She was briefly distracted by a rather unusual looking group of people who seemed to be arguing with the front desk clerk. They seemed quite out of place from anything she had seen in the lobby before, but Mr. Eden's voice drew her back to reality.

"No bold comment from the white knight? That's unusual, Jack. I'd expect a bit of witty repartee."

Cora dared not even grunt. She pulled a handkerchief from her pocket and dabbed at her brow.

"Well, I guess I'll have to wait for a face to face to engage in the pleasantries of another conversation, Jack. So be it. Cross the lobby and go to the service elevator, the smaller one to the far right. Pick up the key card under the floor mat and place it in the slot. Then, you'll be on your way, and we can see to that reunion I promised you."

Cora slammed the receiver down and followed Mr. Eden's directions, grabbing the key card but racing back to her own elevator, which was the only way to reach The Chambers. Her fingers moved with lightning precision as always; the doors closed quickly, and she descended. She refused to look at her watch.

Chapter 25

I spent as little time as possible playing catch-up with Mom and Troy in The Chambers and too much time trying to get them to agree to my plan. When we tag-teamed Mom for the third time, I thought we might win. "Mom, please! I just want Cora to take you to the lobby and get you out of here. You can call Gram, call the police, call the stinkin' FBI for all I care—I just need you out of here."

"Jack, you're wasting your time. No mother leaves her boys in danger. Now let's . . ."

Troy's green eyes were fierce. "MOM! We can't lose you again. Okay? We can't."

"And I can't risk having my boys . . ."

I headed to the door. "There's no time for this! Jori's here somewhere, and I've gotta find her. There's no point in putting all three of us in danger."

My brother sprang to his feet. "Oh, right! And you think I'm going to let you take on dear old Dad and who knows how many of his homemade humanoids all by yourself. No way, Jack. We do this together."

Suddenly a thought struck me. I had a key, but they didn't. I slid it into the slot without warning. "Stay put. I'll be back for you," I commanded and dashed out. My brother's voice rose to a threat level that would have alarmed the Department of Homeland Security as the door sealed them inside, and I bolted down the corridor. The doors to Cora's elevator were opening before I could enter the code to call it, and she nearly collided with me as she struggled to catch her breath.

"Jack, your girlfriend. He's got her. I saw . . . I saw her. He sent you a live video message, and she was in the background; he's threatening to harm her if you don't go to him. There's not much time left." She quickly relayed information about the service elevator, and we traded key cards. "The one you have might take you to the thirteenth floor, Jack, but I know this one will. There's no time for a mistake right now. Take it . . . and hurry!"

"Cora, my mother is in The Chambers with my brother, and they're safe there for the moment. Promise me, Cora, promise you won't let them out unless you have reason to believe they're in danger. I need to know that they're safe. And coming after me is only going to put them both in harm's way."

I could see another adult lecture coming, and I didn't have time for it. "Cora, would you ever endanger a member of your family? On purpose? No, you wouldn't. I know it. So help me protect mine." I jumped into the elevator before realizing I didn't know how to make it go. "Uhhhh, Cora. A little help here?"

She stepped in and pressed some buttons. "It's 1706 to go," she said. "Remember that in case you ever need it."

The entire panel lit up. "Will do. You're a good friend, Cora. Thanks." This time, I was the one who kissed her cheek, and she punched the L button before ducking back out. "Good luck, Jack." I had the feeling there was something more she wanted to say, but she held it in and let me go.

I reached the lobby and quickly ducked into the service elevator. As I slid the key card into the slot and the doors closed, I got a major sense of vertigo. Every panel in the elevator started moving, and before my eyes, this little lift became a throne room for Mr. Eden. I shook my head at the insanity of it; the money wasted on catering to his ego might have fed a starving nation. As the elevator took off, my adrenaline skyrocketed. I didn't really feel afraid. Not yet. All I could think about was that I was walking into a den of lions, and the biggest one hadn't eaten in a year. Within seconds, I arrived, and a mechanical voice droned, "Welcome, Jack Barrett, to the thirteenth floor." I exited the elevator by cautiously stepping into a wide hallway. Two large and impressive-looking doors were located straight across from me, and it seemed that's where I should go. They opened as I approached, and there he was surrounded by his minions. There were eight of them, nine altogether if you counted him. My heart sank because I felt sure they were all androids. What was I, a guy with crushed ribs, going to do against his small but powerful army?

He stepped forward, hat down low, collar up high, as was always the case when we were together. I wondered what he thought he was hiding. "Jack, this is my surgical staff. The nurses just arrived, actually. You were a bit . . . *slower* than I'd expected, but you did make it in time." He tapped his watch and grinned. "Seventeen seconds to spare."

When I saw Jori struggling on the table behind him, my heart nearly came right out of my chest, and I did something unimaginable. I knelt. I hadn't planned it, couldn't believe it was happening, but I subjugated myself to his authority in front of the entire room. And then I pleaded. "Let her go. Please. I'm . . . I'm begging you. You can do anything you want with me . . . *to me* . . . but she's innocent. She never should have gotten mixed up in all of this . . . mixed up . . . with me." I hadn't planned to sound so pitiful, but somehow, I suddenly knew it was the right thing to do. I needed to appear as broken as he wanted me to be. "I'm a loser . . . and she deserves better. Don't punish her for my inadequacies."

"Release the girl." It was a command. "Yes, Adam." And three women, all of whom appeared to be replicas of my mother, spoke in unison and began removing Jori's restraints.

"Jack . . ." he was calling me to look up again, and as I did, he sent a right hook into my jaw that let me know he meant business. "You are definitely a loser . . . and we *all* deserve better." I moved to rise, and he kicked me with enough power to propel me several feet. The duct tape held, but air and I became strangers for a minute.

"JACK!" Jori hobbled across the floor to where I lay sprawled and fell into a heap beside me. Before she could say anything at all, I pulled her into my arms with the little bit of strength I had left and kissed her like I never had before. "I knew you would come," she said and held onto me like she wasn't planning on ever letting go.

The sound of one set of clapping hands—Mr. Eden's—and then he motioned for the others to join in so that a full round of applause was underway. "Marvelous. Better than TV I'd say. Who needs the movies when you have young love to entertain you? Ahhhh, but let's see what happens when they're separated, shall we? Eve One, Eve Two."

The androids were on us like lightning—the one pulling Jori from me sounded like a preschool teacher who'd overdosed on caffeine. "Now, now, Little Lamb. Play time is over," she explained as she forced Jori to stand, taped her mouth again, and held her in place next to Mr. Eden.

I didn't put up any resistance as the other one roughly hoisted me over her shoulder like a sack of potatoes. I needed to continue to let him think he had broken me. "Secure Mr. Barrett, Eve One."

"What about her?" Eve One inclined her head toward Jori while she tossed me onto a table. "Adam, I thought . . ."

"I'm stepping up the timeline. The fight's already gone out of him, it's clear. He doesn't have his brother's spirit. Not yet, anyway."

Eve One pulled a thick metal bar across my chest and locked it down, and Mr. Eden laughed softly as he approached. "You came here, Jack, because you finally admitted what a miserable failure you are. Didn't you?" Eve One was silently locking my wrists and ankles in place, and when I didn't respond, he shrieked and wailed in absolute rage. "ADMIT IT! ADMIT IT! TELL THEM! TELL THEM THAT'S WHY YOU CAME HERE!" His breathing was shallow and rapid now, and then he quieted a bit. "You came here for help. You came to ME . . . ME . . . because you needed someone to make you better than you are."

I looked at Jori, still in the grip of the android who I reasoned was Eve Two. I was afraid to put up any kind of resistance while they had her. "He's right!" I called out loudly into the room and listened to my own voice echo all around. "I have a lot of problems. There are a lot of things wrong with me. I . . . I need someone to fix me. I need . . . Mr. Eden . . . to help me."

"Oooohhhhhh! YES! How I've waited to hear those words come out of your mouth!" He thrust his fist in the air in a sign of victory and turned to look at the others. "You heard him! You all heard it!" He then leaned down over me so his face was inches from mine. "And you're going to get your wish, Jack. In fact, we're *both* going to get something we want."

"What are you talking about?" Okay. The fear thing that wasn't there earlier was now clawing its way up my throat at a very rapid pace.

"You're going to get the help you need, Jack. You've always wanted to be more like your brother, and I'm going to give that to you. You see, I'm going to take the brain out of his body and sell it for a lot of money. There's an idiot out there somewhere who has a son with a diseased brain. And that father, Jack, will pay a very high price to keep some semblance of his son alive. His donation will help me with the rebuilding of Paradise."

He saw the questioning look in my eye though I didn't speak.

"Ohhh, yes, Jack. We're rebuilding . . . elsewhere. One community at a time until we can take over areas that are a bit . . . larger. But it's costly, Jack. Very expensive to do it the right way. *This* facility helps with the financing. It's not really a hotel as you may have guessed. No." He leaned away from me and whirled in a circle of celebration. "This is a safe harbor for husbands who need their wives fixed, dying people who need their organs replaced, parents whose children are unhappy with what God gave them. I see that things are . . . corrected for them."

"So that's how you got Chase here," I accused.

He rushed back to me and began to gloat. "I targeted him—pathetic as he was—he and the simpering mother who was desperate to help him. She gave up one of her eyes, which I sold for a healthy price. Her boy got a physical overhaul courtesy of some of Eve Three's muscular implants, a healthy dose of steroids he thinks are vitamins, a grueling workout schedule, cosmetic dentistry, and some plastic surgery. And I . . . I got *you*. He was our Emissary, Jack, setting the wheels in motion that would bring you, finally, to my door."

"But why go to all this trouble to get me here? Why not just grab me and bring me here by force? Seems more your style." I could feel the edge coming into my voice, and I couldn't hold it back.

"Because I needed you to come broken, Jack. I needed you to come here admitting what a disaster you really are. They say revenge is a dish that is best served cold, and I wanted your temperature at minus twenty."

"You're not much fun at parties, are you?" The sarcastic comment leaked out despite my effort to appear weak. Fortunately, he ignored it.

"Now, let's get back to that father who's going to buy your brother's brain. You see he'll be satisfied with the impulsive, arrogant, rebellious spirit your brother can provide; whereas, I could never be."

"Forgive me if I don't make the connection on how selling my brother's brain is going to make me more like him."

"Oh, it's not, Jack. But with his body in need of some direction once his brain's gone —I thought you'd be the perfect guy to put in charge of it."

"WHAT?" I lost my best actor Oscar right then and there and started yanking at the metal bonds restraining every part of my body. "You're going to put *my* brain into Troy's body?"

"No, Jack. Eve Three's going to do that. I'm just going to watch. Ha! Ha! Ha! No need to be jealous of your little brother anymore, Jack. I'm going to fix things so you can take him over so to speak. And then I'll have what I want. REVENGE!"

"UHhh! UHhh!" I was grunting with effort to break free, and my ribs were protesting each time I slammed them against the bar crossing the center of my body. Nothing had even budged; it was useless. I'm not sure what I thought I was going to do even if I did get loose. The odds certainly weren't in my favor at the moment.

"Goodbye for now, Jack. I'm off to pick up your brother and invite him to our gathering." He stalked away, and I turned my head quickly, slamming the side of my face against the table to keep him in sight. I shouted at him, hoping to draw him back toward me.

"What about Jori? Let her go! You don't need her to make any of this happen."

He paused for a moment, but it was clear he was now a man on a mission, and nothing I said was going to slow him down. "Now, Jack that wouldn't be very courteous of me. I've got contracts on five of her major organs. They'll be airlifted to Asia later tonight, and I'll rake in nearly three million dollars for them. I'd intended to let Eve Three slice her up first and make a little video for you to watch, but plans change. I'm learning to be flexible, Jack.

"MMmmfffffff! Mmmmmmmf!" Jori struggled against Eve Two and tried to call out as Mr. Eden walked by and grabbed her chin roughly. "Your turn's coming, Sweetheart—and very soon. I promise you that."

Chapter 26

Cora had never been inside the gift shop, but she was going to have to have some antacid pills if she was going to make it through the day. As the elevator descended, she submerged her guilt over agreeing to leave Mrs. Barrett and her youngest son locked inside The Chambers. Jack was right, of course, they were safer there, but Cora still felt bad for them and all this worrying had her stomach doing flip-flops.

She stepped off the elevator to tremendous commotion. She'd been considering the hotel lobby a great deal since her last visit here, and the more she thought about the typical "scene" that was repeated over and over again in this location, the more certain she became that it was all staged to persuade anyone who entered the building to believe that this was, in fact, a regular and very busy hotel. And though people were bustling about as always, there was one group of people who just did not fit in. It was the same bizarre-looking group she had seen arguing at the desk before, but the argument had reached new heights. A woman who looked to be about Cora's age but dressed in some type of form-fitting lime green and pink Lycra jumpsuit hoisted a large overnight case onto the front desk.

"Miss, I'm not going to say it again. We are here for the Super Seniors Retreat, and we've come a very long way. Now, I know our group is meeting here in this facility somewhere—you've just got your records confused! Look again."

Cora saw the woman motion to her group, and they all began

moving out into the crowd. A wheelchair-bound elderly man in Native American dress made his way over to Cora. "Hey there, Purdy Gal! I'm fixin' to take me a ride on one a them elevators. You wanna join me?"

Before Cora could respond, a young girl, dressed in a black getup that included a mask, a choker, and fishnet stockings that Cora certainly did not approve of, came to retrieve the elderly gentlemen. "Tomahawk, you're supposed to stick with me."

"Dagnabbit, I was about to run off with my new lady friend here. This mission ain't no fun. We ain't been anywhere 'cept this lobby, and I ain't seen Jack's brother nor anyone that looks like him since we . . ."

"Jack!" Cora spoke his name with such intensity that several members of the costumed group moved quickly in her direction.

Julie knew, just by the way the woman said his name, that Jack was in the building. She spoke quietly and calmly. "I'm Jul . . . er . . . Black Canary, Miss. We're looking for Jack Barrett and for his brother Troy." She tried to keep the longing out of her voice as she spoke Troy's name, but it seeped through.

Cora stared at the group gathered around her now. She wanted to trust them, wanted desperately to have help for Jack, but she couldn't be sure. And then the group parted and Katy Barrett stepped into view with her makeup bag in hand. "If you know something about my grandsons, you're going to . . ." She stopped in midsentence and pulled off her mask. "CORA?" She gasped the name. "Cora Simpson . . . it's not possible! You've been missing for . . ."

"It's me, Katy. Truly. Though I haven't see you in years, you haven't changed a bit." Cora reached out and embraced the elder Barrett woman who immediately began an introduction.

"Everyone, Bill Simpson—is . . . was . . . Amos's and my best friend. This is his sister Cora!" Gram busied herself in her bag and pulled out a spray bottle with some liquid inside. "At least, I think that's who it is, but you can never be sure." And with that said, she pressed a button on the bottle that shot a forceful spray of water right into Cora's face.

"Aaaahhhh!" The elevator attendant cried out and tried to beat back the spray. "Katy, in heaven's name—what are you doing? Turn that OFF!"

"Just another minute now, Cora. Irma, where was that 'off' switch I showed you? I knew I was going to have trouble finding that."

A tiny woman clad in orange and wearing a red cape shuffled forward and pressed a button on the underside of the bottle. The spray ceased. The little woman looked at Cora, smiled, and her teeth suddenly shot out of her mouth and went skating across the polished floor of the lobby. Before anyone could speak, the teeth were retrieved by a large and rather ugly three-legged bulldog who deposited them into the hands of an enormous woman dressed a bit the way Cora imagined G.I. Joe's fairy godmother might look. This woman passed the teeth to the young girl who passed them to the man in the wheelchair who passed them to Katy who passed them to the woman who'd lost them. And that woman, who apparently was Irma, placed them back into her mouth without a moment's hesitation.

"Here's my jacket, Miss. You can use it to dry off." An elderly gentleman, whom Cora thought might appear rather stately were he not clad in a blue nylon outfit with a laughing face on his chest, handed a lightweight canvas jacket to her, and she began to pat down her face and hair. She wondered if he were related to the man in the wheelchair as there seemed to be a resemblance.

"Stop tryin' to steal my gal, Wendell, or I'll have ta scalp ya!" Waldo shouted. He grabbed a tomahawk and began waving it around wildly.

Wendell pointed his arm at his brother, touched the wide plastic belt around his waist, and a blue gas was released out of his sleeve and into the air near Waldo who was immediately taken with a hysterical fit of the giggles.

Gram began inspecting Cora. "Are you rusty around the eyes? Let's see." She grabbed Cora's head and all sense of personal space was violated. "How about your neck, does it still move all right?"

Cora drew herself up and shoved Gram away. "Katy Barrett, what on Earth has gotten into you?"

"Well, I have to do my best to make sure you're not one of those android-robot people. Or maybe a clone. Although I don't know how I'm going to figure that one out." Gram was obviously flabbergasted.

"Katy, it's me. I can assure you, it's me. And there's no time to waste. Jack's gone to face Mr. Eden alone. He made me promise to leave his brother and his mother locked in . . ."

"Mother? Susan's here? She's alive? Ohhh, oh, Cora . . . have you seen her? Do you *know* that she's alive? You have to take us to her right away, Cora. Please. We're going to need to get all the information we can from her if we're going to help Jack."

Cora led them quickly to her elevator. "Well, I haven't actually seen her, but Jack has. He's the one who asked me to keep her safe. And his brother."

"Bet that went over well," Julie said grinning. "You've

got Troy's stuff, right, FAM? I mean, Warrior Princess?"

FAM held up a large backpack from which a green quiver of arrows was protruding. "Thanks to your retrieving them from the boys' locker room, he'll be suited up within minutes, BC. By the way, how exactly *did* you find out they were in the boys' locker room—and how'd you get them out?"

Julie gave FAM a wry grin. "We all have our secrets, Warrior Princess, and that's one of mine."

Waldo had finally stopped laughing. He elbowed Cora. "We're usin' code names to protect ourselves from identity theft while we're here in Vegas. I'm Tomahawk. How's about I call you Ravishing Beauty?"

Wendell slapped his brother on the head. "Old geezer!"

"Codger."

"Am not."

"Are so."

"Boys!" Gram's firm voice silenced them. "Save it."

The elevator came to a stop, and Cora led everyone quickly down the hall to The Chambers, explaining as much as she could about recent events. When they reached the door, Cora slid the key into the slot without hesitation, and the entire group paraded inside. A chorus of exclamations rang out as those who knew each other were reunited while the rest of the group looked on.

"Troy!"

"Jules!"

"Susan!"

"Katy!"

"Favorite Aunt Millie!

"WHIZZER!" Troy's aggravated shout silenced the room,

and everyone looked down to see that his bare feet were covered in dog urine. The dog's tail was wagging happily as he pranced around Troy in repeated circles.

FAM went to grab Mr. Whizzer and pick him up. "He's awfully fond of Troy," she explained to those who didn't know the history. "Here, Hotshot," she tossed her nephew the backpack. "Maybe this'll make up for Whizzer's potty problems. I brought your Green Arrow duds."

"YES!" Troy then realized that everyone was staring at him or rather at his feet. "Yeah, well, I'll . . . umm . . . I'll just be going into the bathroom now and ya know, kinda cleaning up a bit before I get dressed." He slipped a backpack strap onto one shoulder and zoomed away. When he returned, it was, of course, to a chorus of whistles, which delighted him to no end. "Well," said his mother. "If that little girl from preschool could see you now, Romeo, her mother would be eating her words."

"It's . . . uhhh . . . Green Arrow, Mom. I'm the Green Arrow. The Emerald Archer, heroic Robin Hood type. Get it?" He came close and whispered into her ear. "Let's just keep the Romeo thing between us, huh?"

She nodded at him and winked. "Riiiggghhht," she whispered.

"One more addition, *Romeo,*" Julie couldn't resist. From her pocket, she pulled the green leather band that was clearly missing from Troy's right arm. She moved next to him and began strapping it around his bicep. Aware that everyone was watching them, Julie spoke quietly through gritted teeth as he started in with his typical shenanigans. "Stop flexing, you big show off. I can't get it on when you do that." While he loved being the center of attention, she did not.

"You saved it. Didn't you?" he mocked in a playful voice.

"Not a chance. I found it . . . in the locker room." She was twisting his arm now trying to get the band in place, and each time she almost had it, he would flex the bicep with all the power he could muster, and she'd lose it again.

"What were you doing in the boys' locker room, Jules?" he was singsonging at her now.

She looked at him with exasperation and attacked the arm again. "That's *my* business."

He grinned, flexed his muscle, and the band flew into the air. She caught it and gave him a look that sent their audience into fits of laughter. He then shot her a very serious look and explained, "Too much muscle mass. Impossible to tame."

"Right! In your dreams, Troy Barrett!" She resumed her efforts.

"You slept with it under your pillow, didn't you?" He flashed the charming Troy Barrett smile.

"Gross! You think I want some sweaty arm band near me when I'm sleeping?"

"Yes, Jules. I do."

"You're full of yourself."

"Yes, Jules, I am. It's a coping mechanism."

"Well, you've certainly mastered it." She responded with a grin and managed to fasten the band in place at just that moment. "Got it!" She walked across the room then to stand by Waldo's wheelchair. She didn't want to, of course, but she did. "I'll stay over here so there's enough room for you and your ego over there, Green Arrow."

Good-natured laughter followed, and then Gram took charge. "All right everyone, my plan is simple. We take them by surprise and give them everything we've got from the minute we arrive! Questions?"

Troy couldn't believe what he was hearing. "GRAM! You're not serious? Jules and I can go after them, okay, but these guys? You're gonna get somebody killed!"

"Troy Barrett, your Favorite Aunt Millie and I worked long and hard to equip the team with a variety of devices from my makeup bag that will make this mission a success. Some of them have things sewn right into their costumes, and they know how to use them; better yet, we know that no one will believe we're a threat. That's our tactical advantage." She marched over to her grandson. "We're old, Sweetheart . . . we know. Don't make us feel like we're useless."

"Troops!" FAM bellowed. "We take no prisoners. I want you to hit 'em hard and hit 'em fast. Remember, these aren't likely to be real people except for Eden, so I don't want to see anybody holding back."

As FAM completed her instructions, Cora's pager went off and the room fell silent. "He's calling, and he may want to come here! I'll have to get you all to the lobby quickly and then pick him up."

"Susan, Darling, we're coming back for you. Don't you worry," Gram said as she and her friends moved toward the door.

"Whoa! Whoa!" Troy jumped on that comment. "There will be no coming back, Gram. She's been locked up in this place long enough. We're not leaving her here. Not for one second."

Susan Barrett touched her son's cheek. "Troy, it's for the best. When Adam returns, I may be able to keep him here . . . to buy more time for you all to find Jack and Jori. I've made it this far, haven't I? The most important thing right now is that you find your brother."

"Your mother's right, Troy-boy. We talked this all out while you were changing," FAM explained. "It's tough, but it's the right way to play this."

Troy ignored the comment and clenched his fists. "And what happens when he comes back here and finds me gone? Huh? Somebody answer that one for me." He looked at all of them and intentionally tried to shower them in guilt. "What's he gonna do to her? Did anybody think that one through? He's gonna walk in the door, and I won't be here, and he's gonna want answers. Do you know how Mr. Eden gets answers out of people?" His tone was challenging, his fear palpable. "DO YOU? Well, I know! And she can't stay here."

Julie pleaded with him. "Troy, can't you see that you're making this harder for everyone? Someone's in danger either way—Jack or your mom. You can't protect them both."

"I can if they're in the same place, Jules. She has to come."

His mother shook her head. "Troy, I'm staying. It's final. The only way I can help is if I can keep Adam down here. Let me do that."

The pager sounded again. "We have to go. Now." Cora hated herself for saying it, but Mr. Eden should not be kept waiting a second time.

Troy punched the wall. "Fine, but I'll be back for you, Mom! I swear I will." He stormed out the door, and the others followed as Cora whisked them to the lobby, where they quickly unloaded; then, she handed the key card to Troy. "We know this opens the door to The Chambers; maybe it will take you to the thirteenth floor, too. I know he uses a key card to get there, so we'll just have to hope. If it doesn't work—I have no idea how you'll find Jack. Good luck everyone." When she directed them toward the service elevator, Waldo blew her several kisses and mouthed the words, "I'll be seeing you." Cora blushed, patted her hair, and set out to pick up her boss.

As soon as the service elevator opened, Troy slid the key card in place. Once the doors closed, everyone witnessed the incredible transformation of the interior in stunned silence. "Looks like the maids get quite a ride in this place," he said.

"Troy, I don't think this elevator is used by the cleaning crew. It's all a sham—you're supposed to think this is a service elevator—but it's not," was Julie's retort.

"Yeah. Well, I can relate, Jules. You see, I was supposed to *think* I had a father . . . but I guess I never really did because he was actually a psychotic nutcase."

"TROY!" Julie motioned to Gram with her head. The band of travelers had never been this quiet. Gram just looked at the ground.

"I'm sorry, Jules, but it's true. Sometimes the truth hurts; Gram knows that."

"Yes, Troy Barrett, I do," his grandmother responded in a steely voice. "But Mr. Eden *wasn't* your father, and he certainly wasn't my son. Chip had problems, serious ones, but he wasn't the monster we're about to face right now. You remember that because I can assure you I'm trying to."

A tense silence fell over everyone. "Well, then, Sis!" FAM exploded with enthusiasm. "How about those Cubs last year?"

They all winced because FAM only knew one volume, and in an elevator, it just wasn't a pretty thing. Her sister didn't respond but began removing a large piece of metal that was hinged in two places from her makeup bag. It opened up into Captain America's shield. "Irma, I am going to put you in charge of this little baby!" Mrs. Gladfell shuffled forward as Gram refolded the shield partway and handed it to her tiny friend. "You get this to Jack when you see that he needs it. Until then, it's all yours." Mrs. Gladfell silently took the shield and nodded to Gram before resuming her place at the back of the crowd.

"I don't remember Jack's shield folding," Troy broke in.

"It didn't Troy-boy! This is a new one I whipped up. Had to call in a few favors, but it was worth it!"

Gram took over in an effort to spare everyone's eardrums from another unintentional attack by her sister. "It's an amazing device. Besides being collapsible, it's tied to Jack's body chemistry. If he's in danger, his adrenaline will spike, and the shield will move toward him as long as it's in his vicinity."

"Nuh-uhhhhhhh." Troy shook his head in disbelief.

Gram held up a black circular object. "Well, he has to be wearing this on his wrist—but don't you worry. I'll find a way to get it on him."

"I want one!" Troy couldn't resist, and his grandmother's smile told him all was forgiven. The lights at the top of the elevator moved from 11 to 12, and finally, it slowed and stopped before it ever reached 14. "Welcome, Mr. Eden, to the thirteenth floor," droned a robotic voice as the doors began to open. Troy laughed. "Well, his elevator's obviously not prepared to deal with the unexpected. Let's see how his staff handles it 'cause, Folks, we're about to make the X-Men look like candy stripers."

Cora assumed she had made it in time. First, because he hadn't paged her again and second because he didn't chastise her. He had indeed wanted to go to The Chambers, and she had taken him there, of course, but Troy's fears of what might happen there were echoing in Cora's mind. She didn't want to leave Mrs. Barrett alone, and she no longer had a key to reenter the room. Her musings ceased as they arrived, and he left the elevator with only one comment. "Wait here."

The door slid open to reveal Susan Barrett—clad in an emerald green taffeta gown—a breathless vision relaxing on the sofa. Candles were lit throughout The Chambers and soft music played; she had worked at lightning speed to make everything to Adam's liking. The only disruption was the sound of water running in her bathroom shower.

"Susan?" His mind was distracted. He had not anticipated this . . . was unprepared for her to receive him in this way. He suddenly couldn't remember why he had come here.

"Oh! Adam, it *is* you! Thank goodness." She rushed to him and threw her arms around him. "I have to apologize. Those things I said before. . . . I was crazy, Adam. A fool. You've been so good to me. . . . I . . . I just needed time to think. Please forgive me."

"Why yes, yes, Darling, of course. I knew you'd come around." He was flustered, she could tell. Good. Keep him off balance. That was her game. She needed to keep him here as long as possible.

"Adam, I thought we could have dinner this evening. You could arrange for that, couldn't you?" She was leading him over to the sofa.

He shook his head vigorously, trying to clear his thoughts. "Troy. I'm here for Troy. He needs to come with me. Now, Susan. And then, then I can come back, and . . ."

"Well, of course, Darling, but Troy's in the shower right now." She glanced toward her bedroom and tried to remain calm. "He

just got in the minute before you arrived. He's exhausted, Adam."
She moved, catlike, to her bedroom door and eased it closed so
the shower could no longer be heard. Then, she returned and
forced herself to sit very close to him. "Why don't we let him
rest when he's finished in the shower? Let him rest for awhile,
Adam, and then you two can rush off together."

He rose from the sofa and headed for her bedroom door. "No.
No, I need him now, Susan. He needs to come . . ."

She raced over and met him while his hand was still on
the doorknob. "Do you know what we never do, Adam?" She
grabbed one of his hands and put it on her waist, then took the
other and interlaced her fingers in his. "We never dance. I bet
you're a fabulous dancer, Adam." She began moving them out to
the center of the room and trying to force him to move with the
music, but he was resisting.

"No. No, dancing. I . . . I have to take Troy, now." He
extricated himself from her and moved for the door again, but
she met him there.

"Darling, I thought you were going to order some dinner.
What if . . ."

He stared at her, suddenly and with great ferocity. "What are
you hiding, Susan? What have you done?"

She didn't even blink. "Nothing, Adam. Nothing. I just want
to apologize, to show you how sorry I am, and . . ."

He shoved her aside in midsentence, threw open the bedroom
door, and raced into her bathroom to find the empty shower.
And then came the scream. So powerful, so primal it might have
shaken the building to its very foundation. And since he was in
the bedroom, she had no place to run.

"YOU! You treacherous, lying, piece of filth!" He tore the bedroom door from its hinge and tossed it aside as he roared again. "How dare you try and deceive me? After all I've done for you, Susan! After all I've given to you!" He was advancing on her, but she'd slipped out of her heels and was intent on keeping the dining room between them. Her goal, keeping him in this room, would buy her boys more time, and right now, time was what they desperately needed.

"Done for me? You've imprisoned me here! And you want accolades for that?"

"I gave you a palace—all your own." He circled the table, but she countered his every move. "You needed time to understand that we were meant for each other. This was the peaceful place where you would learn that."

"You're insane! You've brutalized my boys, terrorized my family . . . and you think I could ever *love* you?"

He sprung at her but missed, and then he started to shed tears. "You were going to be the *perfect* wife, Susan. And we could have had the *perfect* son. My assistants are going to create him . . . upstairs . . . in just a few minutes."

"What are you talking about?"

"We're going to put Jack's brain into Troy's body, Susan. For you."

She grabbed the lit candlestick from the table and threw it with great force, clipping his forehead. "You aren't going to touch my boys. Ever. Never again! And there's nothing wrong with either of them. They're perfect, just the way they are."

Smoke began billowing from somewhere behind him, and she realized what she'd done. The candlestick had set something ablaze, which meant she had to find a way out of here. He came at her and as she lunged to stay out of his grasp, she tripped, hit her head on the corner of the table, and did not move again. He fell to his knees and pulled her gently forward. "Susan?" She wasn't conscious. She couldn't hear that for one brief moment the voice calling her name was not the voice of Mr. Eden, nor did she hear how quickly his menacing voice returned. As smoke began to fill The Chambers, he shoved her body aside without the slightest care and spoke his final words to her. "You weren't good enough for me anyway." As he exited the room, he ran directly into Cora, knocking her to the ground, or so it seemed. The collision and the fall were intentional on her part. He stormed past her without offering to help her up, just as she had predicted, and that gave her the few seconds she needed to pull the plaque from under her sweater and jam it into place. There was now just enough clearance for someone to get a finger hold on that door. Mrs. Barrett would be able to escape. But then Cora saw the smoke, and she knew that something was very, very wrong.

"WHAT ARE YOU DOING OUT OF THE ELEVATOR?" he raged, turning to look back at her. She immediately stepped in front of the seam of the door to hide her treason. "You don't belong anywhere else. You're not fit to walk the halls! Get down here, NOW! And take me where I need to go."

"No." She could scarcely believe she'd said it.

"WHAT? What do you mean 'no'? No one tells me 'no,' least of all some inferior old biddy who's barely fit to press the buttons in a lift." He began walking toward her, but she halted him.

"Jack's escaping! And Troy. Their grandmother and her friends are here . . . and they're on the thirteenth floor. They might have escaped by now, I don't know. So you can come back here and prove what a man you are by beating me to death, or you can go after them before they get away. Your choice, *Sir.*"

He began to shake, physically, as if he were having some type of wild seizure right before her eyes, and what she could see of his face turned scarlet. "Jack will not escape this place. And if he does, you . . . you will never rest peacefully again. You and I aren't finished, Cora! He turned on his heel and darted the rest of the way down the hall without another word to her.

Cora immediately turned her attention to the door. "Mrs. Barrett! Mrs. Barrett!" She screamed as she tugged at the door. It was so heavy. So very heavy. But inch by inch she managed to tug at it until finally there was an opening she could squeeze through. The smoke was black now and much of the dwelling was full of it. Cora fell to her knees and moved forward. "Mrs. Barrett! Mrs. Barrett!" she croaked and coughed, crawling across the floor until at last, she bumped up against a body she prayed was alive.

Chapter 27

When the large doors opened again into Mr. Eden's thirteenth-floor surgical unit, I expected the sound of his triumphant voice. What I heard instead was the commanding voice of FAM yelling, "CHARGE!" That was followed by a war cry that sounded a lot like Waldo Emmerstine. It could only be Gram and her friends. I didn't know or even care how it was possible; I was just glad they were here.

The room quickly became a free-for-all that I could see only bits and pieces of since I was strapped down to a table. "Ffffzzzzt!" An arrow shot across the room right into the neck of one of the five nurses who had been summoned to assist Eve Three, and suddenly the android lit up like the Fourth of July, started smoking, and collapsed to the floor. I tilted my head to see that my brother, standing clear across the room in his Green Arrow costume, had nailed her. He tipped his hat at me and reentered the fray.

Gram approached from out of the chaos. "Jack, Honey, are you all right?"

"Fine, Gram! Get me out of these things, will you?"

"Well, I'm trying. I just don't see how these come unfastened!" She was bent over investigating when one of the nameless androids came at her. "Gram, look out!"

"Waldo!" She called out—appearing completely unconcerned.

"FFWWWTTH!" A tomahawk sailed across the room and landed smack in the middle of the android's face. She thudded to the floor. "Don't any more of you tin cans mess with my gal, or I'll scalp ya!" cried Waldo, and I saw him pop a wheelie and move on into battle.

Gram was digging in her makeup bag. "Here, Jack. Hold this little pocket mirror in your left hand, Honey." She positioned the mirror exactly the way she wanted it, oblivious to the fact that it was quite difficult for me to hold since my wrist was bolted to the table. Then, she was back in her bag again. "There we go! I knew I brought this little duo for a reason!" She pulled out a welder's mask and a blowtorch and set to work on my bonds.

"Gram, do you know how to use . . ."

"Oh, Jack, there's nothing to it. I saw some guy doing it on TV a few years back. I'll get the hang of it eventually."

And the next thing I knew, I heard the clank of metal and the bar across my chest was shoved aside. Gram lifted her mask for a minute. "See there, I told you it was no problem. Stay still, now." She freed my right wrist next and immediately encircled it with some kind of small black band that was emitting a pulse. "Keep this attached to your wrist, Jack."

"What is it?"

"Well, for starters, you can communicate directly into my hearing aid with it. There's also a small tracking device on the underside that you can remove and attach to Mr. Eden if you get the chance. You never know when that could come in handy. Just squeeze it hard between your fingers and some kind of goo will come out and make it stick. That was Florence's contribution, so who knows if it'll work. Jack, the old girl's not the sharpest tack in the box these days."

"Gram! We are in the middle of a fairly serious situation here!"

She went right on discussing the wristband, as if I hadn't said a thing. "Now, Jack, best of all, Millie's rigged this wristband so that your shield will literally fly right to your hand if you need it. It's some science mumbo-jumbo about your body chemistry. I don't understand any of it, but you've gotta be pretty close to the shield or it's a 'no-go'—that much I remember. Now Millie also said . . ." She glanced into the pocket mirror she'd given me, stopped in midsentence, and swung around to face Eve Three. The android had a needle poised to inject my grandmother with who knows what kind of toxin, but she backed away as Gram notched up the power on her blowtorch and advanced on her like the Terminator. "Sweetcakes, I've mud wrestled with Florence Petrillo in the Panama jungle and won. Surely you don't think you can take me down with that little syringe?" Eve Three was defeated, then, in what I would describe as quite a sad way to go for an android, but a few seconds later, Gram had me free and calmly began repacking her bag.

I hopped off the table to see FAM, only a few feet away, pull out a machine gun. She jammed a cartridge into it that appeared to be full of some kind of golden liquid. "Whizzer!" She called her dog away from Troy, and he came as quickly as a three-legged dog can come. When she inclined her head toward Eve Two, Whizzer got the message. He started peeing all over her shoes, and Eve Two chattered away as if someone was actually listening. "Oh, dear! Oh, my! Pets should not urinate inside. Oh, dear! Oh, my!"

"Yeah, well, Whizzer's got struggles like all the rest of us, Sweetie," FAM called out. "But as long as you're standing still—let's see if we can keep you that way." She set the scope on her gun, fired five blasts in a row of what turned out to be "honey cartridges," and completely encased Eve Two in the sticky golden liquid.

Julie and Troy came racing toward me. "Jack!" Julie's voice was desperate. "One of those women who looks like your mother. She has Jori!"

"I know. And she's dangerous. Very. But I can handle her. Troy, where's Mom?"

"She's still in The Chambers."

"TROY!"

"Jack, don't go there with me! I didn't want to leave her, okay?"

"Boys!" Julie interrupted. "I smell smoke." She dashed to the window. "The building's on fire!"

"And of course, there wouldn't be alarms or sprinklers," I said, "because Mr. Eden wouldn't tolerate unwanted guests showing up before he had time to make an exit. All right, we've gotta work fast. Julie, take the Emmerstine brothers and look for Chase. He and his mother are locked up in this place somewhere. Get them and get out.

"But Jack . . ."

"I'll get your sister, Julie. I promise. Now go."

"Jack, I'm getting Mom."

"Not alone, Troy. Take . . ." but he was gone before I could finish my sentence.

I crossed the room to my aunt. "FAM, take Whizzer and Gram and beat it. The rest of them are on the way out. I'll get Jori and meet you outside."

"Nothing doin', Jackie-boy! When this girl comes to a party, she stays 'til . . ."

"FAM, the building's on fire! Get your sister out of here, and trust me. I'm coming." If you've ever been your aunt's favorite nephew, then you know the look I got. "All right, Kid. You're in charge, but you realize I'll have to do this the hard way. Whizzer—get the bag!" Mr. Whizzer raced to grab Gram's makeup bag, and with no warning, FAM raced across the room, picked up her older and much smaller sister, and carted her toward the doors. "Let's go, Katy! Jack's running this show—and he says it's time for us to exit!"

"Millie, put me down this instant. Jack Edward Barrett, you tell your aunt to . . ." The large doors closed behind FAM, and I advanced on Eve One.

She sneered at me. "I'll snap her neck and spine simultaneously. I can do that, you know. I could do it just for kicks. You make one wrong move, and it's over for the beauty queen."

"You sure you want to make that big of a decision without your boss? Your husband? What is he, really . . . to you?"

She regarded me curiously. "My relationship with Adam is not your affair."

"Are you afraid to answer that question, Eve? Is it because you don't really know?"

"I'm not afraid of anything. I'm not . . ."

The doors opened, and he swept into the room like a black wave of evil. "Eve One, prepare for an immediate departure. We'll be exiting momentarily."

"What about her?" she thrust Jori forward.

"I'll deal with her. Go. Now. I'll join you on the patio." He was clearly communicating something more to her than their next rendezvous point, but I couldn't unscramble the message.

The moment Eve One released her, Jori ripped the tape from her mouth and began hobbling toward me. Mr. Eden simultaneously pulled a small remote control from his pocket. "Ah! Ah! Miss McAllister. Remember this little device? I'd stay quite still if I were you. Not one more step." She froze and leaned against a nearby desk for support. We both remembered the device—or at least one that looked just like it—and we'd seen it incinerate people in the original Paradise village. The smell of burnt flesh came back to me every time I thought about it.

I sighed audibly. "Wow! Really original. I guess I'm a little surprised you don't have some sicko bad guys working in a back room who can cook up some *new* weapons for you."

"Forgive me, Jack, but when you have a device that works so well, why mess with *perfection.*"

"Yeah, well if memory serves, it didn't work so well for you last time—seeing as how you french-fried your kid and all."

He didn't respond to my comment about his former "son," the cloned version of Troy, which I thought very strange. I was still wrestling with the issue of who else died right before my eyes back in the original Paradise village. I had decided it was my father, Chip Barrett, mostly because of that long moment of silence between us after I called him "Dad." I couldn't envision Mr. Eden killing himself, so I decided my father had ended it . . . to save us. But now, with the diary entries I'd found, I wasn't entirely sure. Maybe it was a clone of my father who died in the original village. A clone might carry the personality disorder, right? Or, was this one a clone? I didn't think either was an android because a machine wouldn't show the split personality.

His dark tone refocused my thoughts on the here and now.

"Jack, I'm going to start with a medium charge. One on her and then one on you. Things haven't worked out the way I'd planned here, but I can still kill the two of you, and it won't have been an entire waste of the day."

"Me first." I tried not to cough, but a fair amount of smoke was beginning to head into the room.

"Fine, Jack. Fine. You want it first? You want to be the big hero for your girl? Fine—then let me *give it to you!*" He aimed the remote at me and fired, but a split second before he did, my wrist buzzed—or at least the device Gram had strapped there emitted some kind of pulse. Then, from the far corner of the room, I saw a swatch of orange, a piece of red cape, and suddenly a circular object flew toward me . . . came right to my hand. It was my Captain America shield! I caught it, ducked behind it, and the electrical charge bounced off the shield and struck Mr. Eden head on. He cried out in pain, staggered backward, and dropped the remote, which slid across the floor in Jori's direction. She was leaning hard on the desk for support, but in a fraction of a second, she sent the remote sailing with a swift kick from her good leg. We began moving toward each other—watching him every minute—and when he moved again, we stopped in our tracks.

"I said it was only a medium charge." He grinned. "Not nearly enough to keep a good man down, Jack. Of course," he reached into his pocket. "When you have a device that works so well, you should always travel with two." He removed a second one and pointed it at Jori. "Say goodbye to your girl, Jack."

The swatch of orange was in motion again, the red cape followed, and suddenly the second remote was on the floor, and Mr. Eden was howling in pain. I blinked . . . couldn't believe what I was seeing. There were teeth . . . TEETH attached to the skin of his right hand! But the teeth weren't attached to anyone. It was as if an invisible person just decided to take a bite out of him, and all we got to see were the teeth. And then, I saw her—a tiny woman shuffling quickly over to Jori with one of the remotes in her hand. Emblazoned across the front of her orange leotard was the image of some huge teeth and a large letter "P."

"MRS. GLADFELL? Irma?" No one else I'd ever met was that tiny or shuffled in quite the way that Mrs. Gladfell did. I couldn't imagine Gram bringing her. The woman didn't even speak! But here she was. She had been the one who released my shield.

Mr. Eden managed to yank his hand from the jaws of death and throw them to the ground, and then we all heard his watch. He looked at it, wide-eyed, panicked, and then he glared at me. He didn't speak at first, but I saw hatred burning in his eyes. It was the kind of hatred that people feel when they don't have anything left that's good in their lives. And then he turned his watch toward us, pressed a button on the side, and grinned as he backed out of the room. "The whole building's going to blow in twenty minutes. I can't have anybody finding out what's really been going on here, Jack. You understand that. It might make my future business ventures . . . difficult. Your friends may have made it out, but they'll be picking what's left of you out of the rubble because my special elevator's about to take its last ride, and there's no other way off this floor. Goodbye, Jack." His face lifted a bit more than normal above the coat collar, and the gruesome, twisted grin he gave me made my skin crawl. He turned on his heel, then, and was gone.

Mrs. Gladfell had retrieved her teeth and already had Jori's arm around her shoulder. They were both staring at me. "What do we do, Jack?" Jori's voice sounded confident that I would have an answer. "You heard him; there's no other way off the floor."

I tapped the device on my wrist. "Gram! Gram, where are you?"

"Everyone's waiting on the jet, Jackie-boy, except for your brother and me. Once Millie finds out I slipped out on her it'll get ugly, but a girl's gotta do . . . Listen, we couldn't get that little elevator to come for us, so we're on the twelfth floor; we thought you might need reinforcements."

"The elevator's no longer an option, Gram, and there's no other way on or off the thirteenth floor. We need to get down to where you are—and fast."

"No worries, Sweetheart. You need Ups-a-Daisy, Downs-a-Daisy."

"WHAT? Gram, what I need is . . ." PLUNK! SLAM! PLUNK! Something hit the window hard. We all raced over to see my brother climbing a ladder that was suctioned to the far right window of the room. I moved to open the window next to it, and what do you know? It opened! I thought about how that never happens in the movies as I popped the screen out just as easily.

"Hey, Guys!" Troy spoke as if hanging off the side of a building was a daily event. "Jack, I got Mom out, by the way. She's okay. Now, who's first?"

A brief wave of relief swept over me at the news that my mother was out of harm's way; however, Gram's suction-cup ladder was creating some major anxiety. "Troy can that thing . . . is it even secure?"

Gram's voice spilled out over the com link she'd attached to my wrist. "Jack Edward Barrett, how dare you question him about that? I'm here to tell you that Ups-a-Daisy, Downs-a-Daisy is used by firefighters, mountain climbers, and trained acrobats all over the world. It'll be patented any day now—just you wait and see. I heard all about it on the Home Shopping Network last month."

Troy just cocked his head and looked at me impatiently. "Jack, as long as these gadgets of hers keep working, you don't have a leg to stand on."

I didn't know what to say to that. He had a point. "All right, Mrs. Gladfell," I said. "Let's get you . . ." She shook her head vehemently and gently nudged Jori forward. "Mrs. Gladfell, let's not argue. You need to . . ." She frowned deeply and clicked her teeth together several times as a warning. "Okay, then. Jori—looks like you're first." I helped her carefully step out onto the ladder with Troy, all the while questioning its stability. "Use Troy for support, Jori, and go slow. Troy her ankle's messed up—you're going to have to make sure . . ."

I could sense his impatience before I heard it. "Yeah, yeah, yeah, I got it Dr. Barrett. We'll get her safely outta here."

"Jack, promise me you'll be on this ladder right after Mrs. Gladfell." Jori needed assurance because she knew what I was thinking. If Mr. Eden got away, this was never going to end. Still, I needed her focused on her own safety right now.

"I'll be right behind her. Promise." And I meant it. But I wasn't making any promises about what would happen once I got down to the twelfth floor.

Troy and I saddled Mrs. Gladfell onto the ladder next and, true to my word, I quickly followed. Once we were all securely on the twelfth floor, we found the exit door to the stairs, and I directed them down. "It's too dangerous to take the elevators." I said. "The fire is spreading, and if he plans to blow this place like he said, it'd be doubly risky." We couldn't see a lot of smoke yet, but we could smell it. "Troy, get them to safety." With two senior citizens, plus a wounded Jori, someone was going to have to help them out. He wouldn't be coming with me, which is exactly how I wanted it. He screwed up his face but didn't argue, which was a first in my life. It also told me that the seriousness of the situation wasn't entirely lost on him.

"Jack, take this." He removed a belt containing a small crossbow and one arrow from around his waist. "If you get close enough to him—you need to use this. Favorite Aunt Millie dipped the tip of the arrow in . . . Jack, she says it'll put an end to everything."

I let him strap the belt on. "Troy, you know how miserable I was at those archery camps Dad sent us to. My aim is lousy with a regular bow; I think I only successfully shot a crossbow three times in seven years of camp, and even then I didn't hit anything!"

"I know, Jack. We can't all be me, but take it anyway 'cause it's all I have." He slapped me on the side of the head. "Take care, Bro."

I looked at them all standing there, but I just didn't know what to say. I settled on a wink and "I'll be seeing you." Then, I tore off down the hallway.

I stood in front of the elevator and rested my shield on the floor while I punched in the code, 1151. I presumed Cora was safely outside, but I figured the elevator would still come. Despite my sermon to the others about the danger of using an elevator during a fire, I didn't know of any other way to get to The Lodge. And that's where he was. I knew it, and I wasn't going to let him escape.

"Can I help you, Mr. Barrett?" The doors opened to reveal a pale and gray Cora. She was coughing slightly, and her face and hands were streaked with gray and black. She'd clearly been near the source of the fire.

"Cora, what are you doing here?" I picked up my shield and stepped into the elevator. "You should be . . ."

"I helped Troy get your mother to safety and came back for you. Jack, I'm seventy-four years old, and you're the first person who's ever called me 'friend.' I liked the sound of that; I needed to hear it again. So, *Friend,* I came back. Just got here a moment ago in fact. When I called the elevator, it came from The Lodge. He's up there, and that's where you want to go, isn't it?"

"Well, yeah, but . . . Cora . . . the fire. . . . I'm not sure how safe . . . Look, I just don't want anything to happen to you."

A tear leaked out of one of her eyes. "Oh, I'm sorry," she apologized. "I've just never imagined anyone saying anything so kind to me, other than my brother."

I squeezed her shoulder gently. "Well, now someone has."

She brushed the tear away, and her steely resolve returned. "Jack, there's only one way to The Lodge that I know of, and it's in this elevator. Now we're going to do this together." And without another word, her fingers danced over the control panel and away we flew.

The doors opened to what would soon be an inferno. How could there be so much fire up here already? Cora began to cough immediately and raised a handkerchief to her mouth.

"Go! Head back down. Get out of here!" I shouted. The flames were getting loud though they were confined to the far edges of the room at this point.

"There's no other way out!" she argued. "I won't leave you. That's not what friends do."

"Then stay inside the elevator and close the doors. Lie down on the floor, Cora. There's more oxygen there," I explained. "And hang on to this," I said, and I handed her my shield. She took it, nodded, and I saw her making her way to the floor of the elevator as the doors closed.

I heard a noise then and turned to see him exiting the bedroom with a computer bag in his hand. He was moving toward some drapes that were pulled shut, but he halted when he saw me. Instinctively, he pulled his hat down a bit lower. "Jack. What a pleasant surprise. I'd love to stay and entertain you, but it's time for me . . ."

"You did this, didn't you? Set your living quarters on fire to destroy some kind of evidence, right?"

"My affairs are my business, Jack. No one else needs to be delving into them." He began to cough. "I have everything I need from this place. It's not my main base of operations, after all. In fact, this facility played a very small role in my overall objective; its collapse will be little more than a blip on my radar."

"Are you my father?" Whoa! Where did that come from? I had no idea that question was so dangerously close to the surface.

He stared at me for a long moment of silence and then sneered. "You should be so lucky. My DNA would never dare to create such a worthless piece of garbage."

"Who died in the original village, then? Did my father die there? Because someone did. I watched it happen."

"Your father was an ignorant fool who could barely manage to put his own pants on . . . until I came along. I strengthened him."

"You perverted him." A beam on the ceiling caught fire just above me, and I moved quickly out of the way. Now I was coughing, too. A lot.

"I DID WHAT WAS NECESSARY!" In that scary, Mr. Eden way, he had gone from edgy conversationalist to rage-filled nutball in less time than it took me to blink. "I DID WHAT HE COULD NEVER DO! I began the process of building something that would last. Your father got in the way; when the going got tough, he couldn't stomach the work."

"And by that you mean killing his family, I assume?" The fire was starting to get to me. I could feel my skin heating up past sunburn level.

"He was *weak* . . . like *you*. And now he's dead. It was for the best."

"Are you so sure?" I challenged, holding up the diary. "Because I found *this* under your mattress. I haven't read it all, but I've read enough to know that he's still with you; he's part of you."

He dropped the bag in his hand, roared, and lunged for me. NO! HE'S DEAD, DEAD, DEAD!" And then we were on the floor rolling and screaming. He kept reaching for the journal, but I continually managed to keep it from his grasp. His hands were on my neck. "You and your inferior family have got to be silenced!" I shifted and squirmed under his weight but managed to clock him right in the face with enough power to escape his iron grip. While my ribs were complaining bitterly about the wrestling match and my lungs were threatening to bail completely, flames attacked the lower edge of his trench coat. He beat at them furiously with a couch pillow, and that's when I saw my chance and came at him head on. We were on the floor again, and I turned his face into a punching bag—sending blood flowing generously from his nose. He returned the favor with a forceful jab to the side of my jaw. As the brawl continued, I stealthily removed Florence's tracking device from my wristband and waited for the chance to attach it to him. If he ended up getting out of here, this device would be the game-changer for our side. Finally, I saw my opportunity and grabbed the lapels of his coat in preparation for a major head butt. I affixed the tracker to the inside of his right lapel with my index finger and thumb, and then I let him have it. My head must make for a decent weapon because he hit the ground with a solid thud. The roar of flames turned my attention back to the large set of wine-colored drapes he had been approaching when he first saw me. They were quickly becoming ash and behind them I saw a glass door. There was a huge patio outside of the door and the whir of what sounded like a helicopter told me the rest. I felt sure Eve One was piloting the copter. This was his way out.

"Jack! Jack!" It was Cora, coughing terribly and calling my name. If my lungs were in panic mode, I couldn't imagine what hers were doing. She clearly was no longer on the floor of the elevator because I could see that the doors were open, but the room was so clouded with smoke, I couldn't see her.

"Cora!" I started to make my way toward the sound of her voice when Mr. Eden grabbed both of my legs, and yanked them out from under me. I came down hard, and my ribs screamed wildly. There was white fire on the inside of my body—pain so intense that for a moment I couldn't think, couldn't see. I scrambled to rise, and that's when the beam above us lost its connection to the ceiling.

He jumped back as it came crashing down, knocking me to the ground and then rolling over just enough to pin my legs under its weight. Worse yet, the belt with the crossbow and arrow was ripped from my waist in the process and landed just out of my reach.

"Well, well, well!" He rasped between coughs as he picked the belt up and began to remove the weapon. "This looks dangerous, Jack. Someone could get hurt playing with one of these." He began loading it deliberately. "I was always terribly good at archery. A real . . . good . . . shot, Jack." He took aim and the razor-sharp arrow was pointing straight at my chest.

"Uhhhhhh!" I strained against the beam—tried to pull my body forward and release my legs, but it was no use. I needed some leverage, and I just didn't have it. Was this really how it was going to end? I looked into his eyes—and time seemed to slow down, almost stopping for a few seconds. And though I didn't say anything verbally—sometimes a look can say everything you need to communicate.

I was searching for my dad, the man inside the monster, and miraculously Mr. Eden's finger began to move slowly away from the trigger. His hand appeared to be moving involuntarily; he stared at it as if he couldn't believe what was happening. "Dad?" I coughed out the question.

His neck jerked up from the coat collar, and I could see his head straining to stay in position—to look at me. Mr. Eden was trying to force his face down, back into the shadows where evil strains to hide, but my father's consciousness had managed to wrest control of the body! He had done it because Mr. Eden was going to kill me, and he wasn't going to let that happen. There was an internal struggle taking place in his body that was just shy of Armageddon. It was incredible . . . and frightening. Then, another slowly moving hand pulled the hat up so that I could see more of his face. His body trembled—Mr. Eden was fighting, but my dad was winning!

"Jack . . . Son, I'm sorry. I'm so, so sorry for . . ."

Glass blew at that point. The heat was becoming unbearable; shards went flying all around us, and in that moment, my father lost his hold. The commotion provided enough of a distraction for Mr. Eden to regain control. He stepped toward me, yanked the journal from my grasp, and returned to his position.

"Say goodbye to Daddy, Jack. For good this time!" He tossed the journal toward a pillar that was blazing a few short feet away, and then took aim at me again. "Hope I'm not too rusty, Jack. Let's find out!" His voice had grown hoarse from the smoke, but it retained its malevolent edge. As he readied himself to fire the crossbow, I felt the device on my wrist begin to pulse, which meant Cora was close by, and twice in a day that shield saved my life. It flew from Cora's hands, wherever they were, and charged toward me arriving in my hand just in time to block the arrow's path. "NO!" he screamed. "I HAVE TO GET RID OF YOU! I HAVE TO . . ." Suddenly, there was a huge crash, and three more beams came down from the ceiling, but he managed to avoid being hit. There was no time left; flames began howling all around the room. He gave me an arrogant look of triumph. "Ahhh, well, looks like the fire will do the job for me. So long, Jack. It's a shame you won't be around to see the big plans I've been working on. I'm building a whole new city, Jack. Bigger and better than ever. Too bad you'll never get the chance to visit." He made his way carefully to his computer bag and stepped through

the shattered doorway and out onto the patio. The sound of the
helicopter grew louder, and I craned my neck to see a rope ladder
extending down to the patio. He was going to make it out!

"UHHHH!" I pushed at the beam again hoping the added
adrenaline that comes when you're about to be fried alive would
do the trick. It moved slightly, and I pulled my body forward
some, but it wasn't enough. CRASH! A section of the floor
under his grand piano gave way, and it went falling who knows
how many floors below—underscoring just how desperate the
situation was.

I heard coughing nearby. "Cora?"

She appeared out of the smoke, crawling on her hands and
knees very slowly. "Sweetheart, we have to get you out of here."

"Cora, NO! I'm caught here. You go! Get to the door, to the
patio. They'll see you. Help's gotta be on the way!" And, as if
on cue, I heard the sound of fire engines. Where had they been
all this time? And then I realized that what felt like hours had
actually taken place in only a few minutes.

She shook her head at me and coughed. "Give me . . ." she
reached for the shield, and I relinquished it as she hurriedly
jammed it into the space between the beam and my legs, then
raised herself to her knees and leaned on the shield with all of
her weight. "Pull, Honey, pull hard!" She was wheezing and
coughing so much I could barely make out the words, but I saw
what she was doing. She was providing the leverage I needed to
get free.

I yanked, spun, jerked, and twisted all at once with every
ounce of strength I had left and managed to pull myself out. I
was free! I scrambled up, relieved to find that neither of my legs

appeared seriously damaged, and moved toward Cora. The beam that had pinned me was now lying on the floor between us. "Let's get to the patio," I called. "Cora, give me your hand." I knew there was no way she was going to manage to step over this large beam in her present condition without help, and I had to get both of us out of here fast. She managed to stand, and then looked at me with the most radiant smile as she handed me my father's journal. "I heard what you said about this, Jack, and I had to get it back for you. When you love someone, having their written words with you keeps a part of them alive. It's so important. I've learned that. There's a letter tucked in there, too, for my brother, Bill. Please see that he gets it."

I extended my arm over the beam for her hand. "Cora, you're going to give him that letter, yourself. In person. I'm going to find a way to take you to him. I promise. Now, c'mon. Take my hand."

There were tears streaming down her face. "Thank you, Jack. Thank you for being my friend." She leaned across to take my hand, and that's when the floor beneath her gave way.

"CORA!" I screamed her name and reached out in desperation just as she and much of the furnishings around her disappeared into an abyss. "Cora! NO! NO! CORAAAAAAAAAA!"

"It's too late, Jack! She's gone." It was Troy. I didn't know how he'd entered the room, but he'd seen what had just happened. I moved to step onto the beam, to see how far she'd fallen, but he held me back. "Jack, this whole place could go any minute. She's gone, Bro."

I grabbed his shoulders. "She saved me, Troy! I can't just . . ."

"What you can't do, Jack, is let her sacrifice be for nothing. We *have* to go, and it's gotta be now." He moved me toward the patio, but I was looking back over my shoulder the whole time, ears straining for the slightest sound indicating that she could have survived the fall. There was nothing, though, but the roar of a raging fire.

The patio area was enormous, and the farther we moved from the edge of the building, the more fresh air was available. I leaned over with hands on my knees and pulled some in as Troy fired an arrow down toward the ceiling of a lower building's roof. "What're you expecting to connect with down there hotshot?" I coughed. "And if you think I'm going to . . ."

"Don't question the technique, and don't mess with the master, Big Bro." He tied the line off on our end.

"Troy, you aren't seriously planning . . . this isn't Hollywood! We can't just . . ."

"Jack!" His tense voice drew my attention to the sound of helicopter blades. I had assumed Mr. Eden was well out of range, but apparently, he'd stayed close enough to be sure I was finished. . . . And now he'd found out differently. I could make out Eve One piloting them closer to the patio; he was sitting right beside her and appeared to tip his hat at us. That's when my brother yanked two metal boomerang-shaped devices from his quiver and handed one to me. I ran my finger across a groove carved out of the center as Troy issued a direct order. "The notch goes on the line I just shot down to that other rooftop, Jack. You balance, and you hold on with everything you've got. It's gonna be fast."

"Troy . . . this looks like one of Gram's . . ."

"DO IT! And you've gotta leave the shield behind." I opened my mouth to object, and he silenced me with a look. "I'm telling you, Jack, it's going to take everything you've got just to hang on." Reluctantly, I set the shield aside and watched as he quickly positioned the device on the line. "See you below, Bro." He pulled his knees to his waist and went hurtling downward like a spinning top.

The helicopter had taken an unusual position, a hovering demon watching me. I stared at the occupants. From one perspective, I was looking at my mother and father, yet from another, I was looking at a man and a machine, and they both wanted to kill me. I'm not sure exactly what kind of weapon they fired at me, but whatever it was, it was fast . . . and deadly. Troy reported seeing the entire top floor of the building explode from the very place where I had been standing seconds before, but I missed the fireworks because I was rocketing toward him with my eyes tightly shut. He insists I was screaming in terror like a six-year-old, but I prefer to think of it as more of a heroic shout of triumph. We argued about it as he led me to a waiting taxi and off to the airport; the sound of a huge explosion behind us reinforced that Mr. Eden meant what he said. The building was gone.

Gram had everything arranged, as usual, to make for a clean getaway. She wouldn't be bothered with questions from law enforcement, and I was reminded again of how impossible our story would sound to anyone who hadn't lived it.

I felt sure no one would ever believe the truth, and it made me consider how many other truths might be out there. Truths other people are living with . . . or surviving, that the rest of us know nothing about or pretend we don't. Locker room bullying, the abuse in the apartment next door, or the elderly neighbor who's run out of food. Are these only *possible* truths that people convince themselves aren't reality so the world can seem to be a brighter place? Or are most people like my family? Do they know the truth but convince themselves that nobody else would ever believe it, so they just keep it to themselves? Maybe it's a defense mechanism. Maybe it's part of the human condition. Or maybe it's simply part of the way we survive. Whatever the answer is, I'm not entirely convinced that keeping quiet is in anybody's best interest, and I know I'm going to be wrestling with that question for a very long time.

Chapter 28

Duke Redmer had been flying most of his life. Born and raised in the Land Down Under, he was more at home in the Outback than the city and happier flying a plane than driving a car. Though he'd been living in the States for years, he still retained a trace of his Aussie accent, and he knew how to turn it on when necessary. The American ladies liked that accent, and he hated to disappoint. So, when Favorite Aunt Millie called to him from outside the plane and entrusted Susan Barrett to his care, the pilot gave her a hearty and extra-friendly "G'day, Miss" and helped her to her seat. He tended to the large gash on her head with his first-aid kit and, even after all seemed well, continued to lavish a fair amount of attention on her—regaling her with outlandish stories about her iconic mother-in-law and the merry band of super friends who came with her to Vegas. He was clearly gearing up for another wild tale when Favorite Aunt Millie allowed her thunderous presence and overprotective tone of voice to ward off further advances. "Listen, Sailor, don't you have some flying hoo-ha to go work on or something? This girl needs rest, and she ain't auditioning for *The Bachelorette,* if you get my meaning!"

"Right you are there, Favorite Aunt Millie." Duke responded good-naturedly and tipped his hat to Susan as he headed toward the cockpit.

"Suzie-Q, Katy said to keep you safe and secure, and that's exactly what Whizzer and I intend to do!" FAM barked. "So relax,

Sweetheart. As soon as we get the rest of the team on board, and that includes your boys, we're outta here!" Mr. Whizzer produced a deep throaty growl as he turned in a circle and eyed invisible villains who might be intending to do harm to Mrs. Barrett. He sighed when none appeared and then planted himself at her feet and continued to scour the area.

Though she appreciated the sense of safety the plane provided, Susan Barrett's primary thoughts were for her boys. Why was it taking so long for them to make it to the plane? Isolated in The Chambers for nearly a year, she was starving for interaction. Right now she was engaging in people-watching to keep her mind off Jack and Troy, and this particular group of people gave her plenty to watch. A tiny woman, who had not said a word and who was having a terrible time keeping her teeth in her mouth, was seated across the aisle from Susan. A boy who looked to be Jack's age was sitting two rows back with his mother. Susan had noted the woman's glass eye when she boarded and couldn't help but wonder if Adam had anything to do with that. Julie, who seemed to know the boy quite well, had led them to the plane and was spending a lot of time seeing to their needs. Two elderly men, introduced by FAM as the Emmerstine brothers, had provided a great deal of on-and-off distraction. Susan had expected the men would come to blows several times when the taller one had apparently had enough taunting from his brother. "It weren't my fault them robots didn't take to my laughing gas, you old coot! How was I supposed to know we was goin' to fight a bunch of androids? Huh? You just tell me that."

"You know'd it, Wendell Emmerstine. You know'd it full well, so stop sayin' you didn't! Katy told us there'd likely be a bunch of mechanical people; you just got so carried away with the idea of bein' Laughing Kid, you forgot your gas wouldn't work on robots! Hee! Hee! Ha!" The wheelchair-bound man was giggling with sheer delight.

"She never said a dagnab thing about no robots, Waldo!"

"Did so, did so, did so. You's gettin' that Old-Timer's disease where they forget everything, so of course you don't remember."

The lean older man reached over and smacked his brother on the side of the head. "That's Alzheimer's disease, not Old-Timer's disease, you senile old vegetable, and I ain't neither got it 'cause I still remember what a pain in the keister YOU are!"

"BOYS!" FAM shouted. "Take it outside or button it up. In the unit I commanded, you two wouldn't have lasted the afternoon. Isn't that right, Whizzer?"

The dog emitted three sharp barks and looked threateningly at the Emmerstine brothers.

Wendell quieted down immediately. Waldo, on the other hand, laughed at the dog and waved one of his tomahawks in the air. "Watch yourself Fido, or I'll scalp ya! Hee! Hee! Ha!"

Mr. Whizzer growled menacingly at Waldo, so his brother tried to take the weapon out of his hands. "Nice, doggie. Nice, doggie. Grandpa Waldo didn't mean that. Now, Uncle Wendell will just put the nasty tomahawk away."

"Tarnation, you will! Let go, let go!"

"I will not let go. That dog is ready to attack, you crazy old codger."

"Let him try it! I tell ya, I'll . . ."

The brothers struggled and tussled until, without warning, the tomahawk went sailing through the air and lodged itself into the wall right next to the entrance door through which Katy Barrett and Jori had just stepped. A wisp of Katy's hair came off as the blade sliced past her. Everyone stopped and stared at the near miss, as Irma Gladfell's teeth exploded from her mouth and slid down the aisle toward the newest arrivals.

"Katy!" Susan cried out in horror.

Gram picked up Irma's teeth. "No worries, Susan, risk is my business. Jori, get that tomahawk out of the wall and hang onto it will you?" The young girl followed Katy's instructions and, clearly favoring one leg, turned to head toward a seat when her younger sister came racing up and threw her arms around her. "Jori! I'm sorry for every fight we ever had, and I'm sorry I borrowed your blue sweater without asking, and I'm sorry Dad grounded you for taking money out of his penny jar when I was the one who really did it, and I'm sorry I gave the cat away to that family vacationing from Virginia, and . . ."

Jori extricated herself from the sisterly embrace. "You borrowed my blue sweater without asking? The one with the pearl buttons? Julie! Is that how it got that hole in the right sleeve?"

Julie began biting the nail of her right index finger. "Well . . ." She began shifting her weight, and her eyes darted this way and that until, suddenly, a green-clad figure filled the aisle just outside the cockpit door.

"Any fair maidens in need of rescuing on this plane, 'cause my bro and I just happen to be in the business!"

"TROY!" The collective cries of the ladies was thunderous, and they moved toward him in one giant mass, pulling at him and hugging him and kissing him. Mr. Whizzer began howling

'Well, he's gone. I mean he got away, everyone. I'm sorry.
lly sorry. But, you know without you guys, there wouldn't
: been any chance. I mean we were goners before you all
ved up. I'm . . . uhhh . . . I'm not really sure how to thank
 all, but you certainly deserve to know that you played an
ortant role in everything that happened here today, and
hermore, I'd just like to say that . . ."

iram erupted without warning and jumped from her seat into
aisle waving her Blackberry in the air like a madwoman. She
 clearly been texting during Jack's speech. "Ohhhhh! That
wheeling, good-for-nothing, old crone, Florence Petrillo!"

Gram! I'm trying to say something, here."

he bustled up the aisle toward him and whispered in his ear.
blic speaking's not your gift, Sweetheart. Let's just have you
k to saving the world. Now, go hug your girl."

ack sighed and headed down the aisle where Jori was waiting
him. Apparently his appearance wasn't about to deter her one
"You, Mr. Barrett, look terrific to this girl." She pulled him
 an embrace and squeezed way too hard.

Gentle hugs! Gentle hugs!" He said in a high-pitched tenor
:ed upon him by the pain. "The ribs, the ribs, the pain, the
n!" became a chorus he was forced to repeat.

'Ohhh, Jack, I'm so sorry!" Jori countered. "Here. Maybe this
l work better." She put her hands on both sides of his face and
led him into a major kiss. Right there—with the whole plane
:ching—and she wasn't stopping!

He could not imagine anything more embarrassing! His brother,
 grandmother, and his *mother* were watching this! He tried to
 her into letting him go, but he couldn't make words come out

and was trying desperately to make his way through
to reach Troy but was having no luck.

"Easy, Ladies, easy. There's enough of the Emeral
go around. Everybody can have a turn. Let's not rush

Jack, hidden behind the mob scene created by h
arrival, stepped into the cockpit and gave Duke the
was time to go. As he backed out of the pilot's refuge ai
make his way down the aisle, he saw that Troy had tak
Mr. Whizzer was on his lap, and Julie was wiping of
which had apparently been showered by Whizzer's
upon their reunion. Everyone had quieted down, and tl
staring at Jack now. Tears were rolling down his moth
and Gram and FAM were seated together beaming a
pride. The others were all giving him their undivide
and Jori was standing in the far back aisle looking at
was the most amazing guy in the whole world.

"Uh, hey!" He was at a dead stop; he literally had n
to say or do. How did Troy handle the attention of cro
time? Jack instantly regretted any moment he'd ever b
of his brother being in the spotlight. "I . . . uhh . . . I g
look too good, umm . . ." He looked down. His clot
tatters and the duct tape around his ribs was sugge
had as rough a ride as the rest of his body. The skin
was sooty black and blistered in some places, and I
his face didn't look a whole lot better. He'd been i;
taste of blood leaking into his mouth for awhile, bi
he was acutely aware of it. They were all still star
probably waiting for him to give some kind of victory
he might as well get it over with.

quickly with her lips still attached to his face. "Err . . . Jor . . . my mom's right . . . here. . . . Jor . . . MOM . . . the . . . plane . . . Jori . . . parent in vicinity . . ." She finally released him, pretending she hadn't heard a word he'd just said. "I think you're incredible, Jack Barrett. I hope you know that." She pulled him into the seat next to her just as Gram made it abundantly clear that she and FAM were indeed related.

She banged on the cockpit door and shouted in a voice that told everyone she meant business, "DUKE! Get this baby in flight; Florence and I have issues!"

Chapter 29

Within a few weeks, life had settled back to as normal as normal ever gets for our family. FAM and Mr. Whizzer were off to work with earthquake victims in some remote corner of the world. We'd see them at Christmas, she promised, if all went well. Chase and his mother were back in their old house, and some social coaching from Julie was really starting to help him. He hung with our group now and then, but it was always awkward for me. I wanted to forgive him. I thought I had forgiven him. But the feelings of betrayal kept creeping back whenever he was near, and I still hadn't figured out how to shake them . . . or how to entirely trust him. We both knew it; we both understood it, and neither of us said a word about it. Jori had introduced him to a girl who worked at the hospital gift shop, and there seemed to be some promise there. I really hoped things worked out for him.

My mother was handling a multitude of questions about her sudden reappearance by playing the avoidance game. To former close friends, she said she had needed time away, and if they could accept that without asking any more questions, then the friendship could resume. If not, time to move on. She'd also had coffee with Duke Redmer twice, and on this particular Friday evening in November, they were out to dinner—just as friends— she was careful to say. Whatever. I didn't know how I felt about that. When your father's dead or nuts or sort of dead and sort of nuts, and your mother's been missing for a year and now she's back, but she's having coffee and dinner with a "friend" who just happens to be a tough-guy, Aussie pilot—well, there's not a manual at the public library on how to handle that kind of situation. I looked.

Troy was leaving for a weekend archery camp in northern Minnesota and was set to hit the road within an hour. I wasn't wild about him going alone, but Jori had convinced me to keep quiet. She's the only one I told about Mr. Eden's final words to me. He was re-creating his village, somewhere else, and I had to believe that when the time was right, he'd come looking for us again. I was fairly certain he knew I had escaped, though I couldn't be totally sure. But what about Mom and Troy? They weren't safe as long as he was out there. I *was* sure of that, and no argument from Jori would change my mind. As far as I was concerned, her safety was in question as well, and I was going to have to make some tough decisions very soon if I really wanted to protect her.

I hadn't told anyone about the tracking device I was able to secure to Mr. Eden's lapel. Eventually, I'd need help figuring out how to detect it, but for now, I wasn't going to discuss that with anyone. I needed everyone to feel some sense of security again, and though I didn't think Mr. Eden would be re-entering our world immediately, I was certainly planning on entering his. For once, I was going to take the offensive against him.

I opened my nightstand drawer, fingered Cora's letter to her brother—thinking I would tell Jori about it—and then changed my mind. I was determined to deliver that letter to Bill Simpson, and then I was going to tell him a story he needed to hear—about his sister, Cora. I didn't know why he had joined forces with Mr. Eden, and I'd long since stopped wondering. But wherever this new village was, I felt sure that I'd find them both there. And I'd made up my mind to put an end to everything they'd built or ever intended to build. Once and for all.

The long silence told Jori where my mind was, and she came over and squeezed my hand. "Jack, maybe Mr. Eden's over his preoccupation with your family. Wherever he is, whatever he's doing, maybe he'll be content with Eve One and just do his thing without involving any of you."

I withdrew my hand immediately. "And you could live with that? The knowledge that he's out there somewhere, destroying lives? But it's okay as long as they're not *our* lives, right?"

"No, Jack, that's not what I meant!" She moved to sit on the edge of the bed and sighed. "I suppose I was just hoping that he could be happy with his own little community of androids somewhere—and that maybe he'd forget about all of you. I suppose it's just wishful thinking."

I gazed out the window into Mrs. Norman's garden. "Jori, if there's anything you should have learned by now about Mr. Eden, it's this; he plays to win. Wherever he's rebuilding Paradise, when it's ready, he'll be back. For that village to be perfect, in his eyes, he's either going to have us living on the inside or dead on the outside, and the trouble is, I don't know which one's his objective anymore."

She came up behind me and put her arms around my waist. "What are you going to do, Jack?"

"I'm going to stop him, Jori, and this time I'm not waiting on him to come to me. I'm going to find him first."

"How? He could be anywhere."

"Yeah, well, I'm going to find him no matter where he is." I peeled her hands away and walked over to my dresser, opened the top drawer, and pulled out the journal. When I handed it to her, she looked at me curiously. "This is a journal my father was keeping. I found it under Mr. Eden's mattress, and I think there are clues inside it that are going to help me defeat Mr. Eden once and for all. My dad's not dead, Jori. He may be trapped in that body, but he's not really gone."

"Jack . . ." her tone was tolerant but unbelieving. "I know you want to believe that your dad isn't really gone, but . . ."

"He saved my life, Jori. Mr. Eden was a nanosecond away from firing Troy's crossbow at me. He had it aimed straight at my heart, and my dad wouldn't let him fire it." My voice cracked. "Jori, he's still in there, and I'm going to figure out a way to save him. I couldn't save Cora, but I am going to save my dad."

A door slammed downstairs with enough force to interrupt our conversation and bring all of us racing to the family room. Julie stormed into the room, and an uncomfortable silence immediately settled as she locked eyes with Troy.

"We need to talk, Troy. You're leaving for this archery camp, and there's something I need to say before you go." Her eyes darted around the room. "In private."

Well, that was all we needed. Gram suddenly remembered something she needed to order online and rushed off in a flurry, and Jori practically collided with me as we both raced for the kitchen. We pulled the shutters over the breakfast bar closed but not entirely. We weren't going to miss this.

I heard Troy sigh—an indication he didn't want to go first. My brother rarely wants to start a conversation that's going to be difficult. Julie, of course, knows him as well as anyone, so she didn't wait on him to initiate the discussion.

"Troy . . . I think I love you, okay? And I'm really hoping that I don't because how could I be so mad at someone and still care so much, and I just have this awful feeling in the pit of my stomach when I think about you going away this weekend, but at the same time, when I think about finding you and Bunny in the math lab yesterday, it just makes me furious because I'd been trying to tell you all along that she was . . ."

I opened the shutters ever so slightly in the midst of Julie's non-stop sentence, and Jori didn't even scold me. Instead, she bent down below me to arrange her own viewing area. We probably looked like a two-headed totem pole, but at least we could both see.

"Julie, let's not go there again. Okay?" Troy led her over to the couch, which, situated on the diagonal in the family room, gave us a perfect view of them. "I've told you a hundred times that Bunny . . ."

"Don't say that name! I can't stand to hear it spoken aloud, Troy!"

"But, Julie, YOU just said it!"

"Well, then I can't stand to hear *you* say it. Little Bunny Foo Foo has nearly destroyed our relationship, and . . ."

Troy let out a new kind of sigh—exasperation. "We agreed you weren't going to call her that anymore. Remember? It's Fewtajenga, Jules. A little German, a little English, a little . . ."

"A little sleazebag!"

"Julie, c'mon. Cut her a break! She was freshman class president, she's on the pompom squad every year, she's a great student. She can't be all bad."

"Troy, are we really going to have this conversation again. She is *after* you! She's been after you probably since the minute the two of you met."

"For cryin' out loud, Julie, Bunny's . . ."

"Aaaaahhhh! No names!"

I opened the shutter wider. Troy threw up his hands. "Okay, okay, I forgot. I won't say her name, but look, Jules. We gotta get past this."

She jabbed a finger at his chest, and the inquisition began. I would have asked Jori to make popcorn, but I knew that would get me in big trouble so I reached for some peanuts Gram had put out in a candy dish. "Just what was she doing with her hands all over you when I came to pick you up from math lab, Mr. Barrett? Explain that one, huh?"

"I've tried! A hundred times, but you won't listen. And you're exaggerating. Her hands were not all over me, Julie. She was just . . . measuring my chest. Mr. Sanders told us to measure the circumference of a bunch of different stuff, and she suggested . . . you know . . . measuring my chest." His eyes dodged hers at that moment—not a good sign. Weakness was clearly evidenced. Julie sensed it and sprang.

"With your SHIRT OFF!"

"She said the material was going to mess up her measurements. Jules, she was just trying to be accurate."

"Oh, Troy, please. You were wearing a cotton T-shirt! How much material was there to get in the way? So some girl just asks you to take your shirt off for her, and you . . ."

Troy stood up and his tone became defensive. This was going to get hot! "I did *not* take my shirt off for her, Julie. She tore it, accidentally."

Now Julie was up. "TROY! How can someone accidentally tear off your entire shirt?"

"Look, Jules, I've still got it. I'll show you that it's in pieces, okay. Maybe then you'll believe me!" He made to leave the room but didn't get far. She grabbed his wrist.

"You mean you SAVED it!" Jori looked up at me and shook her head. Not good. He obviously had made a majorly bad decision on the shirt save. "WHY? Why in the world would you save a shirt that some love-starved girl ripped off you? Is it a memento, Troy? Do you think you're a rock star or something?" Without warning, she began another marathon rant. "When my parents decided to move within the city limits of Davenport, Jori and I begged them to look at houses that would send us to school with you and Jack, but if I had any idea how difficult it was going to be dating the hottest guy in the high school, I never, not even for a minute, would have wanted to do it, but then it worked out and I thought it was going to be heaven, but these girls they're just too much and most of them are so empty headed but you still talk to them and most of the time I'm okay about it, but sometimes it just . . ."

"I used it to wax the car, Jules. It wasn't a memento, okay?" And suddenly, it hit him. The grin that dazzles all who stand before it came out with the eagerness of a little boy who's just heard he's getting a B.B. gun for his birthday. "Wait! The *hottest* guy in the high school?" Now he was going to try to play it cool. "Well, uhhh, who, uhhh, who said that? You know, who said that part about me being, you know, the hottest guy and all?"

Julie grabbed his hands and pulled him to the couch. "I did, you goofball!" She reached up and gently stroked his left cheek. "But everyone knows it's true."

"Really?" He used the puppy dog eyes. There's no hope when he does the eyes like that. They even get to me.

"Really." A new kind of fireworks was about to ignite—that much was clear.

Jori closed the shutters and stood up. She turned to face me and promptly stomped on my foot.

"Owwwwww!" What was that for?

"That, Jack Edward Barrett, was because men are scum; he got out of that way too easy. And by the way, if Bunny ever tries to take measurements on you—remind her, I'm a black belt."

Chapter 30

Eve One carried a glass of wine over and set it gracefully on his desk. He glanced up for the briefest moment and then went back to his paperwork while she moved furtively about the office, lingering near a large framed photograph of the Barrett family hanging on the wall. It had been taken during the holidays. Susan and Chip Barrett were surrounded by their two boys as well as Chip's parents; a decorated tree was evident in the background. "Adam, is this necessary? I don't like it." Eve One pouted and moved across the room from the photo.

He rose from his desk without saying a word and joined her. They stared at the photograph from at least fifteen feet away for several quiet moments, and then he spoke. "I couldn't agree more, Eve One. There's something decidedly wrong with this photograph. Certain elements contained in it are quite . . . troublesome."

"Let's take a new photograph, Adam. Let's take a new one and hang it where this photograph is now. Let's *destroy* this one!" Her tone betrayed a passionate desire that was atypical of artificial life, but Adam Eden's engineers had managed to advance Eve One beyond a typical artificial life form. She moved toward the photograph, but he held her back.

"Eve One, it is not so simple as you assume. In order to truly destroy the photograph, you must destroy the people pictured in it."

"Will you do that, Adam?" She was nearly salivating at his

words. "Will you do that for me? For us? For . . . our family?"

"As I am building up a village, I shall be tearing apart everything that threatens it. The people in this photograph are, indeed, a threat, Eve One, to us and to our way of life. And so they will be dealt with . . . one . . . by one. Starting—with him!" Without warning, he pulled a polished chrome letter opener from his pocket and in one smooth movement sent it sailing toward the photograph. The force of the throw, working in combination with the razor sharp tip of the tool, peeled the film back to the left and to the right from the central point of impact. Jack Barrett's smiling face still peered out from the photograph, but his chest was split in half.

Adam Eden took Eve One's hand in his. "The war, my dear, has begun."